GEO

THE GOOD HEART

THE GOOD HEART

by

James Michael Pratt

SHADOW
MOUNTAIN ®

For lifelong friends with good hearts—
Dr. Miles Hall, law enforcement officer Bill Maxfield,
Dr. Neil Whitaker, and the late Dr. Steven Dean Gray
And for a hero—son, brother, friend, soldier—Luke Stone

Library of Congress Cataloging-in-Publication Data

Pratt, James Michael.
  The good heart / James Michael Pratt.
    p.   cm.
  ISBN 1-59038-368-0 (alk. paper)
  1. Heart—Transplantation—Fiction. 2. African American civil rights workers—Fiction. 3. Politicians—Fiction. 4. Clergy—Fiction. I. Title.

PS3566.R337G66 2005
813'.54—dc22   2004030563

Printed in the United States of America   54459
Malloy Lithographing, Inc., Ann Arbor, MI

10   9   8   7   6   5   4   3   2   1

Acknowledgments

My special thanks to Product Director Jana Erickson who read the outline and proposal for this book and gave me such helpful encouragement and guidance. Thanks also to my editor, Richard Peterson. I am grateful as well to Gail Halladay, Andrew Willis, Chris Schoebinger, Richard Erickson, Laurie Cook, and others at Shadow Mountain, including CEO and President Sheri Dew. All have offered tremendous belief in *The Good Heart*.

"TELL ME, WHERE IS FANCY BRED?
IN THE HEART OR IN THE HEAD?"

The Merchant of Venice

Prologue

HE WOULDN'T TELL HIS WIFE. The threat from Lawton was not something to take entirely lightly, but having been in the political business and working for so long among the dark ops people, he knew most of it was just bluster, intended to put the fear of God in him. He'd have to take it seriously, but it wasn't something he was comfortable sharing with Maggie. Besides, there wasn't anything she could do about it, except worry.

Of course there was the trail of an occasional corpse to consider. It did happen—murders covered up as suicides, accidents that didn't seem so accidental, and then there was Nick . . .

He dismissed that thought quickly. He knew the person issuing the threat, and if he wanted to, he could play a better game at it.

But he had hoped those days were well behind him now. He wanted to forget the entire intrigue. In fact, he couldn't understand how he had played the political game for two and one half decades. He recalled loving it, living for it, but now he didn't relate to it and couldn't understand how he could have been so addicted.

Power. Power intoxicates, he thought.

He turned the volume up on his Surround Sound system. Listening to Aaron Copland's "Appalachian Spring" always relaxed him. Maggie was in the kitchen, preparing a Sunday meal of meatless

1

lasagna, buttered squash from the garden, and a medley of other fresh vegetables, lightly steamed in a blush of olive oil—all good for the heart.

He smiled when he thought of Claire Barlow coming over. It would be nice to see that sweet little old lady. Claire's kind and gentle ways always made him think of what really mattered most in life— love, relationships, helping others. One of the things that endeared Claire to him was her rhubarb pie. That was something else he couldn't understand; before the surgery, he'd wanted nothing to do with it, now he craved it.

Anyway—the threat hidden on his mirror until the bathroom steamed—it was a Lawton game. He still held a card Ron Lawton wanted. Dead didn't give that card to Lawton. It all could wait. In fact it would wait. He had no intention of going back to politics anyway, so it was a moot point.

"That's so thoughtful, sweetheart," he said as he reached out to receive the ice-cold lemonade Maggie carried in to him. He reclined in his easy chair and took a sip. "Can't get enough of this," he said, smacking his lips.

"Love you," she said as she went back into the kitchen.

His heart leapt, and he felt a sudden rush of emotion. It always did that, now, whenever he heard her say those words. That was another thing he'd never experienced before the operation; he had always loved her, but his feelings for this woman had intensified in a way he couldn't yet get used to.

He took another sip and closed his eyes. Enjoying the breeze gently wafting through the open living room window and immersing himself in Copland's melodies, he forgot about his worries. Completely soothed, he let his mind wander back to the events of that morning—a victory of sorts for so many people and a good place to mentally be. Then his mind did as it always did now—turned without bidding to places he'd rather not go. He hadn't learned how to shut off the incessant voices in his head. He was working at it, he wanted to get control, but his heart needed more practice. *After all,* he thought, *I have been this way most of my life. A new heart isn't made overnight.*

Earlier that day. Tallahassee, Florida

The crowd had gathered early, and the pews had filled up an hour ahead of time. Now there was standing room only along the walls of the packed church. News cameras from the national networks were in place, poised to report what was about to happen.

Had anyone told him two years before that he would be occupying this place, in this building, in this city, he would have laughed them out of his office. His life was then the model of impropriety, convenience, manipulation, and diplomacy—an odd mixture, unless of course one considered that his entire adult life had been spent in Washington, D.C.

The human interest angle to the story was even more compelling than the medical miracle—the fact that three men had in common something so unique had captured the public's imagination.

He gazed at his wife, seated in the first pew. Maggie had saved him, and he adored her with a depth of feeling he would never have thought possible. She held their newborn up and whispered, "Daddy," pointing toward him. Mike grinned with pleasure, marveling at his good fortune and his new family. Maggie was seated with Claire Barlow, as well as with friends and members of their extended families. They had all come here to honor him in his new position, but also to hear the story that had recently so captivated the nation.

He stood, and the audience quieted, looking upon him with a kind of awe, such as they might have lavished on a person resurrected from the dead. In a way, that's what he was.

He held on to the lectern to steady himself and began:

"They say a man can't be two places at the same time. It is also said that no one knows another man's heart but that man himself and God . . ."

He had spoken for one and one-half hours, and yet the time spent in this cramped and poorly ventilated chapel had seemed but a moment. He had concluded, but the audience hardly moved. Even those who had been standing, lingered, willing him to say more. He nodded in understanding and added:

"A broken heart doesn't always show itself. Often it is masked by the drumbeat of a thousand other noises. The cacophony of daily voices, clamoring for their needs to be met, making demands, voicing anger; even periodic high moments of temporary splendor will cover the truth of a subtle death going on deep within the broken heart. Only a miracle could have saved me. That miracle was a new heart filled with love.

"Remember the words of your former pastor, Nicholas Caine: 'The heart is for giving and the brain is for getting.'

"God bless you all until we meet again."

1

M IKE STONE CRADLED THE TELEPHONE to his ear and leaned back in his swivel chair, feet propped up on the window ledge in his Washington, D.C. office.

"You'd be surprised how far modest donations to the Senator's campaign go, Pete." He gazed toward the Capitol Building, lost in thought on how fortunate he was to have found Maggie, to have her in his life.

"Hey, what I'm asking is modest in comparison to the good your company derives from this. Tax credits, contracts; you're practically being handed six years on a silver platter. Have we got a deal or don't we? We're friends, but I'm not emotional about this, okay?" he said. Mike Stone stopped talking and listened.

"Anyone who is somebody, politically speaking, will be there—state of Florida and beyond. Look, this feels right, doesn't it? I'm not putting the squeeze on you, am I?"

He motioned to his secretary, Liz, to run down the stairs to the office snack shop and grab him a cup of coffee. He also tapped an empty carton of Marlboro cigarettes. "Psst," he sounded with one hand over the phone handset. He held up the empty carton.

She frowned, rubbed her index fingers together indicating "bad boy," but relented.

"Pete, look . . . I believe you. You've always been supportive of the Senator and the Party. What I'm saying is I'm making you an offer you can't refuse. This may look like Joseph Caine's fourth-term bid for seat as senior senator from Florida, but think about who is announcing his run for the big house." He turned to see who was tapping on his open office door. He waved the man in, turned away from him, and frowned.

"Good. You've got it. And that means Senator Caine, chairman of the Appropriations Committee, becomes cabinet member Joseph Caine, or perhaps, and I wouldn't say this to just anyone, but Vice President Caine sounds pretty darned good too, doesn't it?"

He turned to the man now seated in front of him, nodded respectfully, and smiled. "I got him," he mouthed, using his hands to pantomime a fi an reeling in a big catch.

The man offered a slight nod and waited for the conversation to end.

Stone's secretary slid past the seated man, set a cup of coffee and an unopened carton of Marlboros on the desk. "Light one up for me," Stone mouthed silently. She opened the carton, took out a pack, and opened it. Stone reached for a cigarette and held it to his lips as she used his desktop lighter to ignite it. "Thanks," he mouthed.

"Loser," she quietly voiced in reply.

He winked, took a long drag, blew the smoke toward the window he now opened as a courtesy, and stood looking out over the city below.

"This is Michael Stone speaking, Pete. Have I ever let you down? Haven't I always delivered on my end of the political deals? Believe me there are ways around these new contribution rules . . ." He listened, smiled, and winked at the man seated in front of his desk, then took another long drag from his cigarette. *Man, he's unpleasant,* he thought, turning his back to the seated man.

"Good. I'll see you tomorrow at Eatzees. We'll seal the deal. You're on the inside—Senator Caine's Platinum Club! Congrats."

"Well?" the seated man asked.

"I'm delivering. That makes five on the 'Platinum' level. Two more and we're over the top on our goal for this quarter. The senator's re-election campaign fund is on track. Challenger Bob Dobson may have the right on his side but is being left in the dust as far as the money race goes . . . and to the victor of that race go the spoils."

"Good."

"That's all you can say, Mr. Lawton? Good?"

The man stood and extended his hand. An icy glare always greeted those he dealt with.

"You're not at war anymore, Lawton," Mike Stone said as he snubbed out the cigarette then extended his hand. "You'd look good in a smile," he offered in an attempt to find another dimension to the flatness of Senator Caine's chief political assistant. "The CIA sure knows how to make a man show he cares," he finally said as they shook hands.

"Those will be the death of you, boy," the older man said, gesturing toward the ashtray on the desk.

"Maybe, but I'm not like you, Ron. I actually enjoy life—enjoy politics. I don't carry a look on my face like my job is killing me." He lit another cigarette and took a long drag.

"That's where you need some fine-tuning, Stone. See, looks can kill, if you read 'em wrong. Then again, so can those," he said, pointing to Mike's cigarette. "I'll be calling you."

"I can't wait.'Bye," Mike replied in a polite but totally feigned voice, now eager to see the back side of the man exiting his personal space. "Whew," he sighed as he exhaled a lung full of smoke.

"New chief of staff for Senator Joseph Caine, Ron Lawton," he said under his breath as he blew the smoke more forcefully now.

Political strategist Mike Stone couldn't stand Lawton. In Stone's opinion, Lawton was entirely the wrong man for the job—someone who simply didn't fit the image Mike was trying to build for the persona of Joe Caine—affable, approachable, and above the fray.

"That man is not likable," Liz said as she entered to see if there was anything else her boss needed before she closed the office for the day. "He makes me want to put a sweater on when he walks into the room. It's summertime, and he just gave me the chills."

"If looks could kill, we'd be DOA for the first paramedics on the scene. Not good," Mike answered as he paced, lighting yet a third cigarette. "Not good at all," he mumbled. "I can't understand what the senator sees in that man. I've been working Senator Caine's campaigns for . . . how many years now, Liz?"

"You started in 1984. Reagan's second term. That's how I remember."

"Yeah! Now there was a politician! He almost made me quit my party. This guy," he spat, "I liked what I do before he showed up." He took another drag and blew a long, steady stream of smoke. "He makes me feel like my job is work or something. I don't fight well for men like that. I think he's got something on the senator."

"Huh? What's that?"

"Oh, nothing. It was nothing. Go ahead and close up. See you in the morning."

"You going to make that doctor's appointment I set up for you at nine?"

"Tomorrow morning? You set that up for 9:00 A.M.?"

"Physical, for the life insurance. Your fiancée will kill you," she gestured toward the cigarette, "if those don't. You agreed."

"Yeah. Right," he said as he crushed out his third cigarette in just under ten minutes. "Okay. I've got a few calls to make. See you after the appointment."

"'Night."

"Good night, Lizzy."

He sat, sipped at his cooled-off Starbucks coffee, and gazed out over the Washington Mall. He loved D.C. He loved the connections—the power here. It was real. This was the center of gravity to all that happened in the world, and he was making a difference.

He didn't need political office to feel it. He felt it by helping other men win their power. After all, they really understood who got them their elections won. He'd advised five senior congressmen, four senators, one vice president, and now he was on the cusp of helping this man to the White House. Just a few doors swinging in the right direction, the senator's natural charm, and wham, bam, they could slam the "big house" door on Pennsylvania Avenue behind them.

"The big house," he murmured to himself. He wasn't sure that the senator was really presidential stuff. But he had a pretty good grasp of issues and was tops in politicking, and that was what really mattered. *This new guy, Lawton, taking over for poor Johnson . . .* his mind wandered over the events of the past few months.

smoked three, four, five packs a day? Maybe. But he was killed in a freak accident at his home. Crazy. Former Marine tough guy, and he dies slipping on his garden steps and hitting his head on a decorative boulder he brought back from his last publicity trip with the senator to Iraq. The irony.

Enter Ron Lawton. Out-of-the-blue, and he grabs the top spot on Caine's staff. Something's wrong. Ex-CIA, military special ops as far back as Vietnam, staffer to some Fortune 500 big shot and now, suddenly, chief of staff for a contender in D.C. No "Mr. Nice Guy . . ." Plenty of those in Washington, but this one has danger written in every expression. Wonder if he had a Momma? Men like that couldn't have had a mother.

2

T HE RINGING OF HIS DESK PHONE brought him back to reality.

"Stone here."

He smiled broadly. "Oh! Hey, babe! Yeah, I'm done for the day . . . Meet at your Mom's?" he asked. "But . . ." he started to protest. "Just one hour?" he asked, biting his tongue. "Okay, I'll swing by my place, grab a shower, and meet you there. We'll make Momma happy. . . . You know I love her cooking," he added. "Of course I've quit. Have I ever let you down?"

He laughed. She made him feel like a schoolboy, and kept him in line too. No woman had ever done this to him.

"Maggie, you are turning me into an honest man. You know, my mom would have loved you. . . . You give me no choice. I'm practically without any vices left. No smoking, no hard liquor, and you won't even move in with me! You know how hard that is for a political consultant?" He listened, looked down at the ashtray, and laughed at what she had just added to the baggage he was carrying to the trash can with the label: *Poor character traits and nasty habits, dump here.*

"No one in Washington is going to know me when you get finished," he said. "I *am* religious," he protested in response to a quick comeback by Maggie. "You pray for me, don't you?" he joked. She answered. "Well, then, now I've got religion, too." He rolled his eyes and actually couldn't believe he had fallen this hard. "Part of me hates what you're doing to me, Maggie, but I love it too . . . too much to give you up. You ought to be a political consultant. We could work the right and left," he joked. "Oh! We can be the next Mary Matalin and James Carville—an arch conservative married to a died-in-the-wool liberal . . ."

"Oh, Jimmy's got religion. He needs it. How can you be married to a conservative without being religious?" he chuckled nervously. He listened a little more, held the pack of cigarettes in his hand, examining the evidence of a vice he was very reluctantly dispatching to the trash bin.

"James? You'd like him," he protested. "A lot of fun, until Mary tamed him. Just like you're doing to me. . . ." Maggie answered him. "I'm a baby . . . just forty-five and look what you're doing to me!" he accentuated with feigned exasperation. "Okay. See you in an hour. At your Mom's in Chevy Chase . . . Yes, I know how to get there. Love you!"

After looking at it longingly, he tossed the carton of cigarettes into the wastebasket. *It's a good thing the custodian will dump the trash tonight. I'd hate to be so crass as to dig these out of the garbage in the morning. Oh, well, the cancer sticks were getting in the way of my morning runs anyway.*

He swallowed the cold remains of the coffee cup and tossed it in the metal wastebasket along with the cigarettes, then grabbed his leather satchel and his car keys and turned to face the door. After switching off his office lights, he swung the office door open to the empty reception area where he stopped at Lizzy's desk and scribbled a quick note. Turning to head out, he came face-to-face with a man a clear six inches taller.

"You are on top of this, aren't you, Mike?" the man asked. It was not a friendly tone of voice.

"I don't like this, Lawton. Who do you think you are?" he spat back before he could calm himself.

"Hey, relax, Stone. I forgot this." He held a file up. "I am a loyal player. Aren't you?"

"My record is clear. I'm not so sure about yours."

"Don't know that I like your innuendo, but let's forget it. This is how I work. You do your job, and I'm your best friend. You don't do what you are paid to do as I see it, and you are out—gone, and I mean gone. Comprendé?"

"Hey, Lawton! I'm not some kid you can walk on, and the senator and I have a relationship that goes back twenty years."

"You think I don't know about you? That I don't know everything about you? Where you live, what you drive? Who your woman is? Who your women have been? What you like to eat? Where you get your clothes dry cleaned? I know you, I know Senator Caine, and I play hardball, Mikey. Life is too short for pussyfooting around with careless and weak individuals."

An expletive slipped spontaneously from Mike's lips, and Lawton suddenly lightened up.

"Let's be friends, shall we, Mike? You'll see that I'm the best friend a man can have . . . or . . ." he left the remark hanging and walked down the empty corridor to the elevator, then he turned. "You're eating at Maggie's or her mother's? Please give both my regards."

Mike stood glaring at the man's back. *You arrogant . . .* he swore. *Intimidation. I've got to get to Joe Caine and warn him about this guy.* He was very nearly trembling with rage, and a full minute passed before he could gather himself to follow Ron down the hall.

His desk phone rang just as he was locking the office outer door. He was tempted to let it go but then went back into the reception area, set his satchel on a chair next to Lizzy's desk, stepped back into his office, and picked the receiver up.

"Hello . . . hello?" he looked at the screen to see the caller's I.D. Number unavailable, it read. "Hello?"

Click.

*   *   *   *   *

He didn't have much time, but he wanted to get rid of the lingering odor of tobacco smoke that was in his hair, on his breath, and on his clothes. He had assured Maggie he had quit, and if he had any hope of enticing her into a romantic interlude, he would need to get to his house, take a shower, and change. It wasn't going to be easy, giving up his cigarettes, he knew that. The Nicorette chewing gum and those patches hadn't helped. Tomorrow he'd ask the M.D. for some kind of medication to help him quit.

He smiled, thinking about what he was willing to do for Maggie. No woman had ever done to him what she was doing. He'd met her at a party thrown by one of his few, and best, "non-political" friends, federal prosecutor Samuel K. Gibson, and from that moment Mike had been smitten by her beauty and charm.

Non-political . . . right, he thought as he opened the driver's side door to his Lexus sedan and tossed his brown satchel across to the passenger seat. He backed out carefully—the support columns in this underground parking garage had a nasty habit of jumping out and banging his slightly dented rear bumpers.

He punched his card into the exit gate and waited impatiently for the horizontal, metal arm to rise. His failure to wait in the past had already resulted in one broken windshield and a couple of nasty scrapes on the top of his car, to say nothing of the disdain of the people who maintained the garage.

Mike Stone should have been content. He enjoyed his work and loved the new woman in his life. He'd reached a point in his career where he was at the summit of his political powers. After a lifetime of politicking, he'd reached the top of Mt. Everest. If Senator Caine didn't make it to the White House, someone he'd coached eventually would, and he'd tap into that, do a good job, and by fifty-five be on the speaking circuit for ten grand a pop a couple times a month. He'd worked too hard for that, and he wasn't about to let anything or anybody stand in his way.

And Maggie Sanders? That was a pleasant thought. Thirty-six years old, smart, a little sassy, and way beyond what he deserved, she was a picture-perfect partner for the savvy insider to the powerful and elite. *It doesn't hurt that I love her either,* he thought.

The irony was she was a cardio-vascular specialist, a surgeon, one of the rising stars in her profession. She had even assisted dozens of heart transplants. Inscrutable on the surface, Maggie had a compassion few could see. Her clinical professional persona didn't reveal it at work, but at home, at play, she had heart. And, if there ever was a woman fitting of the praise "pure in heart," Maggie was the one.

I adore her. I flat-out adore her. And she's chosen me? The thought continued to amaze him because he knew he didn't have her fooled. Maggie wasn't one of those you could "pitch and close the deal," especially given his nicotine-stained character. In fact, there was so little of that to work with in her, he wondered if he wasn't simply some sort of challenge for the woman who had stolen his rotten heart.

Maggie is simply the epitome of a total woman, he happily thought as he drove along, breaking the posted speed limit. Devoid of compromise, and lacking discernable egomania—she was unlike any beautiful woman he had ever known. *And she is beautiful,* he thought as his heart skipped a beat inside his chest. She stirred him, and he was now more grateful than ever to just be alive.

Even Joseph Caine, senior senator from Florida, had taken a liking to her. At last week's New Year's Ball, he had danced not once but twice with Maggie, making Mike just a bit uncomfortable. It was no secret Senator Caine was a womanizer. For the sake of political schmoozing, Mike let it go. Besides, Maggie wasn't the type to be fooled by a slick operator like Joseph Caine.

Returning from the dance floor after her second dance with the senator, Maggie confided to Mike, "He's dreaming if he thinks I'd ever fall for his nonstop line of bull . . ." She didn't actually add the expletive to her declaration, but there was no mistaking her disdain for the smooth-talking politician.

"I thought you were patriotic, Maggie. I'm shocked," Mike had laughed as he held her in his arms before saying goodnight.

Maggie, impeccably honest, and Mike Stone, totally ready to feign, fake, falsify, or fool in order to do his political best, were the ideal couple, he reasoned silently. *And in time, if she does cure me of my bad behaviors, causing me to lose my clientele, I can make some good money doing what all cured politicos do—write a "tell-all" book about their clients. Maggie, the heart doctor,* he thought with a smile.

Mike Stone wasn't concerned about keeping a man like Joseph Caine in line. Mike had a few secrets that could destroy Joseph Caine, and a dozen other men on the Hill, if he wanted to. He kept them safely stored in files he alone possessed—files hidden so deeply that no one, outside of an interrogator the stature of a brainwasher from the classic John Frankenheimer flick *The Manchurian Candidate,* could ever get to them.

Of all the people he knew, Maggie was the only person he thoroughly trusted. He had come to believe she was someone he could let his fine-tuned mental guard down with. He had always thought he was good at keeping the lonely side of himself hidden. And if anyone needed a heart surgeon, he realized it was old Mike Stone.

Self-serving, ladder-climbing, back-scratching to get what he wanted, Mike only stopped short of back-stabbing.

Well, okay, back-nicking, maybe, he thought as his twenty-year career passed before him. He crossed the Roosevelt Bridge, turned onto the George Washington Expressway, and headed for his town house in Northern Virginia. Deep in reverie, all he had to show for the past twenty years were connections; one failed and short-lived marriage; too many nights passed out on friends' sofas; or too many mornings waking up in places he was embarrassed to think about. He certainly didn't want Maggie to find out about any of it.

I wonder how much Lawton knows. The thought caused him to wince. Not that he couldn't talk his way out of anything Lawton might reveal about him, but he just wanted a new start . . . with Maggie.

Momma would be proud, he thought as he considered his rise from backwater hick to state of Florida political insider in the state capital of Tallahassee and now Washington, D.C. *'Cept for those certain other things boys don't talk about, Momma would be proud,* he reasoned.

He often found himself thinking more about her now. Maybe it was the guilt. She hadn't been able to care for herself, didn't even recognize him anymore. *I had to put her into the care center. It was a good place, best in Tallahassee. Expensive, too,* he reminded himself, to assuage the guilty feelings eating at him. *She knew I loved her. I'm sure she did.* She had died six months after he had moved her into the care center. He fought the emotions that would well inside as he wondered if it were her congenital heart condition or his selfishness that had caused her sudden decline and death.

No time for that now, he reminded himself as he came to at the Tysons Corner exit, suddenly realizing he had been driving with his mind totally gone, far from these Northern Virginia streets and suburbs. He wondered if he always did that—if he simply put the car on autopilot as his mind raced far beyond on issues, people, campaigns, and now love.

Mike had never desired a woman's respect like this before. He had a mountain to climb to even get close to her character. *But she said she loves me.* The thought made him feel like a kid again.

Nice to be liked. Nice to feel loved. And that is worth the climb, he silently posed as he made four right turns, three left, and then drove straight into his town-home drive at The Gardens.

Grabbing the car keys, he allowed his mind to stay on her. He hurried through the door and tossed his keys and cell phone onto the sofa as he headed to the shower. He'd be twenty minutes tops and out the door again to the D.C. Beltway and on to the exclusive neighborhood of Chevy Chase across the Potomac in Maryland.

Out of the hot, soothing shower, he quickly shaved, flossed, brushed, gargled with mouth rinse, and splashed on some cologne, hoping he had successfully killed any trace of cigarettes. It had been two weeks since he had assured Maggie he had given them up.

"You may be wicked, Mike Stone," he said to the man in the mirror, "but you are one good-looking devil!"

*   *   *   *   *

He was halfway to elite suburban Chevy Chase, Maryland, when he realized he needed his future mother-in law's address. He had been there twice, but Maggie had always navigated. Now he couldn't remember if he was supposed to take the first or second Chevy Chase exit. It was either before or after the stunning spires of the Mormons' religious temple that towered above the forest green where the Beltway curved to the northeast.

He reached into his briefcase and moved his hand past the Senator Caine Contributions file to the inside pocket where he kept his small address book and suddenly realized, *No file!* This was the last file he had kept from his personal storage locker.

Panicked, his mind raced to mentally retrace where he had it last. He had just stepped out of his office into the foyer, picked it off Lizzy's desk, and then put it into his briefcase. He went to flip the light off and turned to see Lawton standing there. Ran into him in fact, in an unpleasant "face to face."

I had my little fit over him nosing around, then Lawton left, and then I went back into my office to answer the phone.

Lawton held a file in his hand, but that was the one I'd prepared and left for him with Lizzy. She must have left it in the wall "Outgoing Box" by the door. He saw it, reached in, and then played his mental game with me.

But the contributor's file? I know I put it in my briefcase, he reminded himself. *Better go back to the office.*

He punched a number into his car-cradled cell phone and soon Maggie answered.

"Maggie, honey, I'm sorry I'm running late."

"So what's new? That's why I told you six so you'd be here by seven o'clock."

"I don't deserve you."

"Just remember that, buster. What's going on?"

"Oh, a file. I'm missing a file, and halfway to your Mom's I realized it. It's pretty confidential, and if the wrong person were to get hold of it, it could hurt Senator Caine."

"Well we wouldn't want the future president of the United States to look bad. He doesn't have anything to hide, does he?" she allowed with a trace of sarcasm.

"All politicians have things to hide, Maggie. It's just part of the game. Listen, I have to go back to my office. I promise I'll get there before seven." He coughed as he finished.

He'd been coughing more and more as he tried to quit smoking. He was sure all the smoke-free air he was breathing was going to do him in.

"You're not cheating on me are you?"

"Another woman? You kidding?" He laughed between hacks. "Sorry, honey, but it's all the pure air. Hard on the lungs," he wheezed.

"You'd better not be smoking, Mike."

"Cross my heart and hope to die."

"Well, you'll need to cross your heart if you don't give up tobacco. By the way, Mom is cooking her favorite rhubarb pie, and the chicken oriental is out of this world. All good for the heart. So don't take long. It's better when it's fresh and still warm."

"Love you," he said. *I hate rhubarb pie,* he mouthed silently.

He ended the call and focused on the file. He was sure he had placed it in his briefcase.

Did I set it down in the foyer when I went in to take the call? I left the car unlocked in the driveway. Could have sworn I took the briefcase inside.

He thought back to the drive from his office to his home and remembered watching headlights in his rear-view mirror, which seemed to have been following too close. The driver behind him had driven a little erratically, swerving into the other lane and threatening to pass before pulling back in behind him as Mike made his way across the river, onto the expressway, and then through the streets to Tysons Corner. But his mind had been so far away on other thoughts, on other things that he had brushed it off . . .

That lousy, good-for-nothing . . .

3

Ron Lawton lived for the game—the intrigue and power over others. He had always found life a bit boring after the military and then ten years at the CIA. Thirty-five years of carrying guns in the service of flag and country had become a way of life. It had been the only life he had ever known. He'd abandoned his hometown, family connections, and previous friends years before—in fact he was sure they thought he was dead. But that was another story.

He had found he liked guns as a young soldier in the waning years of America's involvement in Vietnam. He also found he didn't mind the death and carnage of frontline combat. *After all, killing is the legitimate business of war,* he reasoned. The better he became at soldiering, the more he wanted to be near "the action."

He trained with every weapon in the military arsenal. He was expert in all of them. After 'Nam he worked his way up the ranks, into Special Ops, and retired after "twenty-five" with the rank of major. The CIA was looking for his kind of talent, along with a man who was willing to forego family ties and had no desire to settle down. Men like that were expendable but also necessary for easy changes of identities. Over the last ten years, he'd been known by a half-dozen aliases, and "Ron Lawton" was merely his latest.

Guns . . . they made him feel safe. In fact, he felt everyone should own one or two. He didn't trust people who didn't know how to use guns; or worse, *when* to use them. As a result, his circle of friends was small, and he liked it that way.

This new job, working for Senator Joseph Caine, was a hoot. He was playing against minor leaguers; people who could be knocked off with a spit wad, let alone a gun. *Mike Stone is so stupid he didn't even realize he was being tailed. The lousy jerk! A lot of good that man can do me to get this guy Caine into real power.*

And real power was in an office where "Executive Orders" could be written; the president's Oval Office, at 1600 Pennsylvania Ave.

In the hands of the right man, a new country could be forged with Congress barely paying attention, he thought. *Laws created at the president's whim with the stroke of a pen. Now that is power,* he reflected as he retraced the streets he had driven while following the bumbling Michael Stone.

The *Fortune 500* company Digiwatch, Inc. was the upcoming darling of Wall Street. Digiwatch was Lawton's true employer, and the company had a lot at stake—the entire communications industry as it was known, in fact. New digital tracking technology that set off codes in microchips allowed the tracking of virtually any document, including newly printed books, all packaging, even postage stamps, and this meant all companies using Digiwatch technology could offer the American people an unparalleled sense of safety.

It will revolutionize security and that is something this country needs more of, he silently mused. *Especially now, with a century-long war on terror ahead of us.*

Ron Lawton saw himself as a patriot and soldier—anything was justified for the flag and the cause. Since first entering the military he'd been paid to kill, spy, sabotage, derail, injure, and defame, but always at some paltry, government GS pay scale. He was tired of offering the "guts" and letting the people with real power have all the "glory." It was time now to make some *real* money.

It's my turn, he reassured himself. So he studied the upcoming politicians, their views, their backgrounds, and determined Joe Caine, along with one other former U.S. senator and ex-governor by the name of Jackson Lyon, had the best chance over the next eight years of making a successful run to the White House.

Senator Caine looked the part. Maybe he didn't know the difference between a microchip and a potato chip, but he was smooth, he had natural charm, and he could be taught technology.

The rest of Lawton's rise to the top of the political pyramid was easy, and to Ron Lawton, fun. Blackmail was his professional forte. It didn't take him long to discover something on both Senator Caine and the other man of power within the American Alliance Party, Jack Lyon, the kind of dirt that was so devastating that either man—and especially his new boss Senator Caine—would do anything to keep it covered up.

Ron Lawton knew that a politician's chief of staff did all the hiring, firing, and otherwise running of the man's life. He was determined that Caine become president; or at least vice president on the independent ticket.

Ron Lawton also knew how to eliminate the competition. Mr. Johnson, Caine's late chief of staff, was one who had needed elimination. Setting up the "accident" had been a no-brainer. The irony of it all especially appealed to Lawton. *How ironic,* he thought, *"Iraq" even sounds like "a rock." The dumb cluck.* Remembering, he smiled as he made his way through the busy streets of Georgetown where he had a dinner engagement.

While running Digiwatch's security and external intelligence department, he had been accused of running people into the ground at the company's Philadelphia headquarters. Ron had been the political and technology/intelligence consultant to the CEO and took a special interest in the activities of Bob Thornton, the then vice president of Digiwatch International's technical sales.

Bob Thornton had said the magic words that made him disappear—permanently—when during a discussion of the possibility of granting technology sharing licenses to a German company, Thornton had opposed Lawton's decision to deny the Hamburg-based company's request. Lawton was no Boy Scout, but he was loyal to the flag. He had his limits and standards, and there were some lines even he wouldn't cross, national security being one. He had deemed the licensing agreement to put national security at risk, and when Thornton had responded to Lawton's declaration that he was "pulling the German license" with "Over my dead body," well, Thornton had simply gotten what he asked for.

Poor Bob, Lawton said to himself as he pulled into the parking lot of the Marriott on 22nd and M and went into Lu Lu's Mardi Gras Club.

*   *   *   *   *

Maggie Sanders had never wanted to fall for a political type. In her opinion, such men were so consumed by the race, the game, and the struggle to achieve or maintain power that they had no time for a caring relationship away from the political arena. She was revolted by it all.

Her father had died from a massive heart attack while working as a well-paid lobbyist for a powerful pharmaceutical consortium. She blamed his premature death in part on the pressure the pharmaceutical companies had put on him, and she hated them for it. In his passing, she had also found her life's calling: the pursuit of a way to help people live longer. She had agonized, watching her father struggle to live with a bad heart. She would have done anything to make it a healthy heart, but she had been powerless.

That frustration had led her into the study of medicine and the spectacular career she was now enjoying as a successful and respected cardio-vascular specialist.

Maggie's father had been a political hack from his college days. He'd been a congressional aide, had worked in local politics, had risen to be a member of a senator's staff, and finally parlayed his Washington, D.C. connections into the very lucrative job as a lobbyist. But she knew what it had cost him in terms of his health and hadn't wanted to marry a man with that kind of political bug; something she viewed as a viral obsession that ate a person from the inside out. Politicos smoked too much, drank too much, and had too few scruples.

Her aversion to politics had driven her away from the nation's capital. She opted to go to school out West and had graduated at the top of her class at Arizona State before going on to Harvard Med School, where she also distinguished herself, earning a prestigious fellowship at Harvard Medical.

All through the years she had tried to make herself attractive and to find a man who interested her. Desperate to marry, she had been engaged twice, only to realize that she wasn't in love with either of the men, but only in love with love.

Mike Stone had taken her totally by surprise. By then she had given up on finding a husband. She wasn't even looking. If it was ever to work out, she figured love would have to find her. And when it had, she was ready to surrender. Immediately smitten by Mike Stone, she decided it didn't matter what he *did;* but it did matter to her what he *was.* With enough finesse and maneuvering she figured she could work the lure of politics out of his system and get him into a sane line of work.

Maggie and her mother stood at the cutting table in the kitchen, putting the finishing touches on dinner.

"When that boy of yours gets here, I am going to have a word with him, Mag."

"Mom . . . you can say anything you like to Mike. He's political. Words roll off him like water off a duck's back."

"Well, I'm still going to set him straight on a few things. When your father and I got married in 1965, I expected some tough years of school, and we had those. Then I got caught up in all the excitement of the bright lights, parties, rallies, the political causes, and all the charming people."

"Mom? I don't need this—"

"Listen, honey, just one more time. I want you to find love, real love. Not what I settled for."

"You didn't love Dad?"

"Oh, I loved him. I was excited every time that charmer walked through the door. He had a magnetic personality and an aura of strength. I won't lie to you that I didn't feel love. But love can erode if the career rather than the warmth of each other's arms becomes the *raison d'etre*. When nurturing the marriage takes second place to career and ambition, all sorts of things can go wrong. Love is what ends up suffering."

"Mom," Maggie interjected. "I have a handle on this man."

Her mother shook her head. "He reminds me of your father," she answered. "That man loved politics more than he loved me, and you'd better be cautious, honey."

"Mom!"

"I've been at peace since marrying a man with a real career. Bud has always been—"

"Mom! Bud this! Bud that! I just want a quiet dinner and want you to get to know him better. We aren't going to convert him from an entire life, everything he has ever known, overnight!"

"I'll bite my tongue for as long as I can. Bud should be along in a few minutes. I sent him out to the store. He's a good man. I wish you'd give him a chance, Maggie."

"Mom, it's not like I know him and am ever around here long enough to create a relationship. I'm a doctor! I have schedules, and I'm thirty-six! He didn't enter your life until I was already gone from home. I'm happy for you; I really am. But please, Mom . . ." she turned away to hide the moisture that was stinging her eyes.

"Oh, Maggie. I'm sorry. I don't want to upset you," she said tenderly as she reached from behind to rest her hands on her daughter's shoulders. Maggie pulled away to the guest bath and rinsed her eyes.

She wasn't sure her mother wasn't right. Mike was transparent. But in that transparency she thought she saw a heart worth loving and a man worth living with. She knew her mother would be crying by now, feeling sorry once again that she had spoken out so strongly. Maggie knew her mother meant well, and she tried to put on a smile as she came back into the kitchen.

"Mom . . . you were saying?"

Maggie's mother turned to her with reddened eyes. "I'm so proud of you, Mag. I just don't want you hurt. And, honey, please . . . I did love your father. I'm sorry."

"Okay, Mom. Let's just forget it."

"I just want Mike to understand that you've been through this once, as a child, and I don't want my daughter to have to go through it as a wife."

"I know, Mom."

"Okay, then?"

"Yeah. Okay."

*   *   *   *   *

Mike Stone was livid. He had driven through a pouring rain back to his office. A thorough search of his desk, the wastebaskets, Liz's desk, and the floors had revealed nothing. A similar, frantic search of his home turned up nothing as well. By now he was convinced Lawton had somehow sneaked the file from him while his back was turned. Perhaps the car that tailed too close had been a set-up to snatch it away while he was inside showering. Or perhaps it had been taken at the office. He'd watch where Lawton placed his hands from now on.

The more he thought about it, the more he realized how dangerous this man was.

He knew he wasn't dealing with an average control freak. Lawton was an operator. He knew his spook work and enjoyed getting to people. He'd have to do a little research on Lawton, see where it led him. Hopefully he could find some dirty laundry and then expose him to Joe Caine before Lawton had the senator up to his eyeballs in compromise.

"Fine. He's proved his point. He can get files, confidential files, away from me. I'm going to chill and see Maggie. I'll deal with this tomorrow."

Do I always talk aloud to myself? he thought as he closed the front door to his house behind him and headed back to the car. *I've been living alone too long. I'd better start watching that too. He's probably bugged my office, car, and who knows what else?*

He backed out of the driveway, checked around to see if he were being watched, and then headed toward his dinner date in Chevy Chase, Maryland. *He's not going to get rid of me this easy. I've played this game too long. He's not the only one who has a few dirty tricks in his bag.*

*   *   *   *   *

"Hello, Senator." Lawton said, standing up to greet Caine. "Thanks for meeting me here at one of my favorite hangouts. I've got us a special table in the back."

With Lawton leading, they made their way through the bar to a booth in the back of the dimly lit restaurant and sat down.

Senator Caine was dressed casually. He'd come alone—no special protection or aides. He was asked by Ron Lawton to try this way of meeting outside the office. No big scenes. Inconspicuous meetings. No press, no publicity. Lawton had told him he'd soon explain why.

Joe Caine wasn't sure he liked it. He was used to the limelight. He attracted attention on purpose. To have his face and name on the front page and in the headlines as often as he could was the measure of his success. A publicity hound, maybe, but men won elections that way.

"Okay, Ron, what's this all about? I had to break away from an office softball tournament, and the press was there. Why couldn't we meet later, at the office?"

"Because this place is clean and the matter urgent," Lawton said quietly.

"What in the Sam Hill do you mean, *clean?* My office is clean." He looked around him in an attempt to point out the mess people left at their tables.

"Not that kind of clean, Senator. This kind of clean." He scribbled a note on a pad of paper. "Bugs. Wiretapping."

"Nonsense," the senator bellowed.

"Please, Senator. Hold it down. People. You know . . ." Lawton glanced at the nearby diners.

"Precisely," Caine whispered across the table with a controlled hostility. "That is why I always use my office for confidential interviews."

"Like this one?" Lawton pulled out a tape player and turned it on.

Even with the volume turned low, Senator Caine immediately recognized a conversation he'd had with a lady friend the other day.

"Put that away! Where did you get that?" he demanded.

"Senator, you need to be more careful. You think you are the only one who knows your mind and heart about the White House?"

"How? Who? It's against the law!"

"Oh, come on, Senator. Against the law?" Lawton said sarcastically. "Since when are you not above the law? Above bending it a bit?"

"You are treading on thin ice, Lawton."

"Senator. In all the years Sherman Johnson worked for you, did he ever once warn you about this kind of spying going on against you? Did he?"

The senator watched the man across from him with a furtive glare. He wasn't sure what Lawton might have on him now. How far back had he dug? What did he really know? " was utterly loyal, trustworthy, and impeccable in his discretion."

"You mean he looked the other way?"

"I mean . . ." the senator caught a a cuss word leaving his mouth and realized he was losing control. He calmed himself, took a deep breath, and smiled. "What else you got, Ron?"

Lawton reached into his satchel and pulled out a file. He placed it on the table before the senator.

"What is that?" Caine asked.

"A log of contributions to your campaign. Know where I got it?"

"From Mike Stone, I suppose. So what?"

"How confidential would you consider this, Senator?"

"Very."

"This is the kind of information that if the press were to get hold of it could upset those on the list. It could scare off potential donors, maybe even sink your bid for reelection to the Senate, and later the White House."

Caine sat poker-faced, not allowing his expression to reveal what he was thinking.

"Senator. I got this from Mike Stone. I got it from him while he wasn't watching. The man is inept. I not only got it from him once, but twice within one hour!"

"Am I supposed to be impressed?"

"Senator, I called the meeting this time. You are in danger of not only some very inept people in your campaign operations, but of people who want to destroy you."

"And you are just the man to save me?"

"I specialize in 'fixing' things. It's what I did for the military, for the CIA, and for your biggest contributor, Digiwatch. I am your best ally and friend."

"I'll bet you are, Mr. Lawton. So what's the agenda for this meeting?"

"Food. Got to fuel our operations. Let's eat, lighten the mood a bit, and then talk."

"You come very close to offending me, Mr. Lawton."

"Joe, please call me Ron. I'd rather you show the personable side. Voter's love that." He smiled.

"Okay Ron, or Ronnie? You like Ronnie? Is that personable enough?"

Lawton laughed but didn't answer because the waitress had appeared. He retrieved the file and put it back into his satchel. She took their orders and disappeared into the back.

"I just want to do what you want me to, and do it right. I guess I'm a very careful man. I apologize for being as forward as I was. I probably will never live up to Sherm Johnson in your eyes, but I will protect you, Joe—from others and from yourself. You can count on it."

4

MOM, HE'S HERE. Now, Mom; remember, light banter. Light, as in nothing about his work, my work, or your expectations. Hobbies, television shows, movies, those sorts of things are legit. You know, neutral."

"I wasn't born yesterday. Oh, good, here comes Bud, too. Hi, honey." She gave her husband a peck on the cheek as he stepped into the kitchen from the garage and set the groceries on the counter.

"Francisco's," he said, smiling as he pulled a bottle the from the bag. "The best. Alcohol-free, but what the heck. Let me chill it. You go ahead. I'll be right in."

"Isn't he sweet?"

The doorbell rang again.

"Yes, Mom. I'm very happy for you," Maggie replied, walking toward the front door. "Remember . . ." she mouthed back toward her mother.

"Well, hell-Oh! What happened to you?" Maggie asked as she looked Mike up and down.

"What? Something wrong?"

"You look like you've been in a bar fight. Outside of that, nothing. Well, come in, don't stand out in the rain."

"Oh, yeah, well, I had this little problem and . . ."

"That file?"

"Yeah. Looked everywhere. All over the office, outside of the office, in my yard at home, in my town home, in the street. I didn't even pay attention to the rain. I guess I look like a drowned rat."

"You need some downtime. Maybe the men's room," she hinted. She swiped her hair to signal him that maybe he should have a look.

"Oh, yeah. Sure. This way? Oh, hi, Mrs. Zerkel. Nice to see you again."

"Hello, Michael. Glad you could make it."

"Right. Thanks."

Maggie gestured toward the bathroom. "It's Terkel," she whispered to him.

She watched him go, then turned to see the icy glare of her mother. "Mom, don't start."

"I don't have to. Kind of says it all, doesn't it? I think I'll help Bud chill the wine."

"Ugh," Maggie breathed. She waited for Mike to come out of the bathroom. She could hear the blow-dryer now. *A couple more of these obligatory, get-acquainted family dinners, and Mike and I will be off the hook.*

*   *   *   *   *

They'd finished eating. During dinner Lawton tried to lighten the mood a bit by regaling the senator with stories from war, activities of the CIA that he knew the senator had no inkling of.

"I suppose when a man becomes the president there are many things he'll learn about the secret goings on of his government. I hope you don't mind me sharing some of these stories with you."

"Not at all," Joe Caine lied.

"Senator, I want to earn your trust. The only way I know how is by employing my skills and knowledge. A man of your public stature deserves the utmost protection and loyalty from those who are his subordinates."

"Now you are starting to make sense, but it concerns me that you could be as full of hot air, as—"

"Your other advisors? A politician? Yourself, if I dare make that leap?"

"You aren't afraid of me are you, Ron?"

"No, I am not."

"Most people feel intimated by me. I use that to my advantage. Why should I trust a man who can't be controlled?"

"Because of the information I have. You know I have studied your life, Senator. I have investigated it thoroughly."

"That gives me great comfort," he replied with sarcasm.

"I don't work with or for people who don't have some sort of dirty laundry. After all a person wouldn't be human without a few missteps in his life. Wouldn't you agree?"

Senator Joseph Caine was silent. He watched Lawton's eyes. In the eyes you see the soul. He had learned that from his brother, Nicholas. It was one of the few pieces of advice and counsel he had listened to from his older brother, a pastor and his polar opposite.

Now he viewed with suspicion his new chief of staff replacement for Sherm Johnson. Lawton had revealed his knowledge of a bit of dirt Caine had thought he had swept under the rug decades before. This former CIA operative apparently knew some dirty tricks and rules of play that even he, a major player in the Senate, wasn't familiar with. What else did he know about Caine that might be embarrassing?

"Anyway, you have nothing to fear from me," Lawton summed up. "I'm a team player, and you are the captain," Lawton assured him. "Your past, your present, and future are safe with me."

"Fine. Are we finished? Because if we are, I need to head back to my office to take care of some important, unfinished business. Tomorrow's a pretty busy day for me; co-chairing the Intelligence Committee," Caine lied. He was actually on his way to pitch in a softball game—a night game on the Mall near the Washington Monument.

Caine's true passion was baseball and bringing another Major League Baseball franchise back to D.C. Staying "in the game" was one way he reminded himself of his love for the sport and promoted his developing image as a man of the "middle-class," one connected to a life above politics.

"Just one final request, Senator. As we speak, Mike Stone is at his future mother-in-law's house having dinner. But right about now, he is probably having a mild heart attack."

Joseph Caine gaped at Lawton, trying to gauge whether he was telling the truth or speaking metaphorically.

"You are asking, 'How does Lawton know'?"

"Go on."

He held up the file. "I can deliver this in person or we can invite Mike down here to meet with us. If he sees both of us together on the issue of sloppy security for your confidential files maybe we can make a new man out of him."

"Fine. Call him."

"Oh, one other thing, Senator. Mike Stone has other very confidential files that combined with Jackson Lyon's could make your life a bit messy. I'm on to it, but you might want to grease the skids for me a bit."

Caine acknowledged the request. He'd have a talk with Mike Stone about the illegal contributions—the names, numbers, sources. The files could be a major embarrassment, not to mention a legal liability; even possibly criminal with the new statutes in place regarding "soft money" donations.

Both he and Jackson Lyon—his foremost competition for the American Alliance Party nomination for president—wanted Mike Stone to either fully secure those files or give them up entirely where they could keep them safe. *If anything should happen to Mike Stone— heaven forbid—and those files end up floating around, it could be a disaster for all of us,* Caine mused.

Lawton called Mike Stone's cell phone.

"Stone here."

"Mike, the Senator and I are having dinner in Georgetown at Lu Lu's Mardi Gras Club. You know the place?"

"Yes," he answered coldly.

"We need to talk. Can I expect you in thirty minutes?"

"No."

"Great," Lawton replied, knowing the senator would be impressed.

"I said, NO!" Mike emphasized. It had turned into a battle of wills.

"So we'll see you here in thirty minutes?"

"NO!" he replied and hung up.

Maggie's mother was burning a hole through Mike as she dealt with age-old anger about this sort of thing—politics taking precedence over family.

"He'll be right down," Lawton assured the senator. "Shall we order some wine, relax while we wait? I have a few other matters that we can clear up."

Senator Caine raised his hand and snapped his fingers to get the waitress's attention. "Your best wine, three glasses, chilled please."

Lawton knew he had built credibility now. If Mike Stone didn't show up, then the campaign clown would offend the senator. If he did show up, it would show Lawton was a strong leader.

Either way, Ron Lawton would win.

5

Senator, Mike Stone is here to see you." She glanced through the office door and saw Ron Lawton standing in the senator's office. "Thank you," she offered quietly. "I like surprises."

Lawton grinned. He still had the touch with women.

And he had taken quickly to Beth Benoit, Senator Caine's personal assistant. She was a statuesque, thirty-something, blonde woman, who exuded a certain sensuality that Lawton had immediately picked up on.

"Glad you liked it. See you tonight," he mouthed.

Caine noticed the exchange but said nothing. "Very good, Beth. Give us just a moment, then send him in." Senator Caine nodded in the direction of Ron Lawton, who moved quickly into the private study adjacent to the Senator's desk. Before Caine closed the door on him, the senator quietly said, "No office dalliance, *s'il vous plaît,* Mr. Lawton. You are new, but Beth is not, and I need to keep her more than I do you."

"Noted," Lawton replied as he took his place.

"Senator," Mike Stone offered with a courteous nod as he entered the spacious senatorial office.

Senator Caine continued busy at his desk. "I thought you were

36

coming to meet me at Lu Lu's Mardi Gras Club last Friday night. I waited an hour after Ron Lawton placed a call to you."

"With all due respect, sir, you were misinformed."

"You did not tell Lawton you would be down to Georgetown in thirty minutes? That you were breaking away from your private engagement to meet me?" Caine didn't look up. "I gave up a softball tournament and good publicity too," he said, nodding to the ball and bat bag he kept open to view in the corner of his office.

Silence was Mike's answer. *Smells like, feels like a setup,* he thought.

"I see. So Ron is lying. Lawton is a liar?" He looked directly at Mike now.

Mike again didn't answer but did raise an eyebrow with a look that said: What's this really about, Senator?

Senator Caine motioned for Mike to come close enough to his desk to receive the file he held outstretched.

"I'm glad to get this back and to know it was in safe hands."

"Indeed," Senator Joseph Caine answered. "Mike," he said, as he stood and walked around to the front of the desk. "I'm troubled. How long have we worked together?" Joe Caine went to the ball bag and took out his favorite Louisville Slugger and held it in his hands, enjoying the feel of the smooth, lacquered wood.

"Twenty years."

"In that twenty years you have served me well."

"Thank you."

"But lately this, along with other indiscretions, have caused me some concern about how well you are handling my private affairs associated with my campaign."

"Lawton is pitting you against me. I don't need his bull! You can come out now, Ron," he added.

Lawton entered the room. "Good morning, Mike."

A glare from Mike was all he got for an answer.

The senator leaned against the front of his desk as Ron Lawton settled onto the sofa, positioning Mike between the two men.

Mike squared himself in front of the senator, jaw clenched, meeting his gaze directly. "To the point, Joe," Mike demanded.

Senator Caine looked to Lawton now.

"You're sloppy, Stone. Can't be sloppy when a man is headed where Joseph Caine is headed," Lawton said.

"And you're here to straighten me out," Mike said, without turning to face him.

Lawton offered a slight nod but said nothing.

Mike waved the file of contributors in the air. "So you stole this from me, and I'm supposed to be impressed?" Mike continued to stare at the senator, who was now looking away, out the office window.

"Something like that. Except I waved it in your face, and while you looked away made sure it was back in your possession and then while you were in your house getting ready for your dinner date with your sweetheart, I lifted it out of the satchel you left in your unlocked car that I tailed so closely a blind man could have spotted me."

Mike rolled his eyes.

"Well, Mike?" Caine asked, turning back to look at Stone.

"So the spook from the Agency got me. So I can't trust Lawton. So you feel I failed a test. So where now?"

"Oh, I can be trusted," Lawton sneered. "This isn't about me, Stone. It's about weakness. It's about carelessness. Weak and careless people don't survive in this present environment. We're playing hardball here. For keeps," Lawton answered.

"I've heard enough. Senator, good day," Mike said and turned to exit the office.

Ron Lawton beat him to the door. "I know you aren't trying to hurt the senator, Mike," Lawton offered in a patronizing tone. "But I am sworn to protect him. We simply can't risk working with sloppy people. My feeling is you get three strikes and you're out. I gave you three swings at bat the other night, and guess what?"

Mike felt an uncontrollable anger rising and gave Lawton a get-away-from-the-door look. Lawton returned the look with a toss of his head, answering the challenge with his own make-me glare.

"Mike! Listen! This is for your own good. Humble yourself, man!" the senator growled.

Humble myself! From the mouth of Saint Caine himself, Mike fumed. He glanced at his wristwatch. "Senator, I have an appointment in exactly thirty minutes on the other side of town to pick up a check for your campaign. Would you like to do it? I think you should, because I just quit."

He moved again toward the door, but Lawton stepped in front of him, blocking the way. "Don't attempt to push me around, Stone. You don't know who you are messing with," Lawton said in a low, menacing voice.

"Yeah, I think I do, Lawton. You are a manipulative, backstabbing scum who will run over anyone to get where you are going. This man is dangerous, Senator!" he declared with firm voice. "I would watch my backside if I were you," he said as he and Lawton continued to face each other, eyeball to eyeball. "I know you, Lawton. You aren't fooling me."

Mike spoke to Caine while holding Lawton's gaze, "Senator, you can call me at my office. I will box up all your documents and have them ready for Gestapo Lawton here to pick up. Good day."

Ron Lawton smiled, opened the door for him, and stepped aside.

After Mike left the office, there was a moment of silence during which Senator Caine returned to his desk. He sat down and said, "I wish you had let me handle it, Lawton."

"Senator, Stone is a loser, someone you can't afford to have around. All business relationships end at some point. And I am just the man you need. Senator Caine, you are in the Majors and batting a thousand. I intend to see you to the Oval Office," Lawton said.

Senator Caine looked up from his desk and nodded to the man standing before him. He wondered if Mike Stone wasn't right, characterizing Lawton as a Gestapo man. Gestapo was the secret murdering arm of the Nazis. They eliminated anyone in their way.

He eyeballed Lawton.

Lawton didn't flinch.

I wonder what else he has on me that he's not letting me know, Caine thought. It occurred to him that Mike Stone still had that other file, along with Lyon's, and he feared where that information might lead . . . even to a dark night long ago—best left buried in the past.

Lawton finally nodded his head and said, "I think I'll go pick up that check. Good day, Senator."

"Yes, Ron. You do that," he answered.

Lawton turned to leave.

"Oh, Ron," the Senator called.

"Yes, sir?"

"This is a tough town. It can be cold and sometimes heartless, and it's a place where you have to know who your enemies are. I'm sure you know that, though. I just wouldn't underestimate Mike Stone."

Lawton shrugged. Mike Stone was a sandlot player, not someone to take seriously. Lawton had handled better men than him without trying. *Heartlessness is a virtue of the strong, not the weak,* he reminded himself, then offering a patronizing smile, turned and walked away.

6

Sunday—Tallahassee, Florida

I T IS SAID THAT LUCK is just opportunity disguised as hard work. Well, I don't know what I did to deserve to be so lucky, for in your service I have never worked at all. It is I who was disguised, by a beneficent God, for most of you can never know the man I once was or the evil that consumed me."

Pastor Nicholas Caine took a deep breath and struggled for composure. The chapel was filled to capacity with people gathered to hear his farewell sermon after having served as pastor of First Congregational Church of Tallahassee for thirty years.

"Not so, Pastor Caine," a man called loudly from the back of the standing-room-only crowd jammed into the lobby.

The handsome, white-haired churchman looked up from the rostrum, smiled, and humbly said, "Thank you. There are things . . ." and once again his voice succumbed to emotion. He decided to let that thought go and went back to his prepared speech on "luck"—his own.

"But if there were a luckier man alive, he would need my wife, Grace, my dear brother, Joe . . ." he paused, nodded, and then pointed to his handsome sibling, seated in the front row pew. Joe quickly stood and turned to face the congregation. Athletic, fit, and dressed in a dark suit, immaculate white shirt, and red tie, he looked every bit the part of a United States senator, and he responded to the acknowledgment with hands clasped in the salute of a champ before sitting back down.

Both men were in their sixties, but they each possessed the rugged good looks of a Hollywood leading man and a youthful appearance that belied aging and caused people to be easily drawn to them.

" . . . and luck is knowing all of you as friends," he continued, gesturing broadly to the sea of upturned faces before him. "Yes, if there were a luckier man alive he would need everyone here for the friend you are and have been to me, to Grace, and to our children. We thank you."

At this, the congregation stood as one, applauding and loudly cheering him.

"God bless you, Brother Nicholas Caine!"

"We are praying for you, Pastor!"

"We love you, Nicholas!"

Elderly Claire Barlow, the church's biggest financial benefactor, was seated in the pew with Grace Caine, Nicholas's wife of forty years, who now helped aged Claire to her feet. Moisture raining from her eyes, Claire simply raised a shaky hand to her quivering lips and blew him a kiss.

"These are for you, Pastor Caine." A perky ten-year-old girl bounced to the pulpit and handed him a bouquet of spring flowers. "I picked them from the garden. Mommy says you like lilacs. She said they remind you of the first Easter."

He stooped to look into the delicate girl's face, stroked her silken locks with a gentle caress, and kissed her softly on the forehead. "Thank you, sweetheart. I do love lilacs, but these are special. Every time I look at them, they will remind me of you!"

He set the bouquet aside and motioned with his hands for the audience to be seated. "Please . . . thank you all so very much. I'd like a final word. Please . . ." The congregants quieted and slowly took their seats as the hall once again filled with the reverent hush appropriate to the solemn occasion.

"Allow me to read a verse, my last reading before you from this pulpit. It is taken from the Old Testament book of Ezekiel: 'A new heart also will I give you, and a new spirit will I put within you: and I will take away the stony heart out of your flesh, and I will give you an heart of flesh.'

"There are three kinds of men in the world. Those with good hearts, those with cold hearts, and those who are heartless."

He paused to take in a deep breath and to speak in heartfelt but silent prayer to his Maker. *Please, Lord, let me reach Joe.* He looked again out over the vast congregation. "I once was a lost man."

"Not so, Pastor!" an aged gentleman shouted from the balcony, and a murmur swept through the congregation.

"Please . . . hear me out," the preacher continued. "Hear me out, please . . ." The chapel again quieted. "Lost men are heartless men," he emphasized. "Of all the saddest of God's creatures, we must pity most those without the heart to know guilt or remorse and who are blinded by selfishness and worldly honors. In pursuit of these things, such men walk over others and never count the cost. Such are evil men, and by that measure, I have been an evil man."

Pastor Caine scanned the congregation then directed his gaze again upon his younger brother.

"Cold-hearted men," he began in an earnest yet gentler tone, "are not lost but delusional and hyper-rational, telling themselves there is no God; that there is no personal responsibility for their actions. Lacking conscience and convinced the brain does all the work, these poor souls make decisions based only upon 'I, me, and mine,' injuring others as they do. Thinking, but choosing not to feel, cold-hearted men live at a frantic pace, in a desperate pursuit of whatever it is they think they are missing in life. With no time for meditation, prayer, introspection, or reflection, they live as a dog, forever chasing its tail. Remember one and all: the head is for getting and the heart is for giving.

"But there is hope through our Lord's mercy who balances the scale of justice once the deluded mind opens his heart and soul to light. When he begins to think with this," he emphasized by pounding a closed fist upon the center of his chest, "he truly learns to live! It is through the heart that men see with new eyes of kindness, truth, and goodness. I once had a cold heart."

He paused again and smiling sadly, looked once more at his brother, whose eyes were downcast.

"Then there is the 'good heart.' The man or woman who has a good heart thinks from the center up and not the top down. He or she feels life's great questions, then determines the wisest course through the brain. The good heart is what I wish and pray to come upon every man, woman, and child who can hear my voice today. It is only through the miracle of a good heart having been implanted within my breast that I am alive and speaking to you today, for which I thank the Lord Jesus."

So saying, he finally gave way entirely to his emotions as he looked tearfully into the faces of the people he loved and would miss with all his heart.

The choir stood in the loft and began at the direction of Miss Gabby Lott. "All the hopes that sweetly start from the fountain of the heart . . ." they sang.

With the congregation standing to join in, the choir sang a medley of Pastor Caine's favorite hymns. Then the choir concluded: " . . . all the bliss that ever comes to our earthly human homes, all the voices from above sweetly whisper: God is love."

Pastor Caine's voice caught in his throat, and he nearly despaired being able to force from his lips what his heart was filled with. After a moment, through fractured and broken vocals, he was able to say, "Joe, no matter what happens, I love you, and may God favor you with his loving grace."

Senator Joseph Caine, always in control of every moment, wiped quickly at his eyes, then stiffened and nodded to the pulpit with pursed lips and a furrowed brow, as if to say: *Well said, Brother. You needn't fear! Carry on.*

Nicholas Caine's eyes searched his brother's, hoping this moment might awaken Joe to a genuine remorse for the dark secret he had kept hidden for so many years. But instead of seeing in Joe's face the guilt, shame, or the change that radiates from the eyes of a man having a spiritual awakening, he saw only the body language of one still in denial. "God bless you, Joe," he finally said in a voice filled with honest warmth.

Looking out once again over the audience he added, "I expect this will be the last time I will occupy this place of honor. And there is one person here who has honored me more than any other in this life, next to my dear wife. I revere her as the dear mother she is, and she alone understands the deeper meaning implied in Ezekiel's verse toward me."

He gestured toward the front row. "I would like to invite Claire Barlow to the pulpit. Claire?" His brother, Joe, quickly rose and extended his hand to the frail little woman, assisting her to her feet and then escorting her to the steps leading to the podium.

Pastor Caine stepped down from the podium to the floor of the chapel and took Claire's free arm as she reached out for his. The three of them slowly ascended the four steps up to the rostrum, where Nicholas and Joseph Caine stood on either side to balance the bent little woman as she stood for a moment in silence, gripping the oak pulpit.

Claire Barlow was one of the few who knew Nicholas's dark

secret—the truth about his pre-pastoral past, knew what had happened on a night of revenge in 1969 to her son, a civil rights activist and newly ordained minister. It was a secret she had long ago buried.

Inclining toward the microphone she began: "Nicholas Caine is like my son. Nicholas has a part of him that has lived on for these thirty years, since my boy, Jimmy's death. Pastor Caine's life is a changed life from those days. He carries with him something that only my boy could have given him, and I am so proud of this man and his wife. I pray for our brother Nicholas Caine and his family daily, and though my boy is long since gone, I see him every day I look into the eyes of Pastor Caine. It was said by our Master's disciples two thousand years ago, 'He who was dead lives!' And so it has been with my Jimmy. Thank you. Thank you for treating my son's gift with the dignity it deserved and for living in honor with the offering so freely given."

With that, she turned to the pastor. "God bless you, Nicholas Caine," she said in a voice filled with sincerity and love.

Tears streamed freely from the eyes of the retiring pastor. He brought the little woman into his bosom as Senator Joseph Caine reached arms around them both.

"Good, Lord," she whispered in muffled awe as she pressed her head against the heart of Nicholas Caine. "I can hear him!"

*   *   *   *   *

The two brothers wandered out to the gazebo in the flower-bordered yard that Nicholas and Grace kept so meticulously cultivated.

"Our little getaway," Nicholas offered.

"Nice," his brother, Joe, responded. "Very peaceful. Tranquil. How long have you had this place?"

"Going on twenty years now."

"No!"

"Yes. Bought it right after the election that sent you to Washington. You haven't slowed down since."

"It's been that long?"

"It has."

Joe tried to grasp what his brother, several years his senior, was saying; that in essence he had been too busy to notice, to care, to come and visit.

Joe said, "The kids, all grown up and gone?"

"Kathy is at Florida State. Steve's up at the University of Maryland."

"Why don't you send that boy down to D.C. to get to know his Uncle Joe? He can come to work for me. Intern!"

Nicholas shook his head. "No, he's not the political type. Medicine is his thing. He wants to be a doctor—a heart specialist. Which brings me to something, Joe."

He paused awkwardly for a moment before saying, "I guess I don't know how to bring this up."

"An old political axiom answers that statement."

"What's that?"

"Then don't. If you don't know how to bring it up, let it lie."

Lie, the retired pastor thought. They both sat quietly and sipped on the iced lemonade. "Right off my own trees," Nick pointed.

"Hmm," Joe replied as he smacked lips. "Refreshing."

"Joe, I hope I didn't put you too much on the spot—this morning at the service." They were relaxed, both lost in thought. An unusual thing for the ever-on-the-go Senator Caine. "More?" Nick asked as he lifted the pitcher of iced lemonade.

Joe used his index and thumb almost touching to indicate the amount. "No liquor, no iced tea. Man, Nick, you really know how to throw a retirement party."

"Gave it up thirty-five years ago. You know that, Joe."

Joe shook his head. "You gave up a lot of things for this life. What ever happened to my rabble-rousing brother? The rough Army vet? The one who was always shooting someone's window out with the BB gun, or harassing the girls, and—"

"Don't go there. Please . . ." Nick asked softly.

"I feel bad about those days. I wish I could bring him back," Joe offered.

"He brought himself back, and a day doesn't go by that I don't try to honor him."

"Then let's do it!" Joe declared as he stood. "Here's to Jimmy Barlow and civil rights of the sixties!" He raised his lemonade glass.

Nicholas Caine's heart seemed to leap. With uncontrolled moisture in his aging eyes he raised his glass and said, "Here's to brother Jimmy Barlow."

They sipped slowly and sat without conversing as dusk settled upon Tallahassee and the crickets began to chirp and fireflies showed themselves.

"You know," Joe finally said, "I guess as my pastor, or should I say ex-pastor, I owe you," He twirled the ice that remained in his glass. "I know you took an oath of confidentiality, but you were going to say something about Jimmy's death . . . and Meredith. You know, 1969. I mean earlier, when you said you didn't know how to bring the subject up."

"Yes. That's right. But you owe me nothing. Serving you, others, has brought me the deepest joy I've known, and I was made a new man when I got the new heart. I was literally born again. The old cold heart was thrown in the dumpster where it belonged."

"That new ticker has served you well, brother."

"Yes, it has. Just yesterday my doctor said I have the heart of a twenty year-old. Imagine that. A heart that beats seventy times a minute beats forty-two hundred times an hour and over one hundred thousand times a day! I wish you could know how I changed . . . from the inside out . . . experience it, Joe."

"Oh, I've watched. I'm proud of you and a little jealous, too. You kept your wife. I've had two. You keep a low and happy profile while I've had all the limelight and glory. I am a troubled man, yet don't know any way but up. Until I reach . . ."

"The White House?" Nick asked.

Joe stared into his empty glass, spun the remaining ice, and then brought the glass to his lips. He chomped down on an ice cube and crunched loudly and saw his brother wince. He chuckled. "You still hate it when I crunch ice, don't you?"

"Well . . ." Nick demurred.

"Admit it! You always hated that about me."

"What?"

"The loud crunching. My favorite treat. Lemon flavored ice! Ha! I always loved bugging you with it, too!" he laughed.

Nick smiled. While growing up in Tallahassee they had enjoyed annoying each other with displays of irritating habits.

"It's an ambitious goal," Nick said, referring back to their previous topic. "It will take all your attention."

"What?" Joe chuckled as he finished his last ice cube.

"1600 Pennsylvania Avenue."

"Oh, that." Joe nodded.

"You've got to have a First Lady to live there."

"I'm working on it," Joe replied.

"Got a good political advisor? What's his name?"

"Mike Stone, the best." Joe didn't mention that Mike had just resigned. He had determined to let Mike simmer down a bit, then bring him back onto his campaign, but outside of Ron Lawton's direct control.

"Have you got a good chief of staff?"

"Ron Lawton? Don't know. Comes from some people I trust, and they vouch for him. My gut instinct tells me he lives for the fight. I guess so."

"You need to be careful, Joe. A lot of people will want your head."

"Ha!" he chuckled. "What else is new!"

"People will do anything to get their man in the White House. You know that."

"Sadly, Nick, I know it all too well."

They fell silent for a moment. Then Nick said, "Joe, if . . . if you ever want to talk. I mean, about Jimmy Barlow. Well . . . I'm here."

Joe didn't respond immediately. But after a moment, he said quietly, "The older I get, the more I wonder if we did the right thing. It wasn't intentional after all. What happened to Jimmy or . . . you know . . . what happened."

"I know," Nick agreed.

"Well," Joe brightened, "I've got to catch a flight bright and early."

They both stood, and Nick gathered his younger brother into his arms. Uncomfortable in the awkward embrace, Joe quickly pulled away.

"I'm always here if you need to talk," Nick assured him.

Joe nodded. "I'll let myself out through the side gate. Give Gracie my love—and send that boy Steven down from the U of Maryland to see me in D.C."

"I'll be praying for you," Nick called.

"I'll be needing those," Joe answered back with a smile and wave.

I'll pray for both our souls, Nick contemplated as he slowly made his way to the house.

7

MIKE HAD BEEN KEPT BUSY for a week, sending some of the Caine files over to Ron Lawton's office; slowly, one at a time, of course. He wasn't about to give up every file or all the information anyway. In order to keep the ex-CIA spook, Lawton, off balance, he was modifying every file and then shredding the orginals.

Having worked hard, Mike had a proprietary interest in the contacts he had developed over many years, and he wasn't about to give away any of that to a "Nazi" like Lawton. By literally "using his head," Mike in essence would keep all the contents safe, secured, and beyond Lawton's grasp.

Lizzy knew her hours were about to be cut back and offered to quit to make it easier for Mike.

"Are you kidding? You are the only other person on the planet who can handle my business if something happens to me. In fact, I want you to take a couple of weeks off, full pay, and when you get back I'm giving you a raise."

"Huh?" she asked, startled.

"A raise," he repeated.

"As in more money per hour?"

"Yes, sweet Liz. More money. We aren't going out of business. We are going to show that dog Caine that we not only don't need him but we can grow. Get ready, we are about to really take off."

"But I thought you said 'small was more controllable and profitable.' I'm confused."

"Small, as in number of clients. But Joe Caine isn't the biggest fish out there. We can easily handle two more Joe Caines or one bigger than Joe. I've got more than one card up my sleeve," Mike replied.

"Gosh," Liz mumbled. "I'd be confused, but then you are Mike Stone, the epitome of the paradox."

"Well, we are gonna tell those illegitimate sons of female canines in very diplomatic terms where they can take their business. You know the definition of a diplomat don't you, Lizzy?"

"Yeah."

"And?"

"Is this quiz time?"

"I just want to know if you've still got D.C. moxie, sweet Liz. We'll need it more than ever."

"How much?"

"Moxie?"

"No, the raise," she laughed.

"Oh. Well, can you repeat the Diplomatic Creed?"

"Yes I can. Here goes: 'A diplomat will always tell another where to go in such a way that he or she actually looks forward to the trip.'"

"Ka-ching," Mike said, pumping his arm in slot machine fashion. "You hit the jackpot for the grand total of $22.50 per hour!"

Lizzy put her hand to her mouth and began to tear up. "Mike, I don't know what to say?"

"How 'bout a hug and then a kiss right here?" he said, pointing to his cheek and turning his head to receive it.

Liz gave him a peck on the cheek and said, "I don't know what Maggie has done, but she has had a very, very good influence on you!"

"Okay, enough. We are leaving, turning out the lights. I want you to finish up this next week, and then I want you and your husband to take off for two weeks," he said, handing her an envelope.

"What's this?"

"A little 'thank you' for being there for me all these years. I haven't treated you right, Lizzy. I've been so caught up . . . well." He pointed to the envelope and nodded. "Go on, open it," he urged.

Lizzy was like a little girl. Mike Stone was a good boss, but this was unusual even for him. She nervously played with the sealed, legal-sized envelope and finally opened it. She pulled out a travel brochure with two all-expenses-paid vouchers for Cancun folded inside it.

"Mike!" she gasped. "I love you! Thank you, thank you, THANK YOU!" she squealed excitedly.

Mike was grinning at her. "Just enjoy it, and remember, we have a lot of work ahead of us. Get a good tan, relax, and be back three weeks from now ready to take on the world."

"You got it, boss!" She gave him a hard squeeze. "Mind if I tell Troy?"

He held her close and whispered in her ear, "Use the cell phone. I'm a bit worried about bugs in the office."

She pulled away, a puzzled look on her face. "You mean, as in surveillance?" she mouthed.

Mike nodded his head and scrawled a note on a pad: "I'm having this place swept for minicams and recording devices. Lawton is a low-life. I'm sure he's done something. He knows too much when nothing is revealed. So we act like everything is cool but finish up our lease. We'll be moving at the end of next month."

Lizzy read the note and nodded.

"Call me if you need me," he said aloud. He gave her a peck on the cheek and left for a much needed rest.

It was a tough decision to make. He'd never taken more than a one-week vacation. His work had always been too important, and besides, it was fun. Going after the opposition Republicans and Democrats was a game, war, chess, business, a match of wits. He couldn't imagine doing anything else.

But meeting Maggie Sanders had changed everything. No other woman had ever melted the Stone-cold heart like she had done. His feelings for her were deep, and he knew that if he was going to make her happy, he was going to have to stop his insane pace and devote more time to their relationship. She was more than he deserved and was ready to give her all to him. So he needed to take a break— reexamine his course in life.

Mike Stone was a borderline alcoholic, and he knew it.

He also knew that with Maggie's determined help he could stop drinking, get a grip on his life, and really try health for a change.

He'd fooled himself into thinking that playing racquetball three times a week, jogging two mornings a week, along with lifting moderate weights would offset the smoking, drinking, and absurd pace that his on-the-go life demanded of him.

He couldn't fool Maggie. When the tests came back from his life insurance exam, they weren't as good as he had hoped. His cholesterol levels worried her, along with his elevated blood pressure. Just looking at him, no one would have said he was out of shape, but his insides revealed a man ten years older than his chronological age.

Maggie had wanted him to undergo a complete body scan, but he had put his foot down. *She needs to take me as I am and quit trying to make me into her personal idea of super husband,* he thought.

But he could never quite look Maggie in the eyes and tell her what he had earlier determined. He was the proverbial putty in her hands. She was doing more to reshape him than anyone else ever had. There had been others who seemed to care about him, but not like Maggie cared.

Maggie worried about Mike, particularly about his loss of work with the senator. Not that the money was needed. She was doing well in her practice, and until now Mike had had only himself to think about his entire adult life. He claimed to have several years of income in the bank, but had simply never taken the time to do anything with it. So she trusted that he could afford to take this time away from work.

She had asked him directly to take an entire year off, to focus on health issues and do what work he needed to from the house they were buying in Florida. To get out of the D.C. area, she had taken a job offer at the University of Florida Med Center. She would serve there on the teaching staff as well as keep up her practice, performing heart/lung transplants.

She was excited about the change. It would be a good start for her and Mike to leave—for him to get away from the pressures of political life and for her to rid herself of the familiar surroundings that haunted her, not to mention away from Mom.

She loved her mother, but Maggie didn't need her meddling in the beginning years of her marriage. She'd seen other marriages negatively impacted by the unhelpful interference of well-meaning in-laws. And she also didn't want the constant reminder of how her father had let them all down by his devotion to politics.

So this job at the University Hospital was for the both of them.

Mike had a tough-looking veneer, seemingly as cold and hard as his last name. But what Maggie had sensed was that deep inside, Mike had a good heart. And given the business she was in, who would know better?

She would go straight to his heart and turn it around. Maggie Sanders would become Dr. Maggie Stone, the love doctor.

8

Washington, D.C.—Three weeks later

I'VE ALREADY TOLD YOU; Mike Stone is out of the picture, and those files are the property of the man who paid for them; namely Senator Joe Caine!" Ron Lawton was now fully agitated, pacing the floor as he talked loudly into his cell phone.

"What do you mean, you can't help me?" he almost shouted. He looked out his apartment window at the famous Watergate complex where he now lived. "Don't put me on hold. Hey, what the—" The person on the other end had hung up on him.

Lawton cursed at the phone and paced some more. He couldn't let anything happen to the files Stone had and the very private, highly confidential information they held. *Those contributors would be ruined, and nearly 50 million dollars in future contributions would be lost as well,* he fumed in silence. *If anything should happen to Mike Stone; an accident, sickness—anything that could keep the files in limbo-land—they could surface outside of his control. It always starts with out-of-control information,* he groused. For Mike Stone to use them against Caine, or for someone to get them away from Stone's control, would be politically ruinous and sink his own ship along with Caine's and Lyon's.

"I need those files!" he declared loudly, striking his fist against the desk.

Lawton stood, walked to the window, and gazed out at the

apartment complex nestled on the Potomac next to his. *Watergate,* he mused. He had known G. Gordon Liddy just before the break-in in '72. Lawton himself had been recruited and then backed out. *Dodged the bullet by listening to the little voice that time,* he pondered in reverie.

Lawton loved the idea of living within the shadow of history. He wondered how his old friend and Watergate bungler Liddy was doing these days.

Maybe I should pay him a visit. Get the senator on his radio talk show. From Watergate break-in mastermind to bestselling author and radio show host. Hummm. Maybe I ought to—

The phone rang. "Well, Lizzy. How thoughtful. I was just about to pay you a personal visit," he said into his cell phone. "Yes! Now listen carefully because I'm repeating myself. It is the American Alliance Party— 'AAP Private Donor Files'—I'm referring to!"

She put him on hold again. He thought about how Caine would soon be announcing his run for the presidency as the AAP candidate. *Maybe that would be the most powerful venue to make the announcement. Give old G. Gordon the scoop.*

Lizzy came back on the line.

"Yeah, that's right. I need the files on ex-governor of New Mexico, Jackson Lyon, as well." He waited again. "No! Not those files. The contributor files for the ex-governor! Are you stupid or am I?" he yelled into the handset. *And you'd better not intimate that I am, Lizzy, if you know what is good for you,* he thought angrily.

"As you may recall," he said sarcastically, "Lyon was a U.S. senator, then governor." He was put on hold again.

Even though Lawton was officially working for Joseph Caine, he had won the full faith and trust of Jackson Lyon, based on Lawton's previous work in corporate security and intel at Digiwatch.

Lyon was a retired, one-term U.S. senator and two-term governor of New Mexico, and he had been building his power base and resumé with one goal in mind.

Handsome, articulate, and charming, Lyon was enjoying a nice run of favorable public opinion, showing up on all the television and radio talk shows, espousing "conservative independence" and beginning to persuade voters that the time had come to look outside the two established political parties and embrace him as a third-party choice.

Lyon had attracted significant national attention and had garnered growing support. But Lawton saw Lyon for what he was—simply a peddler. Lyon had latched onto a popular viewpoint, and he was going to parlay the country's mood all the way to ultimate power. His mantra was honor, duty, country, and the Constitution, and he was selling himself to the American public. A retired Marine Corps colonel, Vietnam vet, and hero of lesser known wars, Lyon didn't always apply those values to himself. He spouted them on the airwaves and in the public arenas, but Lawton knew Lyon didn't always walk the walk, only when it suited him and his ambitions.

This Lizzy girl is asking for trouble. I'm sure Mike Stone has put her up to this stonewalling.

"Yes, of course I know his name! Jackson Lyon. Now where is it!"

He'd have to put the fear of God into Lizzy, and he knew just how to do it.

"Look, I'll give you the weekend to find that file, and if you don't turn it up, I'll come down there and start from scratch. And, Lizzy, I promise, you won't like my scratch!" He snapped shut his cell phone and fumed.

Jackson Lyon was headed for a showdown with Joe Caine for the nomination of the new American Alliance Party. For the first time in history, the climate was right for success by someone outside the traditional system. Disaffected Democrats, Republicans, and

Independents all felt their parties had moved away from traditional moorings and had left them without a home. Both men had correctly read the political sea change that was taking place and aimed to ride the wave all the way to the seat of ultimate power in Washington, D.C.

Conveniently, the showdown would be staged by the very men who would appear rivals in a matter of weeks. One would run for the office of president and the other for vice president. To Lawton it didn't matter which one—Lyon or his present boss, Caine—made it to the Oval Office. All he had to do was make sure he was on the right train when it pulled into the station. For now he needed to dig a bit deeper into Lyon's and Joe Caine's personal histories. He was sure there was information there that would be useful to him—information about both of them.

And you just never know, he thought. *One of those rich donors might just take a liking to me,* he grinned.

He paced in thought by the picture window that opened a view to neighboring buildings, shops, the common area, and the Potomac River. *Lizzy Price has the files I need; files with names, dates, places.* He smirked and looked out the window to the Watergate Towers next door. He knew the weaker hand could be played against the stronger one when it came to the Lyon and Caine contest for the AAP Convention nomination for president this summer.

Dirt stuck better that way.

9

Tallahassee, Florida—Claire Barlow's home

CLAIRE? IT'S NICHOLAS CAINE. I just came by to see how you are feeling," he said through the open screen door. "Hello . . . Claire?" he called, as he opened the door a crack. She had hearing difficulties, and he knew he was welcome to enter.

Something good always happened to him when he came here. He felt a sense of homecoming, of joy and warmth. Much of that could be attributed to the love that radiated from sweet Claire, but he wondered also if it didn't have something to do with Jimmy's heart, telling him he was "home." The feeling was tangible, and his heart literally accelerated whenever he dropped in on Claire. Intellectually, it didn't make any sense, but that didn't make it any less real. However it worked, he was glad about it. He took it as a sign from God that he had been forgiven, a view that Claire had shared with him. "Claire?" he called again, in a gentle tone, not wanting to startle her.

Claire Barlow was an enigma to most people, but Nicholas knew her true story. This modest bungalow of clean white siding with two baths and three bedrooms had always been called home. She'd raised two children here—Jimmy, who became a minister, and Georgia, who often visited her mother with the grandchildren in tow.

A wraparound, covered porch, furnished with wicker rockers and soft-cushioned seats, was the social focus of the home and the place where Claire spent most of her time. There was always a supply of ice-cold lemonade on hand, that and her homemade shortcake.

"Is that you, Pastor?" Claire called from the kitchen. "I'll be right out. Set yourself down on the porch. I'm just finishin' some rhubarb pie. Would you like some?"

"You know I'd love some. Matter of fact, that is why I came by!" he laughed.

"You are such a tease. How's my boy?" she said with a smile as he leaned down to give her a peck on the forehead. "Here, you take these and set them over on the table will you? I got some of the church ladies comin' by shortly. We are quilting for the Capitol Children's Home Benefit next month. I expect you to be the highest bidder, Pastor Caine."

"You know I will be, Claire. Claire, I've come to talk with you about a matter that is personal. May I sit and take some time before the ladies show?"

"Just let me scoop you out a slice of this pie. And pour some lemonade."

He nodded. She couldn't be slowed, he realized. Her tired-looking and sometimes frail body was hard put to keep pace with her still youthful and energized mind.

She watched in anticipation as Nicholas Caine took his first bite of pie.

"Oh, my . . . Claire!" he pronounced through a smiling mouthful. "I've died and gone to heaven."

"Yes, I bet someone will have me makin' it there, too," she giggled, delighted with the effects she had on her friend Pastor Caine. "I just loved to watch Jimmy eat and enjoy home cookin'. You are just like him. You seem to eat two plates of all his favorite foods; meatless lasagna, and slowly steamed summer squash—lightly buttered—when we hold those potlucks at the church. I've been noticing that for years."

"Strange thing you should mention that, Claire. That's what I've come to talk to you about." He cleared his throat and set the plate down. Taking a sip from the lemonade, he smacked his lips. "Just right."

"Do you want to see how my roses are coming?" she asked, always eager to please and be the gracious hostess.

"Well, I think I had better chat with you about what I came to address. It's about that night." His eyes welled up every time he broached the subject in any form. He and his brother, Joe, had never talked about it in any other terms but those two words. Everyone who was connected with the dark spring evening of April 1969 knew about the meaning behind the words that revealed a night so long ago, when a boyish prank turned deadly. Whenever Nicholas tried to bring the topic up, he was always readily forgiven, and that was the end of the conversation. Even with Claire.

"Jimmy was my pride and joy, Nicholas. May I call you Nicholas?"

He smiled. Claire always asked that question out of respect. For more than twenty years she had been asking if she could use his given name instead of the more formal "Pastor Caine."

She waited for a response.

He looked from the porch into the neatly kept yard, as if solace awaited him there. He blinked at the moisture gathering in his eyes and nodded his head. "Yes," he finally assured in a whisper. "Yes, I wish you would please call me Nicholas," he answered as he always had. "It makes me feel more like . . ."

"My son?"

He nodded.

"You and Jimmy have had a spiritual bond that two men rarely enjoy. Usually that bond is the result of a brotherhood, growing out of shared experiences—friends who serve, play, or go to school together. I see it in a lot of our boys who go off to war and come home. They seem connected. That is how you and Jimmy are."

"I know," he meekly answered.

Now Claire was the minister, and Nicholas was the parishioner. "Jimmy made me promise before he slipped into the darkness that you would get what you needed, not what you deserved. He knew you were changing and had a sick heart. I don't know if someone told him, whether he saw the news story about your need, but he knew. He also knew he was going to meet his Lord."

"Thank you, Claire. I have some more I've never told anyone. And though I feel I have done all I can to make up for what happened, I still feel something remains for me to do. I can't put my finger on it. But I know there is."

"Well, you have honored me, my family, and the memory of my son. What more could I ask? Jimmy would be so proud. You took up his cause. My goodness, Nicholas—you bring me such joy!"

"Thank you, dear Mother Barlow. And thank you for your support and financial donations over the years. I have kept my promise. I've never told a soul about you and your generous financial contributions to so many causes, but the good Lord has touched a lot of people through you."

"And through you and my good boy's heart," she replied as she stood and reached out her hand. "May I show you my roses now?"

He wiped at his face, then took her tiny hand and placed it on his left arm. As they strolled, he talked some more about his regrets. He offered his story in soliloquy as they made their way through rows of fragrant roses . . . and the thorns.

10

Washington, D.C.

Senator Joseph Caine was not without a soul, only nearly so. Over time, he had developed a selective conscience—one able to conveniently remember and forget at the same time.

It was an annual ritual for him to visit the Vietnam Memorial Wall. He always went on the same date, the anniversary of one of the truly unselfish days of his life, when he had earned a Silver Star for heroics in a battle that had cost fifty-four men their lives.

In Caine's mind, those men had stayed forever young. As he looked at their names etched in black polished granite, the nineteen- and twenty-year-old men seemed to come alive and stare back at him. For the old soldier, names meant faces and places, and he could always see their images, asking him to not let them down or forget them.

He could have forgotten them on that terrible day in the highlands of South Vietnam. He was supposed to have turned his company over to a new commander. Of the men in his company, thirty-one were white boys, a lot of them Southerners; and nineteen were black sons of mostly poor families scattered through America's inner cities and small farming towns. His company master sergeant was African-American, and the best organizer and leader of men he had ever known. The rest were Hispanic. One wasn't even an American citizen but a Peruvian who was drafted when his college deferment ran out and he naively remained in the U.S. instead of going back to Lima, Peru.

Carlos should have gone home. He should have run. But Joseph Caine knew the kind of man Sergeant Carlos Zuniga had been. He had stayed and accepted the promise of future citizenship in exchange for his military service.

I sure would like old Calvin Grubbs on my campaign now. He'd know what to do. Sergeant Grubbs never took any prisoners.

Joe found meaning in this annual visit. It was the one truly religious moment he experienced each year. He supposed this sense of reverence was what real religious people feel all the time. He didn't know for sure but guessed also the feelings he experienced at the memorial wall were the kinds of feelings his brother, Nick, found daily in his Christian ministry.

Hello, boys. I've tried to do all I can to keep my promise. I've been in politics since coming home in '70. I determined that someone had to remember you, not let all this be in vain. I hope I didn't let you down in '69. I was told that our losses were an "acceptable sacrifice." I was ordered out that day. I was supposed to leave the fighting to my juniors while a new man was to be brought in on the next supply chopper. I was supposed to go back on that chopper to Pleiku. I guess you all know I didn't. I stayed, and we turned the battle from a loss into a victory—your victory.

He wondered if dead men rejoiced over mortal victories—if somehow the survivors of battles became proxy heroes for the fallen. If so, then why do survivors always mourn their supposed heroics?

He stood quietly facing the wall, lost in thought, ignoring other groups and individuals who were gathered there to pay their respects.

I have stood by the vets all these years. I hope somehow you know that it was you that put the fire in me to try to change things. See, a lot of us old war veterans are politicians now, and we've had a few wars since Vietnam. But your sacrifices taught us to never allow the waste of war to go on without complete victory. We haven't lost any wars since, boys. I don't think we can.

He closed his eyes, picturing their faces, remembering their personalities, and recalling their idiosyncrasies. He wondered what might have become of them, if they had survived the war, and he experienced the same sadness he always felt being there.

After a time, he looked at his watch, then thought: *Well, see you all next year. I hope to make you proud with my run for the top spot, commander in chief.* He saluted, did an about-face, and walked away from his annual rendezvous.

He was to meet with the president on an Appropriations Committee matter this morning, and the walk from the monument to 1600 Pennsylvania Avenue would do him some good.

He wasn't sure if the annual visit to the Vietnam Memorial changed anything, but for a moment each year he felt better about himself. He felt good about that day when he had been willing to give his life up for his comrades. The medals and honors were nice, and it didn't hurt that he had them on his record as he headed into the battle for the presidency.

Jackson Lyon had more medals than Joe, and three tours of duty under his belt, plus the governorship that had been added after his distinguished service in the Senate.

Ron Lawton will need to get his head squared away and keep his promise not to divulge certain indiscretions I've made over the years, he thought.

He wondered if Lawton knew about another time that haunted Joe and his brother, Nick. It had ultimately cost a man his life, and then of course there was Meredith and the accident.

His life had nearly gone up in smoke and all in a twenty-four hour period.

Well, as Nick had told him, *it's all in God's hands now.* And maybe, if there was a God, Joe was finding redemption through his service to country. He'd like to think it wasn't all self-serving. *Of course it's not all about me. How could it be? I am doing it for the people,* he reminded himself.

As he walked toward the White House, he reminded himself of all the good he had done for his country. He took satisfaction in believing that he was part of some master plan of someone else's design. *Maybe those two people, Jimmy and Meredith, gave their lives in some cosmic plan that will allow me to see my path more clearly, course correct myself. Maybe . . .*

*   *   *   *   *

Mike Stone was in withdrawal, and it wasn't easy. Giving up cigarettes, booze, and even coffee had made him edgy and miserable. Maggie had demanded a thorough "inner house cleaning," as she put it. To work on it, he decided to put himself under self-imposed house arrest for a couple of weeks.

Maggie promised to come by early each day to make a morning juice on her way to Fairfax County General, leave him his fruit and vegetables for the midday meal, and come by to fix him a healthy dinner. She prescribed drugs to help him ease the nicotine craving and emptied all wine and booze from his cabinets.

There wasn't a single, solitary cigarette anywhere to be found. He knew. He'd checked in desperation three days ago. Even took a drag from a cigarette butt he found in the trash. That was disgusting enough to put him back on track.

Still, it all had him depressed. Lizzy was holding down the fort, and he didn't need to go in to D.C. or his office. But that was the biggest withdrawal of all. His work was his religion, his passion, and his purpose in life. It defined him, and any slip from power caused an avalanche of feelings of worthlessness to overtake him, mentally, emotionally, and even spiritually—if that were possible.

Maggie hadn't arrived yet, and he was working out on the tread-mill while watching the morning news. He was eager for Maggie to see him pumped up, willing to make this change, and not in the dumps that he truly felt on the inside. He had prided himself on being a master of the art of hyperbole and deceptive looks—body language.

He was the living epitome of what Senator Joe Caine had once dubbed the "Stone smile." It was an ultimate compliment, coming from a master of public relations and personal magnetism.

Mike knew what salesmanship took, what PR demanded, and how to market politicians. "They must be always at their best and never show a down day," he reminded the staffs of the political men and women whose campaigns he had managed. He was so good at covering his own internal stresses and discomforts with the "Stone Smile" that he himself sometimes couldn't identify why he felt uncom-fortable around certain people and in certain situations.

He had always thought his own controlling behavior was sufficient to make up for any deficit in other people's personalities or habits. But now there was something about this Lawton. Every time he had been around the man, he had experienced an ominous chill. *The guy has energy all right, but it's dark energy,* he reasoned as he ran on the exercise machine.

"Stone smiles" are phony. I'm phony. Maggie knows it. She's even said as much. Why am I rolling over for this woman? he wondered as he con-tinued the run, which was now causing him to breathe heavily.

Oh, yeah, love. It's that heart thing and not a head thing. She's always yakking about cardio-energetics, memories of the heart, the language of the heart . . . blah, blah, blah. You'd think she was a shrink and not a medical doctor.

Heart-to-heart, she says. *Two hearts linked in the language of love—*

love equals "L" Energy that can be transmitted from each other's heart in some sort of ethereal wave or energy link. Written by some quack named Doctor Pearsall, *The Heart Code* was the bible his very attractive surgeon-fiancée was insisting he read. He glanced at the book on top of the TV and released a heavy sigh.

He really didn't want to think about the heart having power over his head; if he did that, he'd have to confront his conscience—scruples—a sense of right and wrong. If he did confront his conscience there would be feelings he'd have to deal with—heart stuff—and he'd lose his edge as a political adviser. In fact, he couldn't see anything about politics where the heart came into play, except for phony photo-ops at orphanages and with the hurt or disadvantaged. Politics was about power—a head-game—not about humanity; that was for preachers; the good-hearted.

Surrendering to Maggie's insistence, Mike was determined to do five miles a day, tone up for the honeymoon, and reverse the adverse effect of so many treasured vices. He was even starting to conquer the habit of searching the house over for coffee and cigarettes.

Now, a couple of weeks into his exercise regime, he was actually beginning to feel better—not necessarily while exercising, but after-ward, after cooling down, because it was pure agony when he would first start out on the treadmill. Until he got warmed up and found his pace, he struggled to catch his breath, and his chest felt tight—particularly so today. He slowed his pace a bit, waiting for his second wind to kick in.

Probably the jitters from no smokes, he thought, inhaling deeply. He'd finish his workout, shower, get ready for the day, and then he'd feel comfortable and alert. *Whew,* he allowed, suddenly feeling a little light-headed. He stepped off the treadmill and reached for the railing to steady himself. *I'll just lie down on the floor and let it pass,* he thought.

Falling onto his back, he was suddenly gasping for air. His chest felt as though it was being squeezed in a giant vice, and he rolled onto his side to ease the pain. *Heart attack! Oh, no . . . not . . .* He felt faint, losing ability to get air.

"Hello! Mike, are you here?" Maggie called out as she let herself in the front door. "I got the juice made before I came over this time. Got a super busy schedule today." She walked down the hall to the bedroom converted into a gym, calling his name. "Mike? You in the shower?" she said as she turned the corner.

"Oh, Michael! God, no! Please . . ."

11

THE AMBULANCE WAS IN THE DRIVEWAY within seven minutes of Maggie's call. She knew better than to try to drive him to even the closest hospital, Fairfax County General. She would need all the equipment the paramedics had available. Clearly, Mike was just a few labored heartbeats away from the "Big Adios."

That was just one of the many medical student euphemisms for death and dying. Using terms like the Spanish word for *goodbye* helped young doctors cope. By maintaining some distance and being intentionally irreverent, doctors were able to keep their emotions from getting in the way as they administered emergency medical treatment or had to deal with losing a patient. Maggie had engaged in that dark humor in her own work, but given her feelings for Mike, it seemed so . . . inappropriate, that the phrase would now come to mind.

Kneeling by Mike, she administered CPR, kept him alive, made him chew an aspirin, held his hand, and prayed.

He was perspiring heavily and his skin was clammy. "Maggie. Thank God, Maggie," he groaned.

"I'm here, Mike. You're going to be okay. Help is on the way."

She did her best to keep the cardiologist inside of her focused, but it was hard to be clinical now. She had never felt hopelessness like this overcome her during the year following med school, when she had worked in an emergency room. There, patients were simply bodies needing her best work, but none had ever been related to her; not like this. She had never been in love with someone she was trying to save. She prayed silently that Mike would be able to hang on until he could receive full-blown treatment.

The ride in the ambulance to the hospital was one of the hardest things she had ever endured. She had to allow the paramedics to treat him, and twice she had course-corrected one of them. Each time he had asked her not to interfere, and she had responded by swearing, something she never did. The attendants had their work to do and paid little attention when she explained to them that she was a practicing cardio-pulmonary physician.

Mike was in obvious pain, and she could tell there was emergency surgery awaiting him—if he survived until they could get him to the hospital. So she talked to him. By a nod of the head and a squeeze of the hand she got his permission to authorize whatever treatment she deemed necessary to save his life.

Maggie had her cell phone to her ear now. She paged her partner, Miles Hall, one of the best surgeons in the D.C. area.

He returned her call almost immediately. "Hey, Maggie. What's the 9-1-1 about?"

"My fiancé is in cardiac arrest. I'm headed for Fairfax County General now. Are you available?"

"I just finished a bypass. This look like one to you?"

"He has all indications. Miles, I'm scared," she replied with a broken voice.

"Maggie, I'm headed down to Emergency right now. I'll be there for you. Good thing you called now. Five more minutes and I would have been out in my car headed for home."

"Please hurry things along for me. His name is Michael Stone," she offered and then gave all his personal information, from date of birth to lifestyle, before hanging up.

"Pray for me, Maggie," Mike groaned.

She kissed him on the forehead and quietly offered a prayer aloud for his survival. Mike relaxed, breathed easier, and squeezed her hand to say thanks.

Maggie was stunned. She had never prayed for anyone needing medical attention. She always *hoped* that God would heal people, but physicians routinely mocked that possibility by describing the key doctor in a life-saving procedure as being the one in the "Jesus Seat."

Maggie watched Mike's struggle ease and his blood pressure drop, and for a moment she thought he was slipping from her.

"Michael Stone. I'm marrying you. You can't leave."

"Maggie," he whispered through the oxygen mask. "I'm not leaving you." He forced a smile and offered a slight nod of his head.

"I couldn't live without you. I love you," she said.

With that the ambulance came to a stop at the entrance to the emergency room, where Doctor Miles Hall was waiting with a gurney.

Maggie did something she had never done before. She had seen actors portray this moment, had seen dozens of crying loved ones mutter something upward to an unseen force, and as a physician she had always allowed for what seemed people's unreasonable expectations of their God. Now the shoe was on her foot, and suddenly she had empathy for the thousands who must go through this daily at hospitals around the world.

"God, please let Mike live. I'll do anything you want; just let him live," she softly cried.

"He fits the profile, Maggie," Dr. Hall said. "What do we do? It's your call."

Maggie turned to Mike. "Mike, honey? I need to let you know what we have here. Simply put, you need a bypass. The blood just isn't flowing through the coronary arteries the way it should, and there is little hope of stabilizing you unless we do this.

"You have two of the best standing right next to you. We are going to prep you and get you into surgery. Mike, it is very serious, and without this surgery you might not make it. Do you understand?" she asked tearfully.

He nodded.

"I'll be right there with you. This is Dr. Hall, he's the best in Fairfax County. He'll operate. I'll assist."

Mike smiled weakly. "No Mike Stone. Just Mike Clay—putty in your hands," he slurred.

"Let's go," she said as the attendants wheeled him up to surgery.

*　　*　　*　　*　　*

That afternoon

Lizzy Price called her husband, Troy, and asked him to come to the office. The last telephone conversation with Lawton had left her feeling vulnerable and threatened. Troy promised to hurry back from Baltimore, where he was attending a planning commission meeting on behalf of his employer, Bartlett Enterprises, a development and construction firm.

She hadn't heard from Mike Stone, but he had told her not to call, that the office might have bugs in it, the kind with big ears. Lizzy shook her head. In the previous seven years she had worked full-time for Mike, she had never experienced so much intrigue. The mother of two elementary-school-aged children, she had some really solid goals now. Just a few more years of full-time work, then with all their debt paid off, she could become a stay-at-home mom. Uncomfortable with having to deal with Lawton, that prospect was looking better to her all the time.

Now in her mid-thirties, she had first met Mike Stone nearly twenty years earlier, when he was a partner with Bill Maxfield, another young political analyst. Bill was Lizzy's cousin, and she was still in high school, needing a summer job. She came to work for Bill and Mike Stone and fell in love with the excitement of being around all the political insiders. She came back every summer, until she graduated from college.

At one point, Bill tired of the grind and left the partnership, opting for a steady paycheck and a career in law enforcement. Never having married, Bill was now just finishing almost twenty years with the FBI. He and Mike Stone were so different from each other, yet the two were still best friends. Bill often came by, just to hang out and challenge Mike's liberal politics with his own conservative arguments. She wondered if she should call Bill about these concerns Mike was having with Ron Lawton.

But then, she would have to use a new cell phone or some other secure connection. This whole business with Senator Joe Caine's new chief of staff had her going nuts. Lawton was spooky, and she cringed just answering the phone now. No wonder Mike had given her a raise. But it would take a lot more than $22.50 an hour for her to keep this up much longer.

She had done what Mike had instructed her. She had given Lawton only the least sensitive of the files on Caine supporters. The really meaty stuff, containing contact information, confidential memos, and records of donations, she had stored in a rented storage locker near her mother-in-law's home in Sterling, Virginia. Mike had made it clear he had no intention of turning over anything that would compromise his contacts. Now the job was almost finished. After his two-week vacation, Mike would go to the storage locker and take the

files and shred them. The most vital files he kept secured in his head—
a place no one would be able to access.

Wonder if I should report in to Mike? No . . . can't use the phone. I'll use Troy's cell when he gets here.

She called Troy once more and made sure he knew where she was going to meet him. He replied that he was on his way from Baltimore and would make one stop at Lee's flower shop in Chinatown. She smiled and said he didn't have to. He responded with, "Love you, Babe!"

Lizzy felt like one of the luckiest women in the world. She was adored and had the family of her dreams. Now she just needed a little peace of mind. She wanted only to protect her boss and be done with this nasty Ron Lawton. Closing the office door behind her, she turned, and literally bumped into a man who was standing there.

She gasped audibly, then said, "Oh! You scared me! Can I help you?"

The man was young, athletically trim, and casually dressed. He didn't smile. "I was sent down here by Ron Lawton to pick up the Jackson Lyon file," he said curtly.

"Well, it isn't here. Sometimes Mike Stone takes them home, sometimes I take them home. If you will excuse me, I will be on my way and call Mr. Lawton in the morning after I locate it."

The thirty-something errand boy rested his hand on the door frame, creating a barrier with his arm and blocking Lizzy from turning to the right and into the corridor.

"Please move. You are scaring me."

"Not until I see for myself if you have the file."

She didn't take long to make her decision. The file was in her carrying case, but this man wasn't getting a look at it. She swung the hard briefcase between his legs and up into his groin, and when his knees buckled and he reached to hold himself, she bolted for the exit.

Looking back, she saw that the man had already straightened and was glaring at her. He didn't pursue her, but said loud enough for her to hear, "I wouldn't do this if I were you."

She made an unkind gesture with her free hand and then tried to act as calm as she possibly could as she walked to the parking garage. She wasn't going to be intimidated by Lawton's goon.

Reaching her car, Lizzy glanced behind her but saw no one following. She got in the car and quickly locked the doors, wondering how long the man had been standing outside the office door.

Lizzy was trembling. She was not an aggressive person, and the confrontation had shaken her. She decided to get the file out of her possession, and while pulling out of the underground parking garage, she used her cell phone to dial the D.C. FBI office. After impatiently working her way through the maze of electronic options, she finally reached an operator.

"Federal Bureau of Investigation. How may I direct your call?"

She asked to speak to Bill Maxfield and was relieved when he picked up.

"Special Agent Maxfield."

"Bill, it's Liz."

"Hey, Lizzy! How's it going?"

"Not good. I've got a problem." She went on to explain the Lawton craziness she had experienced, about smacking the messenger considerably above the shins with her briefcase, and asked if Bill could meet her at Union Train Station Mall and take the file off her hands.

"Be delighted," Bill answered. "Let me check this Lawton guy out for you. In the meantime just relax. Nothing will happen to that file in a public place like Union Station."

"Thanks, Bill. I owe you. I'm a bit shaken, I'm afraid."

"Well, I usually don't recommend assault and battery, but I think what you did sent the right message to the punk Lawton sent over.

Anything I can do for you, Troy, or Mikey, is a done deal. Say, how is old Mike and that new girlfriend of his?"

"Maggie is a miracle worker," she happily replied. "Mike is breathing clean air, the first in over twenty years."

"No smokes?"

"No smokes, no booze, no cheating at cards . . . at least I think."

They both laughed.

"Hope she doesn't give the old boy a heart attack. Sudden changes can do that," Bill said, still chuckling. "I'll see you at the station in an hour."

"Thanks, Bill. Love you."

"You, too, Sugar."

Sugar. He's so cute. What a good catch he'd make for some lucky woman.

*   *   *   *   *

Troy turned the corner at the city complex, made his way through busy downtown Baltimore streets, and finally entered the I–95 on-ramp at 6:00 P.M. Liz had sounded nervous. She was afraid to go home alone and afraid to stay at the office.

They had agreed to meet for dinner at Union Station across from the Capitol Building and not far from their modest, recently renovated town home nearby. Troy loved the energy of D.C. He could see himself working for a few years to really get a solid track record in building and development, then start his own company here in Washington, settle in, and make a difference in the nation's capital.

He had known Lizzy since elementary school, lost track of her in the early nineties when he went into military service, and then at their ten-year high-school reunion had reconnected. Theirs was a second marriage for each of them, and they were astounded that they hadn't seen it earlier in their lives; the heart-to-heart connection and peace that each brought to the other. For Troy, Lizzy was the model of feminine perfection, and she often said that she wished she had perceived Troy's strengths before she had married a guy who had been so selfish and abusive. She and Troy couldn't have been happier, and they were agreed that maturity brings a realization to old friends of what love is really all about.

Their two toddlers were being tended at Mom Price's house in Sterling, Virginia. Troy stopped by Lee's, a gift and flower shop on H Street in Chinatown, on his way to Union Station. A few flowers, a good meal, some easing of the tension by taking in a movie, a romantic evening, that's what Lizzy needed to pull out of the deep funk she had fallen into while covering for Mike Stone with this Lawton guy.

Troy smiled as he thought about how excited Lizzy had been when she called to tell him about the raise and the cruise Mike had given her. It would be good to get away for a week and just spend some time together.

His mind a million miles away, Troy didn't notice the black SUV that now followed him as he pulled out on H and then turned south on Massachusetts Ave.

From his training and experience in the army, working for four years as a CID investigator, Troy had developed a certain intuition. It was a skill he hadn't needed in recent years, but something wasn't quite right at the moment. He had an uneasy feeling as he parked his car in the parking garage outside Union Station and walked through the parking structure to the elevators. He was anxious to find Lizzy, who he knew was downstairs waiting at the help-yourself, French-style Au Bon Pain Café across from the B. Dalton bookstore.

Waiting for the elevator, he realized he had forgotten the roses and turned to go back to the car. In doing so, he noticed a casually dressed young man, wearing sunglasses and with thinning hair and a sturdy build, standing by his car, apparently peering inside. The man paused for only a moment, then moved on.

Strange. A neatly dressed man wouldn't likely be looking for easy pickings in plain sight in a busy parking garage. Maybe he's just trying to find his car. Troy quickly retrieved the flowers and returned to the elevators.

He took the elevator up to the ground level, went through the turnstiles and into the galleria of stores, which the graceful but aged Union Train Station across from the Capitol had been turned into. He noticed again the man he had seen in the parking garage, standing with his back to Troy at the bottom of the escalator. In his late twenties to mid-thirties, the athletic-looking man appeared to be looking for someone.

Now a little curious, Troy got off the escalator and walked past him but glanced over to a store window to look for the young man's reflection. The man waited for Troy to pass, and then began walking in the same direction a few paces behind him.

Troy stopped, did an abrupt about-face, and walked back to a nearby newsstand and picked up a magazine. The man who had been walking behind him seemed to hesitate for a moment, but then continued on at a leisurely pace in the direction of the café.

Troy had enjoyed his work in Army criminal investigations. He had in fact planned to make a career of it until his father-in-law, Clifford Conrad, CEO over development, offered the lucrative job at Bartlett Enterprises. He couldn't pass it up. Lizzy Conrad was going to have the finest, and Army salaries couldn't touch the near six figures that his new job coupled with Lizzy's created. Lizzy wouldn't have to work much longer, and they'd be debt free with a D.C. town home nearly paid for. He looked forward to her staying home with the kids and being the traditional housewife she had always wanted to be.

But CID, Criminal Investigation Division, U.S. Army, was police work with just enough intrigue that it had been tough to give it up.

He liked the action, the variety of mental challenges the job offered. He had been called upon to do undercover work on a number of occasions. He had tailed people and had been tailed, and for whatever reason, the old feeling of being "tailed" came back to him as if he had never left the Army.

Troy backtracked. Decided to go up the escalator to the street level, around to the far side of the Galleria, and then down the escalator to come at the café from the east side. He wanted to see if he could shake this guy, if indeed he were being followed. He couldn't imagine why anyone would follow him, unless it was some old grudge for having slapped handcuffs and shackles on some mentally whacked-out dude who deserved it years before. But that was something he had long since quit worrying about.

He decided it was probably just his over-active imagination. The guy had peered into his car, but had probably mistaken it for someone else's. Maybe Lizzy's jumpiness at this Lawton business and her eagerness for him to meet her here instead of at home had raised his antenna to other possibilities.

He took a few extra minutes, stopped, bought a heavily fortified soda and some aspirin, and now leisurely strolled to his rendezvous with Liz.

He spotted her at a corner table next to a rail that separated pedestrian traffic from the café and the walkway leading to the bookstore. Her head was down, her face to one side, resting on her arm on the table. There was a cup of coffee near her hand. *Poor thing,* he thought. *She's exhausted from all the pressure this Ron Lawton guy has created.*

He knew that if he ever met this Lawton face-to-face, he would need all the self-control he could muster not to strangle him for causing the anxiety his wife was feeling over the Mike Stone files.

"Lizzy, honey," he said quietly in her ear so as not to startle her. "Lizzy," he said again, nudging her gently on the shoulder. His heart suddenly pounded out a sprinter's beat. He quickly cast his eyes around the mall. The man who had tailed him came into focus. There was something about him, the way he had launched an almost evil glare and smirk toward him that was unsettling. He'd seen that look before. *Where? Who?* It didn't immediately register with him.

He got down to Lizzy's level by pulling up a chair next to her. He patted her back. "Liz, honey," he said as her face slipped off her arm onto the table. Her eyes were open but showed emptiness. The last time he'd seen a look on a person's face like this was at a CID investigation . . .

"Oh, Lizzy!" he cried. "Oh, dear God, no! Somebody! Call 9-1-1! Hurry, it's my wife!"

12

His eyes caught the man who had tailed him. He was now across the mall, walking briskly toward the exit to the parking garage. *Those eyes,* Troy thought as his brain quickly performed thousands of instantaneous neuron connections, looking for the right file. *I know those eyes!* he said to himself.

He couldn't do anything about it until he had seen to his wife's needs. He lifted her off the chair and laid her gently upon the floor and knelt beside her, feeling for a pulse and checking her breathing. Then he saw it! A puddle of blood was forming under her neck and head!

"Oh, Lizzy! No, baby. Don't do this!" he cried. "Lizzy, come on now. Come back to me, baby!" He laid his ear on her heart and looked again at the emptiness on her face.

"Here, let me help. I'm a doctor," a man said as he came to immediate assistance. He knelt next to her and felt for a heart beat. "We've got a pulse."

"Thank God! Please, please . . . save my wife. She's bleeding from behind her head. Here, back here," he said, pointing to her neck.

Troy took a quick look in the direction of the young man who had tailed him, who was now waiting at the parking structure elevators. He was looking in Troy's direction.

"Watch my wife! Please watch her!" he pleaded. "The man who did this, he's headed out. I've got to follow him! Please, help my wife!" he said again, as if in repeating his plea a miracle could be proffered.

Troy's military training now took over, and he raced the opposite way, up the escalators, past patrons, sprinting and shoving his way through the crowd coming in from the trains. He had to get to the parking garage at the upper level to meet the elevators.

Tears fogged his vision and a sudden rage drove him on. In his heart he feared Lizzy was gone, but he didn't want to believe it. He also knew he had to catch the man who had been following him. He needed a clue—anything—and he wanted that man in his strong hands, down on the ground as he bashed him into unconsciousness.

He was breathing heavily as he pushed his way through the throngs coming and going to the parking garage. He arrived at the elevator on the first upper floor. Out of breath, he stopped, panting, and watched the door open. It was full of people, but only two got off. As the door closed, he saw the man who had tailed him standing in the back of the elevator.

Troy raced to the staircase. With luck he could meet the elevator as its doors opened on each level. He took the treads two at a time, gaining the next floor in seconds. He dodged through a line of cars patiently waiting their turn to enter the ramp that led down to the street level.

If the man hadn't seen him looking for him he would continue on to his car. That would be on the same level Troy had parked his. If he had seen Troy giving chase then he'd simply go to a different level or return on a "down" elevator to try to lose him, just as Troy had done minutes earlier in the galleria.

He was in panic mode now. Terrified that he had just been made a widower, needing to be by Lizzy's side, but alert to the fact that he also might have her killer close at hand, his adrenalin pushed him past all fear and focused him on getting that man.

The elevator opened. He was panting more heavily now, not in the shape he used to be, as he watched people pour out. Just women and kids. He beat his fist against the elevator door, let loose with a loud expletive, and then realized the man had probably gotten off one floor below and would head for the staircases. Which end of the parking garage? He decided to take the stairs nearest—the one he had just come from.

Racing down the flight to the next level, he turned the corner to see a heavy wooden object suddenly coming toward his face. He instinctively brought his hand up but not fast enough as the club caught him flush on the forehead, sending him reeling against the heavy metal drainage pipes in the stairwell, and then down to the deck.

The man behind the club bent over him. He had a stiletto in his hand. Taking Troy's wallet and keys, he began to turn his bloodied head to the side for the finishing touch with a sharp and deadly thrust of the three-inch blade into Troy's spinal column at the base of his skull.

"Hey, man! What's wrong with the guy? You need some help? Mom! Call 9-1-1. There is a man down here bleeding," a burly teen called as he entered the stairwell. "Hey, what you doing? You can't just leave him," the boy said as the man quickly straightened, carefully putting his knife away. The piece of wood, a two-foot length of two-by-four taken from some nearby construction repair work, lay within inches of Troy's head. The man shook his head at the teen. "No English," he said in a feigned Eastern European accent. "No English," he repeated and walked briskly away.

"Hey, man? You okay?" the teen asked to the groans of Troy, who now lay with blood pouring down his face. "Mom! Hurry!"

"I called," she answered. "Oh, my! Oh, no. Son, don't move him," she said.

"My wife. That man . . ." Troy mumbled.

"Hang in there, sir. We called 9-1-1 for you."

Troy made an attempt to sit up. "Got to get back," he groaned. He reached for the boy's shirt. "That man. Killed my . . . Oh!" he moaned as he fell back and into a world filled with darkness.

"It's gonna be okay, mister," the young man replied with encouragement. "Mom! Behind you! Look out! I think—" The boy stood and stared at the man in his car as the window rolled down.

"Hey, boy," the man motioned.

"Mom, run, get help!" he pushed his mother down the staircase and then turned to face a black, shiny gun barrel being pointed at his chest from some fifteen feet away. Someone honked from behind the black SUV and then the teen saw it all happen to him slowly, like film frames slowed to single shots through a camera lens.

Frame one: He was going to be shot.

Frame two: He turned to run down the stairs.

Frame three: The man's car was bumped by another from behind.

Frame four: The boy turned back and saw the gun barrel raised again.

Frame five: He heard a muffled blast, and there was the rush of air and the buzz of a bullet speeding by his right ear and smacking against the stairwell wall.

Frame six: He was about to bound down the stairwell when something hit him in the upper back with greater force than he had ever known, and he was thrown down the stairs by the impact and lay motionless. He hadn't heard the second shot.

"Mom?" he whimpered. "Help me."

13

FORMER PASTOR OF THE FIRST Congregational Church of Tallahassee, Nicholas Caine, felt he had finally put to rest his secret agony and guilt. It was the redemptive forgiveness of Claire Barlow that had sealed the book and provided the peace that had so long eluded him.

So ironic! he thought. *God's mighty hand at work even in the course of sin . . .* His long-standing regret over what he had done to help his brother, Joe, win his girlfriend's heart back in '69 had changed him from the crude and coarse man he had been. The man Nick had helped destroy forgave him, and that had driven Nicholas Caine for the last forty years to find a way to make amends.

He found making amends for such a transgression nearly impossible, however.

He had endured years of nightmares—nightmares he had never shared with anyone, especially not his friend and patron Claire Barlow. In spite of her love, Nick had never had the courage to entirely describe the shame he had felt for the evil thing he had done, knowing it would have caused that sweet woman too much pain. Nor could Nick erase the awful memory of his brother, Joe, standing in rage over the helpless Jimmy Barlow. Claire had buoyed Nicholas's flagging spirit. Now perhaps the dreams would cease, and he could let it all rest.

But as he and Claire walked together from the garden back into her house the other day, he retained a nagging and annoying feeling that something additional had been left undone.

It confused him. *Every man or woman, even Joe, has the right to expect confidentiality from private confessions, don't they?*

Although Joe had been cleared of criminal negligence, Nick knew Joe was still carrying the weight of not just Jimmy's death but also what had happened to Meredith. *It all happened so long ago, and Joe was so young. Can Joe still be blamed for surrendering to his raging youthful hormones and making stupid choices?*

Meredith had been engaged to Jimmy, and Joe had wanted her. Driven by blind desire, Joe had been a man out of control, and what had worried Nick all these years was that Joe had never really dealt with the things that had happened, instead almost reveling in Jimmy's death. That was something Nick felt God had condemned and could not forgive without requiring restitution.

If only Joe had followed Nick's advice, confessed his role, and told the truth, Nick would not have had to carry the burden of knowing but not being able to say. Pastor Caine believed wholeheartedly in priest/penitent confidentiality and that a parishioner's confession was sacrosanct. When Joe had finally confessed his part in Meredith's accident years after the fact, he, Nicholas Caine, as a newly ordained minister had told Joe, "It is all in God's hands now." But Pastor Caine had been concerned that Joe had rationalized his involvement with Meredith's death, just as Nick felt Joe had done with Jimmy's unfortunate "accident."

According to the sheriff's report, Meredith's accidental fall at the levy on the beach was corroborated by another witness. Why should he, Nick, have any doubts?

If Sheriff Blaine Lockhart, now deceased, had closed the books on
the investigation, and if the county attorney's office had found no reason to press charges, then Nick felt he would have to simply accept
Joe's story. Of course Sheriff Lockhart's credentials weren't impeccable;
he had been involved in numerous scandals in the course of his career
and prior to his retirement years ago. There was also the matter of the
sheriff's staff, members of which had been suspected of serious impro-
prieties, frequently spoken of in the community but never proved—
offenses ranging from extortion, to the mishandling of evidence, to
winking at the making of moonshine and prostitution. The mysterious
witness to Meredith's fall had never been identified, and some said he
or she had never existed.

The loss of Meredith caused Joe to flee from the city and join the
Army, where he found himself a year and a half later as a company
commander in Vietnam. Coming home from the war, Joe had seemed
a different man. He was more solemn, mature, and focused, eager to
get his career in politics back on track. Joe had always been good at
getting what he wanted, and somehow, Nick wanted to believe that
Vietnam had changed his brother into a less egocentric man.

Nick's mind had made the journey back to that awful night in
1969 a thousand times. Now he felt, with the forgiveness of this beautiful soul Claire, he could put it all to rest, at least his part in the
sordid affair.

"Nicholas, I want you to read something," Claire had declared a
week or so earlier. They entered through the glass slider from the
backyard patio after a walk in her rose garden.

She led him to a coffee table in the living room where she kept a
large Bible, one containing photos of family members and the family
tree, a family heirloom that had been handed down for three genera-
tions. "This is the official King James Version," she proudly declared.
"I want you to read something for me."

She opened the heavy volume to the Old Testament book of Jeremiah. He smiled at the need she felt to explain to him: "Jeremiah was an ancient prophet of the Lord. But his words then have just as much meaning today. And no other man can bear a witness of these true words as well as you can, my dear boy."

He grinned. *Dear boy,* he thought. He was sixty-five years old. Dear boy, she had called him. He chuckled and brought the book up into the light where he could more easily read it.

"I want you to read Jeremiah, chapter 3 and verse 15. Aloud please," she requested.

Nicholas nodded. He knew this verse by heart.

*   *   *   *   *

Nicholas Caine home, Tallahassee

No, Joe! You got to stop and leave it be with me and the boys. This is our fun! Now go, man. That girl, remember she . . ." he said, then mumbled a few more words before he finished tossing in bed.

Grace wondered if Nick would go on. Sometimes he rambled like this for minutes, then would stop abruptly, only to start up again an hour or two later. Her husband had told her what he could of his nightmares, and she had hoped he had finally gotten it all behind him with his retirement.

She knew that he was torn between the man of his youth and the new man he became after his heart transplant. Somewhere between the old and new man was a dark secret that he hadn't shared, even with her. It worried her, but when she inquired about it, he would say, "Gracie, it's all in God's hands. Best to leave it be."

A sweeter, kinder, and gentler man wasn't to be found on the earth, Grace assured herself. Nicholas was truly a giant among men in his characteristic respect and love for others. Why he should be so tormented was beyond her. She had prayed to God to relieve him from the torture and she had even told Nick so. He simply replied, "Sometimes, Gracie, God gives us a 'thorn in our flesh' like the one Paul the Apostle had. God never saw fit to relieve him of it. He doesn't relieve the pain because it helps us remember our dependence on Him. I need Him now more than ever. Do you understand?"

She did and she didn't understand. Having to endure any "thorn in the flesh" for over thirty years seemed excessive, more than adequate to learn any lesson God might have needed to impart. Besides, how sweet and loving did God expect a man to become through adversity anyway?

She expected with Nicholas's retirement from the pulpit that the lifting of the burden of having so many people to worry about would ease her husband's personal pain.

But now he seemed more agitated than ever. Yesterday, during a quiet meal, he brought up the agony and guilt he carried and part of the story about his miracle transplant she had never heard before.

Chronic sleeplessness, caused by memories and vivid dreams, had always plagued him, but now that he didn't have his ministry, he seemed like a lost boy. She was tempted to tell him to go back into the work as a marriage and family counselor, Sunday School teacher, or church deacon—anything to help him feel useful and fulfilled.

Lying there beside her restless husband, she wondered again what she could do for her beloved Nicholas.

He continued to mumble in his sleep, and when she reached to nudge him, he stopped talking but apparently didn't wake.

She lay in the dark, thinking. *Maybe if I ask him to be more open, honest with me. Maybe if I reconstruct, I can help him get all those issues over Jimmy Barlow's death behind him.*

Grace sat up and got out of bed, fishing a pad of paper and pen from her nightstand drawer and moving in the darkness to a divan on the other side of their bedroom. There she turned on a lamp and began to jot down what Nicholas had revealed to her over the years about the event that had impacted his life so strongly.

She didn't know that Nicholas had awakened at her jostling in bed. He pretended to still be asleep but watched her, wondering what it was that she was writing. His mind went to the nightmare that he had just suffered.

*   *   *   *   *

The nightmare always started with James Barlow's struggle to get away. He could see the entire drama through Jimmy Barlow's eyes as the young, black preacher lay there being beaten. And there was the baseball bat. But Nick hadn't used it in the beating.

This always confused him. The men who had ganged up on James at the church hadn't used a bat. They'd just used their own God-given tools—fists.

Nicholas trembled. *So real,* he said to himself silently as he tossed, waiting for sleep to come to him.

Gracie had watched him struggle during the few months since his retirement. Nick had been concerned when his replacement pastor had not been well-received. Members of the congregation had murmured about the young man's failure to live up to the level of Pastor Caine's performance, and Nicholas had pled with the church board members to have patience—to allow the young man taking his place a chance.

Gracie knew that more than that was bothering her husband. She had heard him mutter the words "priest-penitent confidentiality" in his sleep.

Gracie knew that her husband wondered if he had been correct in not trying to get things straightened out with the law—if it had been sufficient to tell Joe, when his brother first came to him thirty-five years ago after his military duty, that God who sees all would take care of the matter. Joe had not confessed to anything regarding James's injuries and Meredith's death, Nick explained to his wife, that Joe had only said he was present and how very sorry he was over what had happened.

From what Nick had told her, Gracie knew Joe had loved Meredith Little with an almost unreasonable love, and she had watched Nick's younger brother fail miserably at marriage since.

Gracie had decided to talk to Claire; to see if she could get Claire to talk to Nick, or to get her to encourage him to assist the new man at church, even if only during weekly administrative meetings. Nick needed a distraction and a purpose, and Gracie was afraid without it, Nick might finally break, maybe even suffer another stroke—like the one that had prompted his retirement in the first place.

She watched her husband sleeping fitfully and yearned for the peace he deserved but couldn't find.

Nicholas hadn't been asleep at all. He wished his tossing hadn't awakened Gracie. She worried too much about him, but for her sake he wished the dreams would go away, leave him at peace. His back was turned to her, and he stared out the large picture window from his bed, peering deeply into the black night sky.

It was black that night, just like tonight.

January 1969

"I've got just the thing to help that lovesick feeling," Nick grinned.

Joe was in one of his critical moods. "You've got to stop that drinking and smoking, Nick. It's going to kill you. You know that enlarged heart of yours is only a few beats from putting you into a six-by-six-foot piece of real estate—permanently."

"Oh, lighten up, Joe. You worry too much."

"I just want you to have a long life. That's all," Joe countered.

"I was talking about your heavy heart, not mine," Nick explained. "What we need to do is get rid of Jimmy the Negro preacher. He's got the newspapers going, filling the white people's brains of this town so full of civil rights horse dung that the good folks of this part of Florida can't remember how to think straight. Some of them are forgetting who's white and who's black. As for that half-breed nigger girl of yours—"

Joe slammed on the brakes and quickly pulled the Chevy Impala convertible onto the dirt shoulder. He reached across the front seat and grabbed his older brother by the shirt collar.

"Don't you ever talk about Meredith that way! She's as white as any girl you know! Besides, those Negro troublemakers have some good points! I'm trying my best to make friends, win votes for when I run for office. And I better never, EVER, hear you use the word *nigger* in reference to Meredith Little!" Joe's fists were doubled, and his face reddened with rage. "Or any other Negro for that matter."

"Wow!"

"Yeah. WOW!" Joe replied.

"You got it bad for that girl, don't you?" Nick said, taking another swig from the whiskey bottle wrapped in a brown paper bag.

"You don't know the half of it," Joe lamented. "I . . ."

Nick watched his younger brother struggling for words to describe his frustration, and then as if he heard the silent thoughts swirling in Joe's head, Nick said, "You didn't."

"Afraid so," was the mumbled reply.

"So marry her."

"I thought she was going to marry me. Then I get slammed with this letter telling me why she can't, how Jimmy Barlow needs her, and how she had allowed her emotions to carry her away."

"Does Jimmy know?"

"Apparently." Joe sat back, closed his eyes, releasing a heavy sigh. "She's got my child, not his. I can't let go. I wish I'd never . . ."

A young, twenty-three-year-old college grad and newly appointed aide to the mayor of Tallahassee, Joseph Caine wanted a way out, but couldn't leave town, or Meredith, without a win. He was already a political junkie, and winning was part of every aspect of his life. It didn't matter that he loved her. That wasn't enough. He HAD to *win* her.

And, he wasn't going to let the Reverend Jimmy Barlow with all his self-righteous magnanimity step up and save Meredith from her shame. Joe wasn't about to either give Meredith up or allow his honor to be called into question—not without a fight.

"So," Nick began as he took another swig from his bottle and wiped at his lips, "You've got yourself in quite a pickle, haven't you?"

"Yeah. I guess you could say that," Joe agreed.

"Why don't you just admit your mistake publicly and put her on the spot? At least threaten to. That would maybe have her reconsider what she is dealing with. She then would be embarrassing the mighty and righteous Minister Barlow by appearing so loose as to be sleeping around, and you could look like the repentant Saint Joseph who only wants to do the right thing."

"Hmmm." Joe weighed the implications.

"Besides, folks like their politicians to show some humility. They'll trust you more if you 'fess up to making a mistake, show your love on your sleeve for the pretty . . . uh . . . half-white . . . uh, slightly Negro, girl."

"Maybe," Joe said, sighing heavily.

Nick lit up the last cigarette from his pack of Camels. "The doctor says I could die within six months if I don't get this heart thing fixed," he spat out as he exhaled a long drag from the acrid, unfiltered cigarette.

"Stop trying to kill yourself. You don't have to die. You must just want to," Joe replied with disgust as he snatched the cigarette from Nick's mouth and tossed it out the window.

"So, Saint Joe," Nick said. "What will it be? You want me to take care of this Barlow troublemaker? Me and some of the boys from the Roadhouse have been thinkin'—it might be fun to break the old white hoods and sheets out from their hiding place." Nick bellowed at the thought.

"You're drunk," Joe said.

"You know, burn a few crosses, run a few of your Negro friends off the road," Nick continued. "Put the fear of the Klan in them . . ." He laughed at the evil implications of having fun at the expense of the Ku Klux Klan.

Not a member of any organized political group, Nicholas Caine was not a Klansman, never had been. But his sympathies weighed more heavily there than with civil rights do-gooders like his brother, Joe. Nick and his wild friends used to act the part back in his crazy high school days, just to have some fun. They never meant any real harm, but the chase late at night of a few Negros with some of the boys from the Roadhouse, then blaming it on the Klan was just too much of a temptation for the lighthearted Nick Caine to resist.

"So, you'd rough him up a bit?" Joe asked. "Then I'd put the word out about my indiscretions with Meredith?"

"Indiscretions . . . that's a good way to refer to the affair," Nick assured. "Nah, we'd just push him around a little, act like we was gonna hurt him. I promise."

"Then Meredith would see that a life with Jimmy Barlow would be hell to pay for?"

"Something like that."

"And I'd come to her rescue and to Jimmy's defense as a righteous believer in equality, so Meredith could see my compassionate and generous soul?"

Nick Caine lifted his hands over his head in mock adoration and said, "Now you are bathed in the glorious light of truth, Brother Joe Caine!" Nick laughed at his own plotting and the fun that lay ahead for him tonight. He'd as much as been given a death sentence by his doctors because of the enlarged and broken-down, twenty-eight-year-old heart he was carrying around inside his chest. He needed something to take his mind off his troubles.

"You won't let anything really serious happen to Barlow, right? You know, some of those friends of yours can get carried away."

"Don't worry about it! We'll just rough him up a bit. Scare him. Put a little fear of the Almighty in him. Hell, I don't have nothin' against Jimmy. Known him for as long as you have. His Mom is a good woman. You know she helped our folks out that bad year of '58?"

"Huh?"

"When we lost the business. Claire secretly loaned Dad the money to get the store back. She always made a good interest on her money. She is really something. I'll bet you don't know she was the major shareholder at Capitol Trust and Loan?"

"What?"

"Yeah, her old man was quite the savvy businessman. Made a fortune in scrap metals before, during, and after the big war. Seems old man Barlow played low-key, collected junk, and everyone thought he and his sons were just barely getting by.

"Well, he had this white business partner, but James Barlow Sr. was the real money behind the Trust and Loan. When he died, it all fell into Claire's lap. That's how she was able to put Jimmy up in that fancy Ivy League school—Harvard—then Oxford over in England.

She may not show it, but that lady is worth as much as a million dollars I hear say."

"So that's how Jimmy has been able to afford to be free to do all this political stuff, the right's movement and such."

"Yes, indeed. And, get this. She built and paid cash for that new church building her son is the minister of. I'm surprised you didn't know, Joe, you being the savvy politician and all. You are supposed to know about your enemies, have some dirt on them."

"You got any dirt on James W. Barlow?" Joe asked. "This could really work! You got to have something," Joe said eagerly.

"In fact I do. Might not be true, but so what? Perception is reality. That's what we used to say in the infantry. Always make the enemy believe you have more than you do, and use it to your advantage."

"You got the devil in you, Nick."

"I, Mr. President, will do whatever it takes to get the job done. Let's roll. We can talk some more at the Roadhouse, you can go see Meredith, and by tomorrow, she'll be yours!"

"You'd make a good politician, Nick."

Nick grinned.

*   *   *   *   *

Gracie was startled at the loud cry that seemed to come from a sound sleep Nick had finally found.

"No!"

"Nicholas? Nick, honey, wake up!" He was perspiring and rolling his head from side to side, but then relaxed his convulsing frame and lay still and slept, as suddenly asleep as he had awakened. He didn't move, just mouthed the words: "Hello, Joe. What brings you here?"

14

BESIDES DRINKING SPIKED LEMONADE and munching on ice, which he enjoyed doing to irritate people he wanted to bother, Joe Caine was also an addict to sedatives, alcohol, and narcotic strength painkillers. The other addictions he'd had in life were baseball and Meredith Little.

He cleared a space on his desktop, got the ice from the fridge next door, set out enough alcohol to poison a rat, pulled the bottle of Percocet from his medicine cabinet in the private restroom off his office suite, and stared into the large tumbler he'd mix his drink in.

He popped an ice cube into his mouth and crunched as he gathered his thoughts, then unscrewed the cap to the Percocet—a narcotic to most, just a mild sedative to him. He filled the glass tumbler half with lemonade, the other half with vodka out of the bottle he kept hidden (which all his office staff knew to keep fully stocked) in his right-hand, bottom desk drawer.

Two ought to do, he allowed as he swirled the ice in his drink, then popped the pills.

He needed to take his mind off the nagging memory that burdened him today. This same depression overcame him every year, after his annual visit to the "Wall." Being there not only reminded him of the senseless waste of so many young lives in a war no politician cared to win, but also of the reason he had run from Tallahassee and to Vietnam in the first place. He was a lost soul for weeks after each of those yearly visits.

His thoughts ran. He had loved Meredith Little. He really had. He still couldn't bear to see the mental image of her, the last he ever had. Now, today, tomorrow, and maybe during any quiet moment, he would lose himself to the past and replay that final evening with her over and over and over. . . . He'd replay it until after a week or so of drug- and alcohol-induced fog, he could finally sublimate again the memory of the stupid prank he and Nick had pulled. A prank that had resulted in mortal injury to a civil rights activist named Jimmy Barlow and the needless death of beautiful Meredith Little.

The memories made him shudder.

Meredith Little was biracial, what was called in those days a "mulatto." The daughter of a strong-willed black man and an aristocratic-looking French mother, Meredith was a black-eyed beauty, with soft, olive skin, dimples, and a brilliant smile that had thoroughly charmed and captivated Joe Caine from the first time he saw her on campus.

Far from feeling any embarrassment over her mixed parentage, Meredith possessed an unusual inner confidence and an easy bearing and natural school-girl radiance that made Joe's heart race almost faster than his body could endure. And every woman who had entered his life since had been unfavorably compared to Meredith.

Meredith's father, a proud member of the military, was seen by white folks in Tallahassee as uppity—a black man who had had the audacity to presume to marry a white woman. Her mother, an elegant and very European woman, was looked down upon by those same people for having the temerity to consort with a black man. So the Littles had faced persecution in the form of gossip, sneers, whispers, and outright insults.

Meredith was also engaged to Jimmy Barlow, and that had made her twice forbidden—and twice as appealing, at least to Joe Caine, who had found her beauty and her inaccessibility irresistible.

If only Jimmy Barlow hadn't gotten in the way . . . it was a thought Joe had never been able to get out of his mind.

The persecution of Meredith and her family had made Joe angry, and he would have protected them if Meredith had only given him a chance. He could have done it, too. Just graduating from college, an aide to the mayor's campaign manager, then to a congressional candidate, Joe was a guy on his way up. He was going places, and he felt marrying Meredith would show the world how white and black could live, love, and overcome the racial bigotry that had plagued the country since the days of slavery.

Only James Barlow had stood in the way. Jimmy was the fiery rhetorical rocket launcher of verbal missiles that had so impressed the idealistic young Meredith. Joe was sure Meredith was only caught up in the intrigue of the civil rights movement, that she couldn't really be in love with a man going into the ministry, barely making wages, preaching from the First Congregational Church's pulpit as its new, young pastor.

Joe made a point of becoming a friend to Meredith's father, who was stationed at nearby Fort Walton. He, Joe, had not been unkind to Jimmy even though they had both vied for Meredith's attention. Until Meredith had called Joe and told him she couldn't see him anymore, that Jimmy had proposed and she had accepted, Joe had been the model of courtesy to James Barlow as well as to the other local leaders of the rights movements. Then he lost it. With Meredith's phone call, he lost all reason for living, if it was to be without her.

Joe's older brother, Nick, was heavy into the "good-ole-boys" groups, fighting to preserve the ways of the South against the do-gooder civil rights advocates such as the "Freedom Riders," the James Barlows of the world, the NAACP, and the Kennedys with their idealistic rhetoric.

Nick was not the person then he is today, Joe reminded himself. *Such a change of heart. Uncanny. It all happened so innocently. That day and night, Barlow's "accident," the coma. Then Meredith. Then Nick's illness . . . Then Vietnam . . .*

"And here I am, still alone," he mumbled as he lay his head upon his hands and went back in time once again.

*   *   *   *   *

January 1969—Tallahassee, Florida

"Here's a toast to Southern boys and their women!" Nick Caine shouted as he stood on the barroom table. It was as dark inside the Roadhouse Tavern and Pool Hall as it was outside this night. The smack of pool table cues against balls breaking up, a Jerry Lee Lewis song playing on the jukebox, and hoots aimed at the scantily clad, white-booted girl dancing on the small stage were the sounds that made Nick Caine come alive.

"I'm back from protecting the great American dream against the Commie hordes! Yes, sir, those Germans make good beer, but they don't make good friends! Whooo!" he shouted as men clinked chilled beer bottles to his.

"Another round to any man who can down his without a breath. On the count of three. One . . . two . . ." He quickly brought the amber bottle up and guzzled the contents as the rowdy crowd laughed and cheered him on. "Three," he finished, wiping his mouth on his shirtsleeve.

"And here's to my little brother, Joe! Future president of these

United States. My commander in chief," he added with a bellow. "More beer!" he shouted.

"Hey, come on, Nick," Joe said. "Better lay off. Let me get you home."

"No, sir, Mr. President, sir," he slurred as he saluted. "You are a politician. And I don't go home with politicians. They make me feel uncomfortable," he laughed.

"You're drunk, Nick. Come on. You'll end up broke buying all these beers for your new friends."

"New friends?" he laughed. "I might be a little tipsy," he shouted above the raucousness of the barroom. "But, I can see Bob Gordon over there from high school. Bob! How ya doin', Bob!" He waved. Bob raised his bottle. "And this fine fellow," he slopped out, "is Mac Zabrinski, WHO, by the way, is the Roadhouse arm wrestling champ for three years straight! Right, Mac?"

"Right you are, Nick."

"See? I got lots of old friends. Maybe more than you," Nick slurred as he climbed unsteadily off the table onto a chair and then onto the floor. He stumbled toward his brother.

"Good night, ever'body! You gotta get a new man to send over to replace me so those Soviets don't overrun us. Sergeant Nicholas Caine is retired! Ha, Ha . . . Hee-ah! Oh, man, does it ever feel good to forget," he said as Joe slipped his arm around his brother. "Bye! See you guys tomorrow!"

"Nick, you got to get some rest," Joe said as he helped him get into the car.

"Hey! You look just like my little brother, Joe. I thought you were the president! I think I'll call you LBJ!" He giggled at his own comedic attempts to keep the night young and alive. "'L' for Little. 'B' for brother. 'J' for Joe. 'LBJ.' Our beloved president of Vietnam and the civil rights wars? You—LBJ-President . . . Get it?"

"You're a drunk, and it's killing you."

"I'm a smoker, a drunk, and a cheat at cards. I'm sick! You know that's why the Army let me out, LBJ," he spat back angrily. "I was gonna make a career of it! I loved the Army! I was a LIFER!" he slurred, proudly pounding his chest. "A real SOB lifer. That was me!" he sobbed. "So they find a little heart problem. Big deal. So I pass out a few times. Bigger deal! Hell—I was tougher, meaner, leaner, better shooter, could out-maneuver, any other man of my rank!" he moaned.

Joe was driving now. He patted his big brother on the shoulder. "Well, you aren't to blame for a bad heart valve or whatever it is. You were the best, I'm sure."

"Yeah," he sighed. "You shoulda seen them German girls, Joe. You ought to join up. This Vietnam thing is heating up! You might miss it if you don't hurry." With that he leaned his head back against the cushioned seat of Joe's new Impala Coupe and slipped into a rest he hadn't allowed himself since he had returned from Germany the night before.

Joe drove on. He turned the radio to the local news station and heard the voice of the man who was conspiring to take his girl from him. Joe's blood pressure skyrocketed as he gripped the wheel tighter. He had just graduated, filled his draft deferment papers out to continue on in pursuit of a master's degree in political science at Florida State, and all he needed to do was convince Meredith Little to follow him there. He'd marry her, run for office someday, and with a woman like that he'd . . .

15

Next day

WHEN YOU SAY WE ARE JUST GOING to put the 'fear of God' in him, what do you suggest I do? See, Nick—I'd rather be ignorant of all this."

"Little brother, you just leave and wait for a call from the Lone Ranger and the boys. We don't think you should have anything to do with this. Comprende? Me and Tonto have some planning to do. Right, Tonto?" he said, slapping high school friend Bubba Brown on the back with a hardy laugh. "Hi, Ho, Silver!" he hooted.

"Beat it, punk," Bubba said to Joe. "We're goin' huntin', and you ain't invited."

"Just don't do anything I wouldn't do," Joe cautioned. "I'm going to track Meredith down."

Nick winked, coughed, hit his hand against his chest a few times, and downed the remainder of his beer mug. "I'll call you."

Joe wasn't against a little show of force to pull out a victory in politics. He wasn't above creative deception and manipulation for the greater good, but he didn't want to hurt anyone physically. He hoped Nick understood that.

He was hurting; deeply hurting inside. He'd never meant to get carried away with Meredith the way he had. He actually felt like he wanted to be the best possible man in terms of the virtues that he knew no one lived anymore. She had him worked up and seemed to enjoy doing what caused him to lose control.

That's what made him so mad now. *How could she give a signal one way and then head in the opposite direction?* he wondered. Now a new life was involved . . . an unborn child . . . and getting it out into the public could ruin him forever; make him a pariah at City Hall, if he didn't handle the situation with total humility. He wondered how to get her to understand that marrying him was the answer.

His political ambitions to become county commissioner and then to win a seat in Congress, could be dashed if this wasn't handled just right. He'd considered offering to pay for an abortion—thought for a time that might be an answer. But he'd decided that would be like telling Meredith he didn't value her as a person. No. He wanted to let her know he loved her. He'd follow older brother Nick's advice. Put Jimmy Barlow on the spot. Be honorable. Act humble. But the whole situation made his blood boil.

He prided himself on being an intellectual, who was not capable of being prejudiced. He had tried to show that he wanted nothing to do with the old school of white racial superiority; something that was a part of the "old South." But he couldn't stand the fact that Meredith would choose a full-blooded Negro man over him. So he guessed he was prejudiced after all. He found himself hating Barlow. Joe's intellect was being overridden by his emotions. His reasoning and judgment were being conquered by his manhood—the need to win at all costs.

With Meredith by his side he knew he could do so much more for the new state of affairs in racial equality. The couple would be viewed as a symbol of true racial harmony, equals, and it would help the civil rights movement even more.

But Meredith had told him she couldn't abandon "her people."

His mind wandered back to four weeks before, the last time she had allowed him to call on her.

"What about love?" he had asked.

"I love Jimmy as much as I do you, Joe. Can't you see? I wanted to have both. I am sorry," she said tearfully. "And I'm confused. But I do love you both."

"Sorry! That is all you can be? You will take our child, raise it as his! Who is going to buy that when he or she comes out whiter than you or Jimmy? Huh? Don't you think you'll have some explaining to do to him?"

"I've already explained. I apologized. I asked for his forgiveness. I even was tempted to get an . . ." she couldn't say the word, " . . . but I couldn't."

"Well, now. Jimmy's the saint and you are the sinner. Can't you see we fit together better than you and Barlow?"

"Jimmy told me he forgives me and that God will too. He talks about God, you talk about politics. His religion is Jesus, yours is a political party. He is a good man, and you are . . . ," she hesitated. "You are, too," she finished.

"So it really comes down to this! You would be slapping your father in the face, saying, 'I'm better than marrying a Negro man like Mom did.' That's what it really comes down to, isn't it?"

"No! That's not fair!" she cried.

"Life isn't fair. If I never understood it before I just figured that one out!"

They had just finished eating dinner near the capitol building in downtown Tallahassee. He called a cab to the curb, paid the fare for her, and slammed the door shut after she got in. Seething, he watched the cab drive off, taking away from him the thing he wanted most in life, then hopped in his convertible and sped off to the coast. The family beach house at Alligator Point was stocked with alcohol. He was going to get completely, utterly drunk, sauced, and lost for a couple of days.

Furious at the rationalization that Meredith had just used to push him out of her life, he thought it was too bad duels between gentlemen were out of style. *I'd win that one,* he thought as he drove out from Tallahassee to the coast.

Meredith was genuinely confused. She wanted to love Joe, but saw the problems for herself in it down the road. Joe's temper, his fooling around with women . . . she'd heard the rumors and had thought that she might tame him. *What was I thinking?* she berated herself, struggling to keep her composure. *I should have never let it get this far,* she counseled herself in silence. *James is such a gentleman. He loves me, and he is as handsome as Dad,* she reminded herself. *He is respected and wouldn't live for anyone but me, God, and the cause. I have to remember that.*

*　　*　　*　　*　　*

Two days later

"Mama? Happy early birthday to you, Mama!" James sang into the telephone. "I was thinking of you and wanted to say 'I love you.'" He listened as his mother reminded him that she expected him to be on time the next night for the family dinner party. She and the family celebrated each other's birthdays in quiet familial togetherness, and always at the family gathering place—Claire Barlow's modest ranch-style bungalow on three acres of prime citrus land outside of town.

"Yes, Mama," James allowed. "I understand, Mama. I am twenty-nine years old now, Mama," he answered. "I got to go now. Meredith expects me for dinner at her folks," he said. "Uh-huh. Fort Walton," he replied. "I love you too, Mama." *You'd think I was just out of nursery school the way she fusses over me,* he thought.

"Got to go now, Mama," he answered. "Going to do a counseling session and then meet Meredith here to go to her folks; make our engagement official." He smiled as he listened to the list of do's and don'ts. "Yes, Mama, I'll be a good boy," he chuckled. "'Bye, Mama."

Smiling, he realized his mother had been right again. Just put your feet on the well-worn path of the Lord and it will take you where they should go, she'd say. Tonight he was making it official with Meredith's parents and he felt like the luckiest man in the world. While the mistake she had made with Joe Caine had come as a shock, he loved Meredith and knew her to be a good person—sincere and honest. He could forgive her, and they would make a good life together, no matter the child she was carrying.

He hoped Joe would just as graciously accept this marriage and let go. James would be a good father, and Joe had nothing to fear about confidential personal matters between Meredith and himself ever being known. After all, the most sacred of confidentialities were shared between the minister and the ministered to.

He'd purchased a dozen roses and was to meet Meredith after seven o'clock. It would be a late dinner party, but he couldn't get out of the appointment he had made.

A man had called, said he was in desperate need of counseling. Said he would take his own life if the minister didn't meet with him today. The man, Ken K. Knight, was new to the area, he said. He didn't know who else to call and was desperate.

"I'm a black minister and you are white, isn't that so?"

"Yes. I don't have a problem with that, Pastor. You are a man of the cloth, that's all that matters," the man had replied.

"Well, good then. I'll meet you here at the Church at six o'clock. Just knock on the back door on the west wing. I'll see you then," he had told the stranger before hanging up. *Ken K. Knight,* he thought. *Isn't it just my luck,* pondering the man's ominous initials.

He picked up the phone and dialed a husky friend, a member of his congregation and newly married man, Andrew Williams. "Hey, Andrew," he said to the young handyman. "We got some repair work we need done. Some leaking faucets. You mind meeting me here around six o'clock?" he asked. "Yes, I know it's short notice, but I could sure use you," he said with a pause. "It will take you just a few minutes. Please come around to the back door." He listened. . . . "six-thirty? Okay, thanks. See you then."

Good. I won't have to be alone at night with some white brother. Something about the call had given him the creeps. He'd seen too much violence in response to the civil rights movement, and after all he'd been through with Reverend King, he wasn't sure it was a safe move to be counseling anyone alone at night—especially not a stranger by the name of Ken K. Knight. *Best have someone else present,* he counseled himself.

James thought about how he had arrived at this place in life. His parents had given him every opportunity they had never had. All he had to do was take advantage of the material benefits they had provided and the things they had taught him, and he had.

He had promised his father on his deathbed that he would be a good son. He had kept the faith on that. He never forgot the birthdays, the holidays, the anniversaries, and he made sure his mother's every need was met. Few knew the wealth the family had amassed during the forties and fifties in the rubbish and scrap business. They had been simple and hardworking folk, his father, uncles, and the others. The Barlows kept things tidy and neat but never flaunted the wealth they had accumulated through hard work and industry. They viewed what they had as a blessing from the Lord and felt obliged to be responsible stewards of their holdings.

It was little wonder that James had gone into the ministry. It wasn't so much a conscious decision and a career path as a natural gravitation. The Barlows had the means to take care of the less fortunate, but also a bent to do so, and that was part of James's ministry. He now administered the estate holdings and made sure poorer folk and those needing a lift, especially the Negro brothers and sisters who had suffered so much, could get breaks at schooling. Mostly anonymously, they had from time to time made business loans at low interest rates to friends of all races; curiously to James now, there was one loan he had never forgotten. It was something between his father and old man Caine. His father had become a silent partner of sorts to Joseph Caine Sr. when his grocery business floundered in the late fifties. *So there is justice after all,* he thought. But now it was Caine vs. Barlow. *Meredith is a gift from God, and I won her hand, fair and square,* he reminded himself.

Pastor Barlow looked at the clock. A quarter to six.

Don't want this fellow Ken Knight to trip in the dark. Andrew will be through as well, he remembered.

He flipped the switch that turned the enclosed patio lights on. The path from the back door led through the patio gate to a broad lawn bordered by orange groves in the back of the church. Parking was in front and on the east side of the building.

He decided to call Meredith and explain that he might be a bit late and not to worry. He dialed her number and listened to the sweetest voice on earth answer.

"Meredith, honey? Just thinking of you. . . . No, I haven't forgotten dinner. Could be, though, I'll be a little late. Seems a man has some troubles and needs to talk to a minister. . . . No, I don't know who he is. . . . I'll call just before I get ready to leave the building to let you know I'm on my way. I love you."

111

16

PASTOR BARLOW SAT AT HIS DESK waiting for his appointment to arrive. He hoped Andrew the handyman would be by just as soon. He hadn't felt comfortable in talking with the man and though he knew he could handle himself, something about the meeting left him uneasy.

He smiled, thinking about the gregarious Andrew Williams and his bib-overall daily uniform. Andrew came in three colors. His overalls were white with a white shirt and bow tie on Sundays and blue with navy blue denim shirt during the other six days of the week. Of course his skin color, bronzed from so much work outdoors, could make him pass for two of three races that made up James's congregation.

Andrew made him feel comfortable. In fact, he called the friendly handyman "Doc Williams" because he made him feel so much better just by being around. His prescription was always the same: A cheerful attitude, do your best, and when you lay you down to rest, turn your worries over to God to keep. "The Lord'll be up all night anyway," Andrew always said.

James leaned back in his swivel chair, chuckled, and was grateful for humor and for men who lived like Andrew, with a light heart. He reached for the photo of Meredith on the credenza and went back to when they first met.

He smiled to himself as he replayed the scenes of first meeting Meredith one Sunday morning. He had to do everything in his power to keep his heart inside his chest and act like a courteous gentleman, disinterested, and dutiful. It had taken him several weeks to get up the nerve to ask her if she would like to go out to dinner with him.

It was awkward being a person's minister and her suitor as well. He wasn't very skilled at the latter and just thanked God that Meredith was decent enough to overlook so many failings he had shown over the months that followed.

He thought he heard a vehicle pull in out back, then the slamming of a car door. *Probably Andrew,* he thought. He waited and then heard a louder thumping sound and muffled voices. He grabbed a flashlight from the desk drawer.

"Hey, Andrew? That you out there?" He scanned the back of the church parking lot and the broad lawn that extended beyond the patio out to the citrus grove. A dirt driveway led from the church to the rows of trees. Sometimes Andrew parked his truck out in the grove. He liked to pick the sweet oranges that any in James's congregation were welcome to. He'd take a crate or two home every couple of weeks during season.

"Andrew? That you?"

He decided to take a quick look. He turned west and headed to the side lot, where Andrew would of course be coming from if he didn't use the back lot approach.

"Andrew?" He scanned the parking lot and then froze as the headlamps on three cars suddenly turned on. The bright lights temporarily blinded him, and he shielded his eyes from the high beams and saw three men step out from behind car doors, wearing hoods and sheets that some still donned in Mississippi and Alabama, but not here.

"Hey, now," he said, as he slowly started to retreat toward the back door office. "We don't need this kind of trouble. You boys are asking for a lot of trouble that can ruin your lives."

"Well, look who's calling us 'boys,'" one laughed.

The church was located on property at the edge of town. Held by the Barlow family for years, it was all orchards and was connected to the main highway a quarter of a mile east by a narrow paved road. James knew that unless a miracle were given him, he'd be beaten at best, killed outright at worst.

"Seems like the nigger preacher don't understand who's in charge around here," another said.

"We don't want no trouble, Barlow," the third chimed in. "We just want you to understand something. We know you been dating a mostly white girl, and we are not in favor of such mixings going on. We've had enough of you Northern-educated black boys comin' back here with all sorts of liberal ideas about 'rights.'"

James Barlow kept backing toward the patio that led to the back door of the church. He knew this wouldn't turn out good, no matter how he survived it.

He turned to run for the door. He might be able to make a dash and lock these hoodlums out. "Lord, if you are there, I need you now."

17

THE BUSY CHAIRMAN OF THE Appropriations Committee, Senator Joseph Caine, had actually dozed off at his desk. He shook himself awake, went to the water cooler and drew a mug full of the cool water, reached into his coat pocket, and downed a heavy-duty, codeine-based painkiller.

His war wounds were a source of chronic pain. But now, with the around-the-clock pressure of maneuvering to enter the presidential race, as well as periodic stabbing back pain where shrapnel still lay embedded near his spine, he had gotten to where he could hardly function without the pills.

He didn't always take the Percocet for pain, though. He took it periodically for another reason. After a strong dose of Vodka and mixers, he sometimes sat alone in his office, long after everyone else had left for the day, just to feel—absolutely nothing.

He used his private bathroom, splashed cold water on his face several times, decided he could use a shave, and went about waking up to the late afternoon business he would need to conduct.

Random memories . . . God messed up when he designed the brain like a computer, he thought. *If I were God I would allow a "delete" key.* He chuckled at his own wit.

Back at his desk, he started reading through the afternoon stack of legislative briefs but found it hard to concentrate.

He turned from his desk and gazed out the window, contemplating the dark memories that had occupied his mind during the previous hour.

"Senator?" Beth Benoit, his office manager, said as she cautiously opened the door to his office. "Senator Caine?" she gently repeated. "I'm sorry to disturb you, but I have a call I think you may want to take."

"Who?" he said as he awoke from his reverie.

"It's Mike Stone."

"Beth, tell him I'll call back later."

He still couldn't shake the melancholy he always experienced this time of year . . .

"Senator?"

"Yes! Beth! What is it now?"

"It's not Mike Stone, but *about* Mike Stone."

He shrugged and shook his head. His body language told her he wasn't connecting the dots.

"Sir, Mike Stone is dying."

*　　*　　*　　*　　*

Digiwatch corporate headquarters—Philadelphia

"Are you sure?" Jackson Lyon asked. "I can't believe it. Mike Stone? When did this happen? "Uh-huh. Well, we'll have to talk to Lawton then. Yes."

He flipped the cell phone off and put it back into the holster on his belt. He was a board member of the most forward looking and dynamic technology company on the planet. And having decision-making power meant he could help tailor, fix this marketing on the micro-scanning, surveillance, and information devices to promote his agenda.

Jack Lyon, former governor of New Mexico and retired United States Senator, knew Lawton well enough to know he left no traces of his involvement in the accidents he engineered. *This is just a casualty of war,* he rationalized. *And a war we must win.* This comforted the ardent defender of the Constitution. *At least where it applies to the new world order,* he reminded himself.

Jack Lyon was savvy enough to know the public didn't like the sound of "new world order." But to his thinking, the new world "cause" was nothing more than America taking its rightful place at the head of nations, instead of acquiescing to a bunch of political has-beens in Europe, light-weights in Asia, or whining, third-world nuisances.

The Constitution was the only document of its kind, and it had made possible the two-hundred-plus-year-old success of the American experiment. Lyon believed in the Constitution and knew that its principles were what had made the United States the free and prosperous leader of world nations it was.

Lyon wanted to be the leader in the march toward that new world order, and he knew how to get there. His mantra was that control and power were secured by the appropriate application of knowledge, and he now had the lobbying and publicity machinery in place to help him reach his goal.

He also had a good right-hand man to run the point in his campaign to become the candidate of the newly formed American Alliance Party, which was made up of disgruntled Democrats, Republicans, and Independents who were looking for reforms that they were convinced the traditional parties couldn't deliver. Ron Lawton was the man for the job—skilled and ruthless but also devoted.

Lyon had it all mapped out. Senator Joe Caine would be Lyon's running-mate, but Lawton would run the show. They had cut the deal. Lawton would serve as chief of staff to either himself or Caine—whichever man won the party's nomination for president. But Lyon would win. He was certain he would get the nod. He even thought that Joe Caine understood that by now.

In shaping his political persona, Lyon had become the poster boy for the Second Amendment. He was unabashed in his insistence of the right of citizens to bear arms. A former Marine hero of three wars, the rifle had been featured in every political campaign ad he ever put out.

Guns in the right hands is a good thing, he reasoned. *Bad guys hate an armed citizenry.*

He complimented the American people on their good moral judgment at every talk show opportunity. He urged them to be ever vigilant during this war on terror—to become "citizen soldiers," always on the side of the law and the military who served the nation.

Lyon had almost singlehandedly succeeded in taking the right-wing gun image of the NRA and turning it into a middle-of-the-road position, accepted now by even the most radical Hollywood and media left-wingers. Movie stars were regular guests at his ranch north of Santa Fe, New Mexico. Shooting Stars, he called his private gatherings. Everyone sought an invitation, and he took full publicity advantage of each occasion.

Now Mike Stone, one of the savviest political hacks in Washington, and a man he had used as an adviser before, was on medical death row. His life was hanging in the balance, and his survival was in the hands of his doctors.

One thing that made Ron Lawton so valuable was his nearly uncanny ability to dig up any dirt on potential rivals or contributors. It had long been rumored that Joe Caine had had a scandalous affair before hurriedly joining the military in 1969—that he had impregnated an African American beauty who met a mysterious and sudden death in his presence. The official records of what had happened had been sealed for years, but had then somehow ended up in Mike Stone's possession. Mike had seen to that, when he had the chance to get to know a certain disgruntled former sheriff's deputy who had an ax to grind with Sheriff Blaine Lockhart. Stone was in the business of collecting that kind of information—information that could be used as leverage in certain situations, information that would be embarrassing if it were to come to light. The files on Caine were said to have been destroyed in a fire at a storage facility, but Lawton had reason to believe otherwise. It was his opinion that Stone still had them and that the information they contained would be of great value to Lyon in his race against Caine for the nomination.

Mike Stone simply had to live; had to survive—at least until he could be persuaded to give up those files.

Lawton, who worked for Joe Caine in D.C. and Jack Lyon in Philadelphia, had checked out Stone's story about the storage fire, and the story didn't wash. So Lawton put one of his hired goons, TJ—an ex-military sleuth—onto harassing Stone's secretary the same day Mike had his unfortunate heart attack.

The fool wasn't supposed to harm her, just intimidate, follow, make his presence felt until he, Ron Lawton, could get her to give up the information he needed. He needed those confidential files on Caine's past and also the roster of big-time contributors to Lyon's and Caine's previous campaigns. Mike Stone was now the only one who could help him—if he lived. If Lawton was able to get the files and then Stone should die—all the better.

That idiot TJ. Shooting a kid, busting the husband's head with a two-by-four. Now Lawton was scrambling to get the young, goof-up assailant out of the country. He pondered all the variables.

TJ knows too much. If he's caught, he could pin this on me. If he left a fingerprint trail or could be identified by witnesses, it could mean big trouble.

Lyon pulled out the cell phone used for calls to Lawton alone and punched in the numbers. He let it ring three times and hung up, then rang twice, then three times, each time allowing ten seconds before the next signal. Lawton would return his call within sixty seconds. It never failed.

Lyon's phone rang. No names were ever used as an added security precaution.

"You heard about the senator's ex-manager?" Lawton asked.

"Heart attack?"

"Right."

"Too bad. What about our problem?"

"Our friend—the errand boy?"

"Yes."

"He has just left for a vacation. An extended leave-of-absence."

"Hmmm."

"Shouldn't present a further nuisance."

"You know, he was very untidy with the way he handled this."

"Don't worry. I'll take care of it," Lawton replied.

"Witnesses?" Lyon asked.

"Taken care of."

"The files?"

"In my possession," Lawton lied.

"Good. Make the problem go away."

Jackson Lyon flipped the cell phone off and waited for the Digiwatch Board Meeting to commence.

Today was an important day in the nation. Congress had just passed legislation that he was sure the President would sign. It mandated that all federal, state, and government contractors adopt a new, personal identification procedure. This to help thwart the mounting threat of terrorist infiltration into security sensitive areas. Digiwatch and two other manufacturers would vie for the multi-billion dollar appropriation set aside to fund the new system.

This first step toward controlling the American people would allow them to see how well Digiwatch, under his guidance, could help secure their freedoms and safeguard their government from attack. As citizens became comfortable with the concept, Digiwatch would make available to American families "free" digital cards or implants. No pressure, just the option to be part of an identification system designed to weed out the evil ones bent on America's destruction. Of course, to obtain such a card, each American would be required to prove, irrefutably, his or her citizenship. *There goes the immigration problem,* Lyon told himself.

To Jackson Lyon and Ron Lawton, this national identification system was a necessary evil, and something that was designed not to burden, but to "free" Americans.

Besides, the money they would make and add to the political war chest from this Act of Congress would ensure the coming election went to them. In Jackson Lyon's mind there was only one thing greater than controlling guns and technology when it came to securing political power—and that was money.

18

RON LAWTON PICKED UP a piece of paper. He wrote in block letters, printing with a black ink pen, slanted left. His natural writing was cursive slanted right. Spanish was one of three languages Lawton had studied as a Special Ops for the CIA during several years while fighting communists in San Salvador and Guatemala during the late 1970s and early 80s.

He wrote in Spanish, using coded references, and addressed the paper he would fax to Felipe Lozano Martinez, proprietor, Hotel Intercontinental Pacifico, Acapulco:

"Estimado Felipe, Tengo el placer de mandarle un paquete. Lo usual. Espero que le vaya bien. Encontrará el pago ya esta hecho por mitad. Notifiquemelo cuando termina el asunto.

"'Leon'"

Pretty obvious, he thought, *using my alias of Leon—the word for* lion *in Spanish.* He liked the idea of using the word so linked to one of his superiors—Jackson Lyon. Jackson Lyon was called "Mad Jack" by war buddies because of the death that always followed his path and the risks he would take.

Lawton admired that about Jackson.

Now . . . he hated doing this to any man on his side—having one of his operatives eliminated. But the man in question could talk. Not that he didn't trust him. The man was a very good trained killer, but he had messed up at the D.C. train station, and his foul-up could cost Caine or Lyon the presidency and expose all the illegal "soft money" donations.

This TJ Mattsen fellow—a good man really—simply had to disappear. TJ had made matters messy with the attack on Lizzy and her husband. Lawton could cover himself with Caine but not with Lyon. Lyon was too savvy, streetwise, and a fighter—deadly, really.

If needed, Lawton would quickly switch allegiance to Lyon—but then even Lyon understood this—and ride that ticket to the White House as the ultimate voice and unelected power under the president himself—chief of staff. The chief of staff knew everyone; it was his job. He also knew all the dirt on everyone; also his job.

By this means more power was accumulated than by any other means. Knowledge was power, and to have total knowledge on all people surrounding the president—the most powerful man in the world, what more could a man ask for?

So he had sent TJ on a month-long, "pre-paid" vacation to Acapulco. "Just while things settle down," he had told the younger man, who had botched the Lizzy Price assignment. She was now unconscious in a hospital bed, and her husband was still alive. Then there was the kid who got in the way. That kid had seen TJ. Lawton would have to have someone else take care of the three of them now.

He positioned the paper in the fax machine and dialed the international number. The fax tone picked it up and in minutes the message was relayed. He pulled the transmitted message out of the tray as it passed through the fax, held it over the trash can, and set it on fire with a cigarette lighter, watching as the flame slowly crawled its way up to the Spanish words:

"Esteemed Felipe, I have the pleasure of sending you a package. The usual. I expect it to go well with you. You will find the payment is half made already. Notify me when the matter is concluded.

"Leon"

Felipe had been a trusted advisor and "business associate" in San Salvador during its civil war with communist insurgents. His business had been to assure that people who disappeared never returned. But Felipe was getting greedy lately. That was too bad. Greed always consumed its most ardent proponent.

As the flames finally obliterated the name *Felipe,* Lawton wondered, in a curious and perhaps morose way, if he'd have to someday handle Felipe in the same way. Fire left no fingerprints. You could never be too careful in this business.

*　　*　　*　　*　　*

Acapulco, Mexico

Felipe had more important matters to see to today, and so he sent his best man to "do the job." He rationalized that his men would never get trained if he had to personally take care of every customer Ron Lawton sent.

Fernando Laporte, known as "Pancho" to his inner circle of associates, was a veteran of the drug cartel wars, and making people vanish was his specialty. He saw this as an easy job. Pancho hated gringos, anyway. He'd take real pleasure in making sure "the package" was disposed of properly. He had a 100-acre rancho east of town and there an underground room dedicated to just about anything Felipe might ask him to do—interrogate, lock up, or finish off. That room was known to him and Felipe alone.

There had been rumors, of course, among some of his day

field-workers about people going there with Pancho and not leaving, but Pancho had made sure those rumors were buried with the last man he had heard speak them.

Waiting at the passenger terminal at the airport, Pancho held up a cardboard sign on which he had written in heavy marker pen: "Hotel Intercontinental Pacifico—Digiwatch Guest." The first passengers now arrived in the terminal. He paid close attention to the type of men arriving. This one would be athletic, serious, wearing sunglasses, no doubt a military look to him. Pancho would go into his "humble servant" role, playing dumb, and enjoying every minute of it.

The last person to exit the plane wasn't a man, but an attractive woman. "Are you the Digiwatch tour guide?" she asked cheerily. She carried a handbag and reached out, handing it to him to carry for her.

Pancho couldn't help giving himself away. His eyes squinting, the surprise registering on his face, he finally said, "Si, Señorita. Here to serve you."

"Well, let's go. I didn't bring any luggage. I thought I'd purchase what I need here at the markets. A girl really doesn't need that much in Acapulco, no, Señor?" Beth Benoit offered with a wicked grin.

"Así es. Una señorita doesn't need much in Acapulco." He followed the woman out the door to the curbside and then pointed to his car, a Dodge Durango. Pancho's surprised face gradually registered the placid look of a humble taxi driver. *I will play the fool for her, but enjoy something more than Felipe has paid me to do,* he thought as he ogled in amazement her extremely good looks. *He has always cheated me. This time I will take my own bonus.*

*   *   *   *   *

The young man in his middle-thirties, well-built and looking like someone who might compete in the boxing ring, exited the plane now that the rest of the passengers had gotten off. He had complained of feeling sick and told the stewardess that he needed just a minute in the lavatory. The minute turned into fifteen before he finally exited the plane.

He made sure no one was tailing him by ambling casually through the terminal, taking a snack at one of the small kiosks, picking up a magazine, and then thumbing through it with the appearance of a person with nothing in the world to hurry him and nowhere he needed to be.

He didn't trust Lawton. There was no honor among thieves. He knew that. He in fact trusted no one and confided in no one, especially not Mr. Ron Lawton. He was a man for hire, good at what he did, and he enjoyed his freedom. Lawton, from the same school of professionally trained killers for flag and country, was an "old man" from the Cold War era. These days it took youthful mental and physical agility to do his kind of work. For now, TJ was just using Lawton's connections until the time was right to move him out of the way.

When Lawton had called TJ and discovered his failed attempt to secure the Caine and Lyon files from Mike Stone's secretary, and learned how he had injured her and her husband along with a bystander at the train station, Lawton had to make a decision.

TJ knew Lawton wouldn't believe him if he turned down the trip to Acapulco to "let things cool off." He also knew Lawton wouldn't be hiring him again for some time. That left TJ with one option. Disappear, but not on Lawton's terms.

The young operative knew all about Lawton and the woman, Beth Benoit, who worked for Senator Caine in D.C. He knew that was Lawton's weakness—getting tied up emotionally with a female instead of just using her.

TJ had friends at Digiwatch whom he had cultivated very carefully. There were men there just as eager to move their superiors out of their place as TJ was to move Lawton permanently out of his seat of control.

TJ had a bachelor's degree in public administration from the University of California at Berkeley and a master's degree in political science that he had earned from Texas A&M during his years in the Army. His resumé was respectable, and he always had a cover for his "dark ops" work, which showed him in high managerial positions for well-known corporations—courtesy NSA.

He had no doubt. He was qualified to move Lawton aside and work as a chief of staff for either Lyon or Caine. He preferred Lyon because the ex-senator was tough and single-minded. And Caine had some baggage that TJ had discovered—baggage from the days just before and just after his service in Vietnam.

He also knew how to get the files from Mike Stone anyway. He knew where they were. The girl, Lizzy, wasn't that careful. The name and location of the storage locker with Mike's instructions were sitting on her desk two nights before her unfortunate "accident," when he had gone in Stone's office to do the "janitorial" work.

He felt kind of sorry for Beth Benoit. She was a looker, and he had enjoyed watching her from one seat over and across the aisle as they flew from L.A. directly to this tropical Mexican city. He could see why and how she had reached Lawton's ice-cold heart.

He might have felt sorry enough for her to prevent what was about to happen to her, if what was about to happen hadn't been designed by Lawton for *him*. Beth's misfortune would send a message to the tough but old guy Lawton that he, TJ Mattsen, Army Special Forces and NSA trained, wasn't to be messed with. He also was a player.

He would take a cab to the Hotel Intercontinental Pacifico, where he had some unscheduled business to conduct with one Felipe Lozano Martinez. Martinez would be offering him quite a payday once the night was through. Then, Martinez and his goon, Pancho, would enjoy an all-expense-paid reservation to the finest underground accommodations at "El Rancho Pancho," just outside of town.

Live by the sword, die by the sword, he reminded himself. That was the only Bible verse he remembered from his childhood on his mama's knee, and it comforted him to know that Jesus was right about the way these opponents would end up. Besides, he figured he was doing the world a favor. These enforcers for hire were not like him. These goons were trash. *The dirty punks who worked drugs need to be stopped,* he told himself. He detested drugs. Addictions had affected his childhood, his father, mother, people in his hometown.

"Taxi," he called out from the curbside.

"Donde, Señor?" the taxi driver asked.

"Hotel Intercontinental Pacifico, por favor," he replied.

*   *   *   *   *

Ron Lawton was flying into Philadelphia to meet with his internal contacts in Digiwatch, and with former senator and ex-governor Jackson Lyon, who would be there for a board meeting. Lawton had also planned a surprise romantic dinner and evening with Beth Benoit. He had cleared it with her boss, the rationale for her coming to Philly being that she was needed to help with information and "contact" gathering at Digiwatch—one of Senator Caine's biggest campaign contributors. But Lawton had additional things in mind for Beth.

She had been excited when he called her with the news that they would be spending a weekend together at a surprise location. Up until now, their rendezvous had been far more discreet.

Lawton enjoyed this dalliance with power, testing Caine's resolve in insisting there be no dating among office staff, and he enjoyed Beth Benoit. She was just the thing to soften his rough edges, and he needed that. He had always yearned for a woman to hold, trust him, and yet allow him room to be the political renegade and clandestine operator he was. He sensed that Beth was the right girl—that he had finally found a soul mate.

"Where are we going?" Beth had asked.

"It's a surprise."

"Then I'll need to pack some things?"

"What would you need?" he chuckled in return.

"Oh, a change of clothes. This is a weekend getaway, right?"

"Right." He was looking forward to being with her.

The two of them had hit it off immediately a few months back, when Lawton was hired as Senator Caine's new chief of staff and he had first met the senator's very attractive personal assistant.

Beth was a flirt and had dated a lot of men. But she had never met anyone quite like Ron Lawton. He exuded confidence and power. There was even something mysterious and a little dangerous about him. But she also sensed in him a kind of vulnerability. She found that unlikely combination of toughness and tenderness, coupled with his rugged good looks, irresistible. It didn't hurt, either, that he was generous and liked to surprise her, such as he had with the news of this unexpected trip.

From the start, she had pierced the armor that shielded a very cold spirit. After just a few dates, Lawton had begun picturing himself providing for her, even having a child or two. For the first time in his life, he felt he wanted to tell someone the truth about himself. Such feelings alarmed him, and, of course, that would never be; his course had been set long ago. He had chosen a life of lies before Beth was ever born. So he would shield her from the nasty, down-and-dirty business he specialized in and live two lives and succeed at both.

He asked Beth to keep him advised on Mike Stone's condition. He didn't really care for Stone, but he couldn't afford to let the man go to the grave and risk having whatever information he had on Caine and Lyon float to light. In fact, in a few minutes he would be at the Digiwatch board meeting and be able to report that the foul-up at the Union Train Station Shopping Gallery had been taken care of—permanently.

TJ had messed that up . . . unless, of course, TJ is starting to get too smart for his former dark-ops britches.

Lawton would put a call in to Felipe and give TJ a chance to redeem himself, tell him that if he would reveal where the files were, he would promise him his life. And then, Felipe could take care of "the package." Then Lawton could relax, although the husband of TJ's target in D.C. and the kid that had gotten in the way would still need to be dealt with. But that could wait. *Stone's secretary wasn't supposed to be killed,* he groused. *TJ knew better. This really complicates things.*

His mind was going back and forth between the necessary dark deeds that he performed to take care of the long-term mission and to the innocence of love. He had always felt people who fall in love were weak. Now he wondered about himself and the vulnerable position he had put himself in with Beth Benoit.

In any case, tonight would be a night to remember. He'd even brought an uncut diamond that he'd liberated from a dying rebel leader during a long ago Special Ops assignment in South Africa. He would present the one-karat stone to Beth during dinner and invite her to create her own design for the ring that she'd wear—making Ron Lawton one of the newest of honorable men in Washington, D.C.

Yes! he smiled in self-congratulatory musings. He was on a roll, the stars were lining up for him, and tonight would be a night he'd never forget.

19

MAGGIE SANDERS STOOD next to Mike's bed in the intensive care unit of Fairfax County General Hospital, gazing into his face. His color was good and his vital signs normal, for someone who had been through that kind of ordeal. The operation had been lifesaving, and now it was time to wait and see. *But Mike is tough. He'll make it through,* she assured herself.

What troubled her was the truth of Mike's long-term cardiac health. His heart was a mess, was in fact failing. It wasn't a simple matter of needing the bypass. He suffered from a degenerative coronary condition, so bad that now in the irreversible stages, his heart needed replacing. How he had hidden it from her and the world was a mystery. He should have dropped dead a year ago.

She smiled sadly and felt the moisture well up in her eyes. His voice came to her mind as she searched the sterile floor by his bedside for the answer.

"I survive this pace based on two things, Maggie. First, my love for you, and second, my love for politics. I have always loved politics, but I had never known real love until I found you. It heals me and makes everything worth it. I have a feeling one is going to have to make way for the other, and sometimes it scares me," he had admitted just a week before.

So now politics will have to go, she reassured herself. When he awoke, Mike would be told the truth by Doctor Hall, that a heart transplant was in his future. He was only a few beats away from his train-wrecked heart going still, and that would mean he was being immediately placed on the transplant waiting list.

Maggie understood the odds. For every heart that became available for transplant, there were more than four times that number of potential recipients awaiting the gift of life. The tens of thousands of people who could donate upon passing away as a result of accidents each year just didn't understand or simply hadn't made arrangements to become a donor.

Now her focus would be on seeking a donor with little time to live, a healthy heart, and a willingness to donate his or her heart upon passing to Mike Stone. A series of miracles timed by God would need to occur for all of that to happen. She had only known of one case where someone had actually given their heart via codicil—a last will and testament, and that person had been another family member. So far as she knew, Mike had no relatives with a terminal illness or injury.

The odds were stacked against Mike. And she had every reason to give up hope—but she couldn't do that. Love wouldn't allow it. Already, even before marriage, she felt it her duty to stand by Mike "in sickness or in health." Besides that, she loved him and couldn't bear the thought of losing him.

"Hey, babe," Mike said, his voice muffled by the oxygen mask. "Am I alive, or are you an angel sent to take me home?"

Startled, she raised her sagging head and scooted near him to give a kiss on his forehead. "Both," she muttered, smiling weakly.

"I am alive and you are an angel," he whispered in satisfaction. He reached for her hand. A slight squeeze reassured her that he wasn't going anywhere yet.

Her eyes welled with tears, and she gently laid her head against his exposed left shoulder.

"So how did it go? I'm going to live . . . right?"

"Rest. Save your energy," she replied.

"You don't look too happy."

"I'm worried."

"Bad news?"

"Could be worse," she lied.

"Well, then. I'll be back at it in a couple of weeks."

She nodded, trying in vain to feel supportive. Her sad brown eyes gave her away.

"Tell me the truth, Maggie."

"Rest."

He nodded then blinked. He wanted to gaze upon Maggie's angelic radiance for as long as he possibly could, but he couldn't keep his eyes open.

He was drifting now, but not before a silently offered deal to the Almighty: *God, I'll do anything you ask, if you just let me live . . . fix my heart. Give me a chance to live and love Maggie. Anything you ask. I'll do anything . . .*

*   *   *   *   *

Life seemed to be spinning out of control for Joe Caine. His chief political advisor, Mike Stone, was near death, and Ron Lawton, forced upon him by Lyon when Sherm Johnson had died, had taken control, and that was a disturbing enough thought. But now the call from Jackson Lyon, revealing Lizzy Price's comatose condition and her husband's near fatal clubbing the other day, meant he had no one to turn to but Lawton for administration of his political affairs. Even Beth Benoit had abandoned him. She had come home from a weekend trip to Mexico and abruptly quit without stating a reason, leaving Caine to hire and train someone new. Of course, Lawton would see to that.

Jack Lyon was an ally but no friend. The two of them were as different in tactics and political warfare as the Marine Corps of Lyon's youth was to Joe Caine's combat infantryman's experience with the Army. Both knew how to fight, but each felt he was more deserving than the other in the race for the American Alliance Party's nomination for the presidency.

Indeed, one man would win the party's nomination and the other, no doubt, would become the vice presidential candidate on the ticket. The country was looking for a fresh start, and with the war on terror expanding daily, two men of military combat experience would make a compelling team.

The possibility of becoming the most powerful man in the world was real! Joe Caine could almost taste it. He knew he was a better choice for the job than Lyon. Now it would be up to Ron Lawton to control things—keep a finger in the dike—to prevent a leak from springing from the dam that held a reservoir of information about his past—some not too favorable.

Joe wondered about several of the ladies he had been seeing—if any of them would likely talk about their affairs. He needed to choose one to be his personal "running mate." No small task given the time available to find a suitable wife. But a man going to the White House needed a good woman at his side, and the American public expected a First Lady they could love.

Maybe with Mike Stone out of the way, pretty Maggie Sanders would give him a second look. Caine was nearly twice her age, but that didn't seem to matter to women who enjoyed powerful men. He didn't want to lose Mike, he hoped Mike would pull through, but if he didn't, candidate Caine would be more than happy to personally console the beautiful Doctor Maggie Sanders.

20

FORTY-EIGHT HOURS HAD PASSED, and Mike was stable but barely able to raise an eyelid to the world that now was an incubator to a new man; or a dying one. Intensive care was open at all hours to Maggie, and she stayed and prayed around the clock. The benefit of being a professional medical practitioner was the knowledge she had. The downside was also the knowledge she had.

She needed faith—something not handed out with the medical degree. She was, like most physicians, innately cautious, even somewhat cynical when it had to do with healing. The clinical reality of the operation of internal organs, medications, and treatments left little room for unrealistic hope or optimism. Given her knowledge of the condition of Mike's heart, she couldn't realistically give him more than a fifty-fifty chance that he would survive another year. Her love for Mike and the bit of faith she had in a higher power upped those odds somewhat, but how much, she wasn't sure. He would definitely need a transplant.

The odds of getting a transplant while on the national waiting list were slim. There were some fifty thousand people waiting now, and Mike might be looking at three or even four years. Possible donors, after all, had to die first. Even if millions signed up for organ donation lists with their state driver's licensing bureaus and other registries, that didn't mean the generous were the people being called home by Saint Peter.

"Hey," Mike said softly.

"Hey, you!" Maggie returned with a smile.

"So . . . am I going to live?" Mike squeaked out.

"Long enough to marry me," she replied through kisses and tears. "You scared me."

"So am I all better?" He offered a weak smile to let her know he had no intention of giving up. "Take my hand."

Maggie took his hand and stroked his pitch black hair back and kissed him once again.

"Marry me," he said. "Don't make me wait. Call Bill Maxfield and ask him to be my best man. And Lizzy and Troy, invite them. Call the hospital chaplain. We can still do this, can't we?"

She blinked away the tears that came freely now. She had just learned about Lizzy, who was in this same hospital in a coma, and her husband, Troy—he had undergone surgery for a broken wrist and a skull fracture. She had seen the report on the evening news and called to verify her suspicions. The boy who had taken a bullet was up and talking, giving a description of the attacker.

All this intrigue seemed so unreal to Maggie. Lizzy Price had been supportive of Mike's new health regimen, in fact the two women had been in touch daily by phone, coordinating their strategy to get Mike off the booze and cigarettes. Maggie had even overheard Mike tell Lizzy in one phone conversation that the office files needed to be moved to a new location—that a guy named Ron was pressuring and threatening him, that she needed to be "careful and watch her back," as Mike had put it.

She couldn't avoid the nagging feeling that the assault on Lizzy, which had happened in a public, well-lighted place such as the Au Bon

Pain Café, wasn't just a random attack but had to be linked somehow to the threats Mike had been getting.

Maybe attacking Lizzy was a way of sending a signal to Mike, she considered. An attack gone too far, but violent nevertheless, just to show Mike that the man wanting the information was really serious about his demands.

Maggie's mind continued to race, conjuring up all kinds of conspiracies and fantastic scenarios. Then she saw the silliness of her day-dreaming. Even in the capital of intrigue, Washington, D.C., people wouldn't be so brazen.

Maggie decided she would hold off telling Mike about Troy's and Lizzy's injuries. It would only upset him at a time when he needed all his strength to recover from his surgery. And she considered again her mother's advice against marrying a man in the political business.

She was brought back to reality by Mike's labored voice.

"Well?" Mike asked with a subdued cough.

"Rest, sweetheart."

"I love you, Mag," he replied.

"I love you, too. I will be back in the morning, and we can make the arrangements. Okay?" She feigned a smile.

"Okay," he said with a nod and then closed his eyes. He squeezed her hand and then let go as he drifted off to sleep.

Maggie left the room and headed down the hall to check on Lizzy Price's condition. Walking down the corridor, she realized how tired she was. She would need to get some rest tonight. It looked like another long day ahead of her tomorrow and an even longer week.

She needed some strength and didn't know where to get it. She pulled Mike's cell phone out of her pocket. She had noticed it at the house when the paramedics asked her to back away, and had stuck it in her pocket for some reason, maybe thinking Mike might need to take an important call.

Wife already, she smiled.

She scrolled down the call list and saw a number and name she recognized. *He'll know what to do,* she decided.

"Hello, Special Agent Maxfield."

"Bill?"

"Maggie?"

"Yeah, uh, Bill . . ."

"You with Mike? I see his caller ID."

"Yeah. I'm using his cell."

"Maggie, I just got word here at the Bureau. My cousin Lizzy, she was attacked and—"

"I know. I saw it on the news. She's here at the hospital. In intensive care."

"Have you seen her? Is she going to be okay?"

"I don't know what to say, Bill. I mean, I can't . . ." she stopped and caught her herself. It was easier being a doctor when you were treating strangers. "I'm sorry. This is hard," she allowed with a catch in her voice.

"Is Mike involved in this? Is he okay?"

"I don't know if he is involved or not, and no, he isn't okay. He's just had emergency bypass surgery, and . . . Bill," she choked on her words, "I need your—"

"Bypass surgery? He didn't tell me—"

"He didn't know. He collapsed this morning, and had to have emergency surgery."

"Where are you?"

"County General."

"I'm on my way. Give me thirty minutes. I'll call this number when I get to the ER."

"Thank you, Bill," she answered softly. "I knew I could count on you."

She clicked the phone off and looked in and saw the doctors testing Lizzy. This was all so surreal. She knew this was a tough town, but beatings, killings? And who would benefit? Joe Caine certainly wouldn't. He needed Mike. Mike no doubt had enemies, as all political players have, but to go this far? To intimidate his staff? She just couldn't see any puzzle pieces fitting.

She didn't like games; and certainly not political games. The more she thought about it, the angrier it made her. She was going to make a statement to whomever had done this. She was going to marry Mike Stone, get him well, and do all she could for Lizzy and Troy Price.

The new heart Mike would need would take all his energy. He would be out of politics for all practical purposes, and at least her mother would be satisfied. Yes, she would marry Mike and get him through this; help him get a new heart, a new life.

And his enemies? she asked herself. *They can all burn in hell.*

*　　*　　*　　*　　*

A week later

"Bill, I don't remember anything between the time I saw that two-by-four coming at my head and when I woke up here in the hospital. How's Lizzy today?"

"Not back. Improving though. We can thank God for that."

Troy bit into his lip and struggled to control his anger. "The boy who saved me?"

"He's at home, recovering under police protection. He's talked, given a composite of the guy who attacked you. He took a bullet for you. Quite the young hero. As for the perp, well, we don't have much on him yet. We think he is the same one who tried to drive a pen knife into Lizzy's brain. He messed up, thank God. It appears he was going to do the same to you."

"Not an amateur?"

"A professional killer, Troy."

"Why?"

"Can you tell me?"

Troy studied the ceiling above his bed for a moment, a blank look on his face. He finally shook his head slowly. "I don't know. I'm still foggy."

"It's the meds."

"Good stuff. Makes everything go away."

"This guy . . . uh, Troy, he's bad and wanted you dead. We are following up a lot of leads, looking into anyone who might have had it in for Mike Stone. Maggie has also given us some reason to investigate Joe Caine's chief of staff, a guy named Lawton. You know anything about him? Did Lizzy ever say anything about him?"

"Well, yeah, she did. That's why I was hurrying to meet her. Lawton had been pressuring her to turn over some of Mike's files. She felt threatened because of the way he was coming on."

"Files? What kind of files?"

"I don't know for sure. All she told me was that they were highly confidential. Mike didn't want her to turn them over to Lawton."

Troy glanced away from Bill who was standing at his bedside and thought again about his wife, lying on the floor in a pool of her own blood. The rage he had been struggling to contain suddenly overcame him. "I'm gonna kill that . . . whoever it was who did this to Lizzy."

Bill didn't respond, but he understood how Troy felt. If it had been his wife, he'd want to do the same thing. But revenge was hardly something he could condone. "Troy. How about you? Is there anyone who might be carrying a grudge—maybe someone you put away when you worked Army CID? Is there anyone like that you can think of?"

Troy took a deep breath and thought for a moment. "Yeah. One. A guy named Jon Gilbert. But he's dead. He used to send me death threats from Leavenworth, until he was killed in a brawl with another inmate. Or so I was told."

"Who told you?"

"I got a letter from someone at Leavenworth. Some inmate said he thought I should know. He said that the guy was beaten to a bloody pulp and his cell burned."

"Sounds like a bad boy."

"Yeah, pretty bad. He'd killed another operative in cold blood after a Special Ops mission. He was what we called 'black ops'—officially didn't exist. Black operatives are—"

"I know. Specialists. Target assessment and elimination."

"You got it."

"So why did CID get involved?" Bill asked.

"He did the killing off-duty, in the apartment of his friend. He caught his buddy with a girl the killer had been dating and went berserk. He claimed he acted in self-defense. You know, both men trained to fight with quick strikes and lethally; just instinct, he said. The trouble was . . ."

"What?"

Troy strained at the vision in the ceiling. "I need the file. I need you to call a friend who was with me at CID. He left the Army and joined the FBI a while back. Not sure where he is now. There's something about the dead guy. I need to know something. The agent's name is Mac Richardson. He'll remember the case."

"I'll find out where he's assigned and call him today."

"Bill?"

"Yeah?"

"Get right back to me?"

"I promise."

Troy visibly relaxed and closed his eyes, and Bill stepped from the room into the hospital corridor and closed the door behind him. He nodded at the uniformed and armed sheriff's deputy guarding the room and turned to walk away. Then he stopped, turned, and took a second look. "Aren't the Feds on this case? I thought the Federal Marshal's Office was handling the security, working the case with D.C. Police."

"Don't know about that," the slender officer returned. "Fairfax County Hospital and all. We're often the ones given the detail."

"Hmm." Bill felt uncomfortable and thought he'd check it out with a call to a friend in D.C. *Better check on Lizzy first and give her mom and dad my love,* he decided. *Then I need to look in on Mike up in intensive care.*

Bill wondered about the assailant's motives—if Mike Stone's heart attack might somehow be connected to the attempted killing of Lizzy and her husband or anyone else who might have gotten in the way.

Coincidence? he wondered. *Lizzy has something the guy wanted, and he decided to keep her quiet, or at least frighten her. Botched murder? Maybe not. Maybe a message.*

He knocked softly on the door of his younger female cousin's hospital room and was surprised when his tearful uncle opened it. Lizzy's mother and siblings were gathered about the bed, crying and holding each other as a Catholic priest stood over Lizzy Price's still body. Muted moans and sobs and the rhythmic whispering of a respirator offering the mechanical breath of life to Lizzy were the only sounds that intruded on the otherwise sacred quiet.

21

The Next Day

$\mathbf{M}$AGGIE HADN'T BEEN ABLE to bring herself to tell Mike about the seriousness of his secretary's condition. She wasn't sure when or if the family would allow the plug to life-support to be pulled, but it looked imminent. It was up to Troy now. He and Lizzy had made a deal early in their marriage that if by accident or sickness either was to ever be in this condition, the other would allow God's will to be done, rather than to employ artificial means to sustain life.

Troy Price was out of bed and trying to change from hospital gown to street clothes. The cast on his wrist extended down to his hand, and with his fingers partially encased in plaster, he was having a hard time buttoning the top button of his shirt.

The frustration of trying to dress himself had done nothing to lighten the emotion he was feeling. He had been struggling ever since he had been informed of Lizzy's condition. His sorrow and anguish were matched by his grim determination to find his wife's murderer, kill him, and then tell his wife one final goodbye, with the news that justice had been done.

"Good morning, Troy. How ya doin'?" Bill offered as he entered the room.

"Not so good," Troy answered, indicating his unbuttoned shirt.

"Here, let me give you a hand," Bill said, stepping behind Troy and reaching around his neck to fasten the top button. Then he helped Troy knot his tie and cinch it up, wondering at Troy's getting so formally dressed to walk down the hall and announce his decision.

Bill shook his head. "I've seen a lot of bad stuff in my life, Troy, but this is more than a man should have to do."

"Yeah." Troy indicated his trousers. "I wore this suit when we got married. Can't wear the coat though with this thing." He held up the cast.

Bill nodded as Troy's face suddenly turned red with rage and he balled his good hand into a fist. "I'm finding him and killing him," he declared.

Bill looked at him without speaking.

"You understand, Bill? I am finding that SOB and I am not waiting for a court of law. Not this time."

Bill looked away—didn't reply.

"My children will be deprived of their mother forever, Bill. I know you'll have to testify against me for saying this, but when you're called to the stand, remember that Lizzy Price was murdered in cold blood. Her murderer signed his own execution order when he calculated and pre-meditated the deed. He attempted to murder me, too, so I could not defend her and her sacred life. I'm going to find him, Bill, and I'm going to make him pay."

Agent Maxfield didn't flinch. He just turned slowly and offered a penetrating glance into Troy's soul.

"Lizzy's attacker has forced me to decide whether his life would be ended. What happens to Lizzy, happens to him; plain and simple. Do you understand what I am saying?"

Bill stood frozen. Twenty-five years of law enforcement instincts overwhelmed by personal feelings, he didn't want to say what he needed to say at this moment . . . not now, not with his heart where it stood for both Lizzy and Troy.

"Bill . . . decide now what you are going to do. We can walk out of here, down the hall where everyone is waiting in Lizzy's room, and then you can take me into custody, or . . ." he didn't finish.

Bill acted his part. He tossed his head to one side toward the door in a "let's go," motion.

Troy turned and looked into the mirror and straightened his tie. Below the bandage on his head, his eyes were still blackened. Given the extent of his injuries and the surgery he had undergone, he wasn't even supposed to be up yet.

Before leaving the room, he picked up the small desk photo he'd asked his mother-in-law to bring to the hospital; a snapshot where Lizzy was giving her first official married kiss to him after their garden wedding ceremony. He took a long look at it, sighed, and then lovingly put it in his shirt pocket, over his heart.

*   *   *   *   *

Later that day

"Mike? Hi, honey! You look so much better!" Maggie smiled, putting her hands to his face and kissing him gently.

"I shaved and brushed my teeth. All on my own. Could you tell?"

"Absolutely. What's up? You getting married or something?"

"Might as well. Know anyone who'd be interested?"

Maggie giggled, feeling a little giddy. "So," she said, "can you slip on some trousers and a clean white shirt and tie I brought?" She held them up for him to see.

"How do the . . ." He pointed to various tubes coming out of his body, the IV drip, and shrugged.

"You can sit up then."

"No, I want to do this right. I want to stand." He slid his legs off the bed and stood shakily.

Maggie took a pair of trousers out of the bag she was holding and handed them to him.

"No underwear?" he asked. "What kind of woman am I engaged to?"

"Oh, hush! I forgot. Just slip the pants on under that gown!"

"Don't peek. We aren't married yet."

"I was with you in surgery. Afraid there is nothing to hide," she laughed.

"Oh, great. I kept myself pure and modest only to be checked out while under sedation. You are a very bad girl!"

"Can I turn around?"

"You'll have to. Can you help me untie this hospital gown?"

She did so, then handed him the shirt.

Mike peered down at the sutures on his chest and abdomen. "Why all the sutures so near my belly button?"

"When you hit the floor, you must have damaged your spleen. Internal bleeding. Either way, you were a dead man without a good doctor in the Jesus seat."

"Maggie, I am grateful to Dr. Hall, but he wasn't in the 'Jesus seat.'"

"What?" she laughed.

He didn't reply.

Mike had his final button on the shirt done up, but because of the tubes he wasn't able to tuck it into his trousers.

"Can you manage the tie? Here, let me help you."

Facing him, she draped the tie around his neck, fashioned an overhand knot, tucked it under his collar, and slid it into place. Then she used the tie to pull his face forward and kiss him. "I love you, Mike," she said.

"I love you and will never leave you," he replied.

"You have a bad heart. It will need to . . ." she said almost apologetically. "I can't help it. The physician is so near the surface. It's like it is all I have ever been. I'm not sure if I will ever just be Maggie Stone. I feel like I will always be your doctor too."

"That's okay with me," he grinned. I've always wondered how female doctors—"

"Hey!" Bill Maxfield called from the door. "Anybody home?"

"Hi, Bill," Maggie replied as he entered the room. She gave him a warm hug and kiss on the cheek. "The best man has arrived. I'll go change and see what is keeping the family and the chaplain. Don't start without me," she teased. "I'll be right back."

"So, how's it goin', Mikey?" Bill began. "You look good in that custom, air-conditioned . . . whatever it is."

Mike looked down at the tubes running out from under his shirt-tail and at his bare feet. The shirt was a little too big, and his pants hung loosely on his hips. "Lost a little weight in the past three weeks. I'm ready to get out of here though."

"Bet you are."

Mike leaned against the edge of the bed and motioned toward the wardrobe. "There are some slippers in there. Can you get them for me?"

Bill retrieved the white hospital slippers and bent to put them on Mike's feet. Then he stepped back and said, "You look like a man about to get married in his hospital room."

Mike laughed. "I've always thought I would get married someday, I just never imagined it happening like this."

They visited for a few minutes, until Maggie swept back into the room.

"Wow! Look at Doctor Maggie Sanders," Mike said, lighting up as she entered the room, with her mother and step-father, Bud Terkel, following.

Maggie was wearing a cream-colored linen skirt and matching jacket over a silky, white blouse. She posed and turned around for Mike to see.

"What do you think?" she asked. "I couldn't decide between this and some green hospital scrubs."

Mike grinned at her. "You look great."

"Hi, Mom," Mike waved to a frowning Mrs. Terkel.

Maggie's mother nodded but didn't approach Mike. She stood off to one side of her daughter as a witness to the ceremony.

"Good afternoon, I'm Chaplain Kennedy," the hospital minister who suddenly appeared announced. "You must be Mr. Stone," he said, stepping forward to shake Mike's hand.

"Please . . . Mike, just Mike."

"Of course." He shook hands with the others and asked, "Is this everybody you're expecting, Dr. Sanders?"

Maggie looked around. "Dr. Hall said he might make it, but maybe he got held up."

"No. I'm here," Dr. Hall said, coming into the room. "I'm not about to let one of my patients go through something like this without having his physician present." He handed Maggie a single rose he had picked up in the hospital gift shop.

"How about the rings?" Chaplain Kennedy asked.

Bill held up the small black box containing both rings.

"Very well. Shall we begin, then?" the chaplain asked. Maggie nodded and moved to stand next to Mike, who supported himself by holding on to the bed rail.

"Dearly beloved, we are gathered here . . ." the chaplain began.

It was over in two minutes, and the newlyweds kissed each other.

"Can we leave for the honeymoon now?" Mike teased.

"Back in bed," she ordered sternly.

"Can't we order a room with a king size or something?"

"Believe me, Mike," Bill chimed in. "You don't need that kind of bed rest. Your heart would stop in a millisecond."

Maggie turned to her mother. "Mom? Aren't you going to say anything to Mike?" she asked the dour-faced woman.

"Congratulations. Now get a real job," she said to Mike, then turned and abruptly left the room.

Maggie gaped after her. Bill, not given to humor, stifled an almost uncontrolled and deeply birthed laugh, then surrendered to a bellow heard throughout the floor. He struggled to catch his breath and wiped at the moisture coming to his eyes. "I'm sorry. I can't help it. I told Mike to get a real job twenty years ago, and to look at her face . . . Man, that was worth a whole lot today!" he chortled. "Get a real job," he repeated. "Whew. That felt good after so many bad days in a row," he said as he held out a small, white box with an elegant bow on it to Maggie. "Yours is coming later," he added in Mike's direction.

"I wonder . . ." Maggie said as she slipped the bow off the package and peeked inside. "Oh, Bill! You sweetheart!"

"Hey, let me see," Mike said.

Maggie lifted the gift from the box. "A new name tag! Thank you, Bill!" He grinned as she kissed him on the cheek.

"Twenty-four carat, too! That's a class act, Bill," Mike offered. "Doctor Maggie Stone," he read.

"Doctor Maggie Stone," she repeated as her lips met his. "Get some rest, honey. I'll see you later and we'll talk about getting you out of here."

22

SPRING ALWAYS BROUGHT the sweet fragrance of lemon, orange, and grapefruit blossoms to Tallahassee. Spring also brought torment to Pastor Nick Caine. The season always reminded him of a warm spring evening so long ago. In spite of the loving kindness and merciful forgiveness extended to him by Claire Barlow, Nick was for those few weeks each year tormented by memories and remorse, in the form of a violent, recurring dream. As if it were a movie, seen through James Barlow's eyes, the dream would be repeated, night after night. And then for months he would mercifully be left alone.

In his dream, Nick never actually witnessed James Barlow's savage beating, a brutal incident that Nick's brother, Joe, always referred to as the "tragic accident." Nick had only pseudo-memories of those events—his but not his. As real as any memory Nick ever had from actual personal experience, they seemed to call from his heavy but very healthy heart.

In Nick's dream, Joe was always guilty. But that was the problem. Joe had never owned up to his responsibility, had always sworn he had nothing to do with what had happened. But then, Nick's younger brother had always had an enormous ability to rationalize, compartmentalize, and use political rhetoric to put his own spin on events.

And in Nick's view, that was what Joe had done with what had happened to Jimmy and to Meredith.

From his first involvement in local government in the early 1960s, Joe had been intoxicated by politics. His love of the pursuit of power was matched only by his desire to possess Meredith Little, a woman he wanted but who the realities of the time had dictated he could never have. Like the effects of too much gin mixed with tonic water, his twin lusts had distorted his vision and deprived him of his usual judgment. And what he ended up doing put Meredith forever out of reach, for both Jimmy Barlow and himself.

Nick owed a tremendous debt to James Barlow. He knew that. James had given him the gift of life and a loving heart. And then there was Meredith's pointless and awful death. Nick worried about his own soul, but also Joe's. Surely a judgment would follow that neither of them could escape.

Now Nick Caine's tired mind swirled with the repeated vision and nightmare of an act his senator brother swore he did not commit. Nick had wrestled with those demons again the entire night, and his wife, Gracie, now begged him to go to see their family physician.

Nick might do that, but for the present, he would have to call Joe today, ask him to come down to Tallahassee, revisit the night that had changed all their lives.

If not for Joe's soul, then for mine.

Nick needed this final cleansing of the slate. He couldn't bear the thought of this infernal darkness coming over him with every blossoming of spring flowers for the remainder of his life. It was too much to endure. He needed to bury the past and see flowers bloom in memory's place. Spring was for hope, renewal, and dreams of immortality—the glory promised by the Risen One, who James Barlow had and now Nick Caine so devoutly believed in.

If hearts always spoke the truth, Nick would let his heart be known to Joe, and then his brother would have to carry the burden. Nick could be free at last.

23

T J HAD MESSED WITH THE WRONG man, and his woman, Beth Benoit. Now TJ would have to pay.

Any other man would have been blind with rage, but Ron Lawton prided himself in controlling his anger, making it work for him. The trick would be to let TJ finish himself off through mistakes.

He did give grudging credit to TJ for saving Beth Benoit from the hired goons in Acapulco. But that wasn't enough to excuse the insult that TJ had paid Lawton. He'd been around too long to let a snot-nosed wannabe like TJ Mattsen jerk him around. No, the kid would pay.

Ron now knew how TJ had found out about his liaison with Beth. Ron had found the bug that had compromised his cell phone calls to Beth. He would have to be far more careful in the future.

TJ had set Beth up to go to Mexico instead of flying to meet Ron in Philadelphia. That TJ had ultimately saved Beth from Felipe and that thug Fernando Laporte only cancelled out part of the debt. What TJ still owed Lawton was the resulting loss of Beth's faith and trust. For that, Ron would kill TJ if he could find him.

Beth had returned to the States the same day TJ Mattsen liberated her from her Mexican kidnappers. She had arrived home totally traumatized by the experience. Mattsen had saved her from actually being assaulted, but she had been taken and held against her will and had then witnessed the brutal killing of her two assailants.

When Ron finally got ahold of her on the phone, Beth tearfully told him he would never see her again. He tried to explain to her, but couldn't find a way out of a snare of his own making. If he was somehow involved with dangerous criminals like those whom TJ Mattsen had assured her were Ron Lawton's Mexican associates, she could never love, touch, or live with such a man.

"I didn't set this up, Beth. Can't you see this TJ Mattsen has some sort of grudge against me? He is the one who did all this, just to make me look bad—get back at me. You can't possibly believe I'd associate with criminals in Mexico. How absurd!" he had reasoned.

"So . . . If I can't depend on you to protect me from your enemies, whoever they are, how can I ever trust you?" she had replied. "We're through! I'm clearing out my office and leaving my resignation on Senator Caine's desk. You fix it with him! Get him a new personal assistant!" she had cried and then slammed the phone down.

Lawton was seething. *TJ is messing with a superior player. The boys in Mexico bungled it, and in this business, you only get one chance to bungle something, and then you pay the price. TJ is about to pay that price.*

Lawton admitted to himself that he had misjudged TJ's resourcefulness and the extent of his NSA and CIA contractor training. The ex-Special Forces and Black Ops man was proving himself to be resilient. In fact, Lawton held a grudging admiration for the young operative. TJ reminded Ron of himself; the way he Ron Lawton, surnamed Horton when he left his hometown of Coldcreek, Colorado, to first join the Army in 1967, had reinvented himself so many times during his younger crusading years—had changed names, gone so deeply underground that not a single family member knew he was alive. Not that he cared.

His biological father was dead. Had died in Korea. His mother was an alcoholic, and his step-father had abused him in a vile way. But Ron had fixed that. His step-father, too, like his old man, was long ago deceased.

TJ . . . In a way, Lawton wished he didn't have to do what he was about to do; the set-up. But TJ would determine its outcome after all. In fact, if TJ made it through alive, he would deserve to live. Lawton would then offer to call a truce and keep something he knew was valuable to TJ. There was something all men needed in this business of dark operations, secrets, and espionage; that is identity. Each needs to hide his true name, his true past, his true personal history.

TJ hadn't been as careful as he should have been in covering himself, and besides, Ron had had twenty more years than the punk to make alliances in the intelligence community.

Too bad, TJ. You better hope for your sake you don't show.

*   *   *   *   *

As far as TJ Mattsen was concerned, the whole bunch of them could take a flying leap without chutes. His last two surnames had been those of friends who had died somewhere in the world doing their duty. He would need a new name now, and a new look.

A scar across my face. That will do nicely. Women love scars. Something about their need to nurse.

He looked into the mirror, picked up the razor blade, and didn't hesitate. He'd anesthetized the area an hour before. No pain, just plenty of blood.

Like cutting through soft butter. Now one across the eye.

He sliced this a bit more carefully. Here, he'd determined, his eyelid should sag a bit.

War wounds. Now a month-long vacation. *Should I call Beth*

Benoit? Naw, that would be rubbing salt into Ron's wound. Think I'll go get killed in Afghanistan and then come back a new man.

*   *   *   *   *

"Hey, man. Wake up!" TJ said, nudging the homeless man he had brought back today from a street corner in D.C. "So I kept my promise, right?"

The tired drunk in worn-out clothes claimed to be a Vietnam veteran—had his cardboard, handwritten sign lying beside him on the living room floor: "Will work for food." It amused TJ to have found a bum who actually was missing all his teeth, who wore dentures. That made it almost too easy.

"Yeah, man. You're a good dude. You want me to get up now and work?" the wino slurred.

"No need. Just stay there. Here are the house keys. Come and go as you like." TJ walked to the door, then stopped and turned back to the man. "I put your bag of personal belongings in the kitchen."

The man's facial expression, though dulled by alcohol, was painted with surprise and bewilderment.

"You mean I can stay?" he asked, rising up on an elbow.

"Sure, why not? I'm headed out of town. I'll just lock the doors. You wake up, do the yard work, and take care of the place. Food's in the fridge."

"Man . . . you must be . . . a vet too!" he slowly but happily drooled.

"I've seen a few fights. Have a nice sleep," TJ offered with a feigned smile.

The toothless man returned a vacuous smile, took another swig from his whiskey bottle, let out a belch, and was quickly out again.

TJ packed light. He took the man's small bag with his dentures, one I.D. card, and other personal belongings, and threw them into the front seat of his car.

Packing light was one of TJ's specialties. He enjoyed not needing anything or anyone. He could buy anything he needed on the road. Money was no problem. He had several credit cards on fake IDs.

He made sure the natural gas line where it entered the house was open, went back in and killed the pilot lights to the water heater and kitchen range, then turned on the valves on the stove. He closed the garage door behind him. All windows were closed. Now natural gas would make its way through the house, take the inebriated, homeless bum on to the happy hunting grounds, and then . . .

Lawton set the timer on his watch and waited in his car for thirty minutes. It was 3:00 A.M., and the tree-lined country lane leading to his rented farmhouse outside of the town of Manassas, Virginia, didn't boast of any other homes for over a mile.

He stopped the car about fifty yards from the house, picked up the survival flare gun he had purchased, popped a round in the chamber, aimed squarely for the living room window, and sped off, seeing only the fireball explode in the rearview mirror.

Too bad about that. TJ Mattsen officially dead. Another casualty of war.

*   *   *   *   *

TJ wasn't going to do this free-lance operation for his black ops contact. He could smell a Lawton setup. It was too soon after the Mexico gig. Ron would either buy into his faked death at the house in Manassas or keep him on his hit list.

Even if he stayed on the hit list, he was confident who would ultimately win. Ron was an old-timer, and his time was past; done—over. The word TJ had received, presumably from one of his old contacts, was that he only needed to spend three days and nights on a special mission in Afghanistan, and that fifty thousand dollars waited for him in the account in Switzerland.

"Yeah, right," he mumbled.

He thought he *would* go to Afghanistan, meet his contact, and then disappear. Paying a local, he'd simply fake his death, give up some blood, stain a shirt with it, and the local would take it back to report his death and dismemberment by rebel Taliban operatives to the contact in Kabul.

But he figured Lawton might not buy into that either. Even if some DNA from the charred corpse in the house wasn't usable for identification, TJ would still have to watch his back.

When he messed with Ron's girlfriend, Beth, TJ knew there would be a price to pay. But he had needed to send a strong message to Lawton—that he, TJ Mattsen, wasn't just some hack who Ron could dispose of at will. TJ was a player—a professional in the covert intelligence game—and he wasn't going down like some two-bit clown wearing a security badge at a shopping mall.

He had Lawton figured for the murdering scum he was from the beginning. He only consented to work with him because he wanted Ron's job. The best way to find a man's weak spot is to work for him, and so the "loyal-soldier" routine was a necessary evil.

TJ had carefully manufactured the resumé of a consummate business and political manager and had managed to study the art in the shadow of men like Lawton for several years.

In his view, he was superior to Ron in everyway. He had mastered the latest techniques in communications, tracking, surveillance, disposal, target assessment, elimination of targets, weaponry, and just plain youthful smarts. If he really wanted Ron out of the way he could make it happen tomorrow. Thing was, a smart operator knew that when the opposition created his own demise, that was the first weapon of choice.

He was a believer in the murder investigator's maxim: You can't track a killer who doesn't kill. Lethal means of dealing with a target wasn't always with pills, poisons, blades, or gunpowder. Sometimes it was simple old smarts. To get the other guy set up and make him trip on his own booby-trap wire.

Besides, when TJ killed, it was the enemy; always the enemy of his country or his own personal enemy, like those Mexicans who would have gladly killed him for the Lawton payment. Lawton was still loyal to the bigger cause, the war against the homeland. For that TJ would give Ron the benefit of the doubt and allow him to bring himself down.

TJ had never silenced someone inside the system. He had a line he drew. He was an American, and he would be willing to die himself before he'd terminate someone who was allied to the cause; unless, of course, they were trying to kill him. When an American was the target, he'd better well be a traitor or trying to terminate him.

So that was the difference between himself and Lawton.

He wouldn't kill just anybody. And because of his higher standards he, TJ, knew that he was a better man.

And the good guys always win, he reflected with satisfaction.

Now he'd keep Lawton waiting. If anyone was going to trip up, it wouldn't be him. He'd stay on the move, monitor Lawton, and let his inside network at Digiwatch take care of tracking Ron and his team.

He wished he didn't know so many of them—Lawton's private Black Ops. He didn't like the idea of going up against someone he actually knew. He didn't care for that at all. He had shut emotion down long ago, but once in awhile they all had shared some bit of personal life history in war and peacetime. He hoped none of them ever came after him. He'd never had to kill someone he understood—someone like himself—someone real.

Jackson Lyon . . . now there was a man who understood friendship; someone who knew how to be grateful to a man who served him.

He hoped Ron wasn't up to speed yet on Lyon's plans.

That could change everything.

For now, he'd lie low and watch. His pay had been so good and generous for years, he really didn't have to work. He rarely spent money—didn't have the time.

TJ Mattsen would enjoy this time off, create his new identity and papers, use his influence on the inside, and wait his turn. The old dog Lawton was about to lose his position at the helm of Lyon's enterprising power plays. Digiwatch would soon have a new internal security chief—a man with more recent battle scars.

24

Three months later

THINK WITH YOUR HEAD, MAGGIE. The heart is a pump.
All a good doctor has to do is the mechanics and let nature do the
rest."

Maggie held the phone to her ear and rubbed at her eyes with the
fingers on her other hand. "Ken, I know what you are saying is text-
book, and I have assisted in a good number of transplants, but I want
to know that my husband's heart comes from a good person—you
know, someone who has taken care of it."

"You mean to tell me, you will turn down this heart donor
because of his criminal past? He is a dead man on life support. Brain
dead! His family has his written last will and testament, giving them
permission to donate his organs to whomever they see fit."

"Ken, he lived a hard life. A dark life. His heart was bad inside
and out and just because it's a 'ticker' you mean my husband should
have it put into his chest? The heart of a murderer and thief?"

"Maggie. Where did you come up with these nutty notions?
You been reading that new age medicine mumbo jumbo about the
cardio-memory?"

"The heart's more than a pump, Ken. It's all found in JAMA. What
makes sense is that neuron cells are now found in the heart, the stom-
ach. . . . What about 'gut instinct'? What about 'follow your heart'?

What if the brain is a collaborator with the heart and stores information there as well? There are plenty of case studies of people receiving a transplant only to acquire also the donor's tastes, moods, habits."

"Maggie! You can't be serious!"

"As good as double-blind studies, these unrelated cases all point to the same thing—that the heart carries something of the memory of the donor. The stories are well-documented and are in the thousands. I just can't set the concern aside. Besides, I haven't lost my identity as Maggie Sanders, the idealistic med student out to save the world. You know me, Ken. If the stream runs downhill, I swim up. I can't help it, and I can't help feeling like I do about the most vital organ in the human body."

"Your husband's bad heart was made that way by his own substance abuse, hard living, and—"

"Ken, please . . ."

"And now you are going to kick a gift horse in the mouth? How do you plan on getting a good heart for Mike? Is his ticker going to last while you screen the life histories of all possible donors?"

Silence.

"Maggie, as a friend, and the one who has agreed to do this operation, I'm only going to ask you this one last time. Most other surgeons would not have bothered, but I care. I have always cared about you, Maggie."

More silence.

Maggie and Ken Miller had once dated for a while, until she realized she didn't actually love him—that she had only been husband shopping. She needed to feel love, and that didn't come from the head.

"Do you want the heart that will be available this week? I can make it happen. The family has asked that I recommend a patient in critical need. The donor, the criminal, wanted to make amends somehow. Isn't that an indication of your need being met for the almighty good heart? I called you because we are friends and because of our professional relationship—and of course because I want you to know I still genuinely care about you, Maggie. What should I tell them about the jailbird's free pump being offered to Mike?"

"Ken . . . I need some time."

"We don't have much of that, Maggie."

"Twenty-four hours?"

He gave her the twenty-four hours.

She hung up the phone.

*　　　*　　　*　　　*　　　*

Nicholas Caine was admitted to the hospital for tests. Just months after retiring, he had seemed to withdraw more and more into a melancholy that only visiting Claire Barlow could shake.

Gracie sensed that left to his own devices, he would soon die. Without a cause and something meaningful to do, he would simply give up. It hurt her to think that she wasn't cause enough—that their marriage of three decades wasn't the focus of Nick's life now, as she had hoped it one day would be.

Without the demands of his ministerial service, Nick felt lost. Her hope had been that he might look to her, that he would find in their relationship fulfillment enough. She had been a faithful and loyal companion and deserved being ministered to and the center of his love and life. So when this last round of headaches, nausea, and listlessness had gone on for almost two weeks, she checked Nick into the hospital for tests.

Then, last night, Nick had suffered a seizure induced by a stroke and was partially paralyzed on the left side. She knew the depression from which he suffered would not help him in his rehabilitation efforts and hoped the doctors could diagnose his overall illness.

Gracie called Joe, Nick's only living sibling and immediate family member, and Joe seemed willing enough to come down, to get out of D.C. He had a senatorial office set up in six key Florida cities, including one in Tallahassee. He would be able to keep in touch with D.C. through it.

"Gracie, I'll come directly to the hospital. How's my big brother really doing?"

Grace tried to say something positive, but her emotions betrayed her.

"Gracie? Are you there? Are you all right?"

"Yes," she squeaked.

"No, you're not okay. Are you at Nick's bedside?"

"Yes," she forced out between sobs.

"I'll be there as soon as I can catch a flight."

"Thank you," she said.

Joe pondered where all this might lead. *Nick's death? Then what?* His concern for his brother was suddenly overridden by a practical consideration. *The Presidency. With Nick gone, no one will have to know about the Barlow incident . . . About Meredith . . . And that means . . .*

That sudden, selfish thought caused him shame but also brought relief. He would do what Senator Joseph Caine had always done— follow his minister brother's advice from years before:

No need to stay up and fret about something you can't do anything about. Get a good night's sleep and leave the matter in God's hands. He will be up all night anyway.

*　　*　　*　　*　　*

Maggie hadn't anticipated an almost overnight deterioration in Mike's condition. Now, days later, she second-guessed her decision to turn down Doctor Ken Miller's life-saving offer of a donor heart from a dying criminal. That opportunity was now lost—the heart had been donated to someone else on the waiting list.

She nervously dialed Bill's number. She didn't know why. *What can an FBI agent tell me?* All she knew was she might be a widow by the end of the week and needed some reassurance, somebody's caring words to encourage her.

"Special Agent Maxfield," the husky voice answered.

"Bill?"

"Maggie. What's going on?"

"I need to talk. I don't know where to start."

"Maggie. Where are you? What's happened?"

"I'm at the hospital. With Mike. I don't know what to do."

"I have a meeting with several assistant directors here at the Bureau. I'll be done in two hours. Where can I meet you?"

"I'm so scared, Bill," she replied. "I'm afraid if I leave the hospital Mike could die. Maybe a nurse would miss a vital sign. Maybe Mike will awake to speak final words. Maybe . . ." she cried.

"Maggie. Just hold on. Stay there. I'll be with you by five o'clock. Is that okay?"

Maggie thanked him and slowly folded the cell's flip clamshell closed. She watched the struggles of a pale man whose muscles were atrophying from so many weeks of heart–failure–induced weakness. He barely could rouse the energy to open his eyes and lips to see and speak to her.

She took his hand in hers. "I love you, Mike. I didn't know I could feel this way about a man. It's not even logical for me to feel this way. My heart has taken over my mind, and I want you to live. Are you leaving me, Mike?" she whispered into his ear as she bathed his pale face with tears.

"I love you, too," he breathed. "I love you, too," his lips formed again as his heavily sedated mind drifted far from where his heart was leading him.

25

BILL MAXFIELD HAD REASONED with Troy and helped temper his desire for revenge. Troy's decision had stunned everyone in the room where Lizzy's life support fate was decided. Now he agreed to hear Bill out.

No one in the family had expected Troy to back down from authorizing removal of life support. Lizzy's parents agreed that a married couple had every right in a prearranged decision such as this. That is, if anything ever put the other one onto life support, the surviving spouse should have the authority to allow the partner to die in dignity.

Troy had put on his best attire to visit his comatose wife. He wanted only to whisper the words of love and closure to their life together as he bent down to kiss her.

But it was Lizzy who spoke to Troy on that day weeks before. He swore she had. "Give Mike my heart," she had said. No one else in the room had heard a word or had seen Lizzy even move her lips. Troy simply but adamantly declared that she had said those words and was not to be taken off life support.

"How did she even know about Mike? His heart attack? She couldn't have known before being attacked at Union Station," a hopeful younger sister stated.

167

"I don't know. But I heard those words," Troy humbly answered. "They came to my ears as clear as her voice ever spoke."

There was silence. Doctor Whitaker, the treating physician, came forward. "Troy. There is no hurry here. Don't feel pressured. But, if you believe Lizzy should be a donor for Mike Stone, I think I owe it to Maggie and all of you here to start that process that will save another's life. There is paperwork, and—"

Troy had turned to the doctor. "How much time does Mike have?"

"Days at worst and maybe weeks at best."

Troy then said to Lizzy's grieving parents, "If she has power to speak, she has power to live. I feel sorry for Mike, but I want her back. If she lives, she's mine. If she dies, Mike gets her heart."

Bill admired Troy for the stand he was taking. He loved his cousin Lizzy, but he loved Mike like a brother too. He told Maggie about Lizzy's request and now she was in a state of disbelief, immobilized by fear and emotion as how to see Mike to either the end or to a new life.

Bill rarely interceded in other people's personal and private affairs. It just wasn't like him. He pondered deeply where all this was leading him.

But after all, Mike always said I was his adopted big brother. And Maggie is in trouble. Lizzy near death is willing to give the gift of life, and Troy is willing to find a man he doesn't know and take a life; perhaps allowing Mike to die in the process.

He picked up the phone and called his contact with Amtrak's Police Division. He had received authorization from an assistant director at the Bureau to establish some sort of federal jurisdiction over Lizzy's, Troy's, and the boy's attacks at Union Station, since it had occurred on government property and because Amtrak was a government-run enterprise.

He had asked Troy to give him a chance to use his federal

resources to track the man down and promised that Troy would always be kept in the loop. He also assured Troy that if he went out on his own and did find and cause the death of his attacker, he, Bill, would be forced to testify regarding what Troy had premeditated.

Bill didn't often look for help outside his own resourcefulness. But this involved people who all were extremely close to him.

God, he whispered under his breath. *I don't expect to get any extra deal from this; for myself, I mean.* He'd never been religious, although he had certainly allowed for a divine presence. Now he wished he were a praying man. *Then maybe I'd know what to tell everyone.*

*   *   *   *   *

TJ Mattsen was enjoying his notoriety as a tragic recluse suddenly taken from this life. The local D.C. and Northern Virginia CBS affiliate had first reported his death from explosion due to a faulty gas line at his home. He especially enjoyed their description of him:

"The landlord said the renter, one TJ Mattsen, was a healthy and physically fit man, somewhere between thirty and forty years of age.

"A loner, as the homeowner called his renter, he was always on time with cash payments, and never talked to his neighbors. No known family for Mattsen has come forth, and investigators are continuing to seek background information to determine who his family might be.

"Although Mattsen's body was literally consumed in the inferno, making identification virtually impossible, authorities are not ruling out foul play, but are considering some information provided them through an unknown source.

"The homeowner made a statement to investigators that just last week he had personally replaced the water heater and kitchen stove at the renter's request, and expense, due to some concerns Mattsen had expressed. The owner, who is a journeyman plumber, says this rental home was in top condition and that he had every reason to keep it that way.

"Right now there appear to be more questions than answers, and it looks as though what may be considered a tragic accident will remain under scrutiny until those questions are cleared up. Reporting from Manassas, Virginia. Back to you in the studio."

TJ smiled, clicked the TV off, and walked outside into the forest darkness at the rented peninsula cottage. *I'm officially dead under suspicious circumstances. I wonder what the "information provided by an unknown source" could be?*

He walked a few yards to a nearby creek, which ultimately flowed into Chesapeake Bay. He took the remaining papers and threw them into a metal wastebasket, doused them with lighter fluid, and dropped a match into the container. He watched the ashes drift around in the bottom of the metal trash can as he stirred the burning papers with a stick. He threw the final document containing any personal history of TJ Mattsen into the smoldering flames.

The last thing he saw as he stared transfixed into the yellow fire creeping up the pages of his Digiwatch Security profile was a name. Now an orange glow, the final words consumed read:

"Hired by Ron Lawton, Security Director, Digiwatch, Inc. Jan. 15, 2004."

TJ carried the can over to the water's edge and mixed the ashes thoroughly into the creek and watched them swirl away. "See you soon, Ron."

*   *   *   *   *

"So TJ has gone undercover," Lawton stated to the man on the other end of the telephone line. Lawton was seated on a plane, waiting for it to pull away from the terminal. "What's Lyon saying about it? . . . He's bought into it? . . . Good."

He clicked the phone off and prepared to relax during the flight to Florida. There he'd pick up a car under a different name, pay cash, and make some hospital rounds.

The phone again.

"Give me an update on Stone," Lawton demanded. "That bad?" he replied. "Yeah. I have it covered," he answered. "No, I don't know when the man is dying. Not yet."

Click. It had been Lyon. A very nervous Jackson Lyon.

Jack Lyon didn't want Stone to die—not with so much information floating around, and, according to Lyon, Stone had "political value." Lawton was dubious about anyone needing to live just because of his "political value." *There are a dozen lined up and willing to take any one man's place in this world,* he reminded himself. *But information? Can't get that from a dead man. So Stone needs a new heart,* he summarized to himself.

Ron Lawton had a full plate. Everything—all his newly won political clout with Lyon and Caine—was riding on making bad news disappear. He wanted the information from Stone's files for all the blackmailing he would have to do, but not until he made it to the White House under either Lyon or Caine. He wanted to be able to use "bad news"—stuff from past misdeeds or illegal transactions—with the top man himself. *Would sort of make me a pseudo-president without all the hassles,* he grinned to himself.

"I like that," he said aloud without realizing it.

"What was that, sir?" the stewardess asked him as she passed by.

"I'd like that drink now."

"Yes, sir." She took his order.

He gazed out the window as the aircraft lifted off, heading to its announced flying altitude of 35,000 feet. His eyes glazed over, picturing in his mind the power he had worked so hard for; deserved, and was now so close he could almost taste it. He thought about Mike Stone, his talent, and how valuable he'd be if he were healthy and could be compromised; bought, paid for.

A healthy Mike Stone is a treasure trove of information about contributors, the powerful men and women who have given their resources to get Caine and Lyon into office and keep them in power over the years, he thought. He had uncovered just enough intelligence to also strongly suspect there might be other damaging information in those files—something Joe Caine would desperately not want to become public.

It's a shame some man has to die just to get Stone his healthy heart.

Then there was Mattsen. TJ remained a big distraction—a distraction that was becoming more like a cat-and-mouse sideshow to the real life-and-death drama tying up Lyon and Caine's concerns— whether or not Mike Stone died with all the information they wanted still in him.

Lawton had seen the news about the supposed death of Mattsen, but he had immediately seen through the ruse. I wonder how he covered up the dental records? He knew Mattsen would try to make a move on his place as political advisor to Lyon at Digiwatch, and possibly Caine as well.

Now he had his own life-and-death contest to add to the list of items he was supposed to make good on.

So, TJ Mattsen . . . The game is on after all.

26

"GRACIE," JOE SAID in a soft voice as his right hand settled upon her shoulder.

"Oh! Hello, Joe. You startled me."

"I'm sorry. I came as soon as I could."

She took Joe's hand in hers. "That is so good of you."

"How's my big brother?" Joe asked, gesturing toward the hospital bed.

"Oh . . ." she said, releasing a heavy sigh. "He comes and goes. He was awake a few moments ago and asked if you were coming. They have him pretty sedated. He said 'Joe' like a question. The stroke he suffered has him seized up on his left side pretty much, and it's made it difficult for him to speak."

Joe coughed, and struggled to control the emotion he suddenly experienced.

"They say he could recover from the stroke. He'll be all right . . . won't he, Joe?"

"Sure! Sure he will! He's been through heart transplant surgery and a lot of tough situations. He should have died years ago and look now! Why, he'll be better in days. You watch."

Joe looked down upon the paleness of his deathly still brother and something told him otherwise, but he couldn't bring himself to believe that Nick could actually die. Nick had always seemed immortal to him. Even when his first heart failed him, Nick had survived. Joe felt Nick had nine lives.

"Thank you for that reassurance," Grace Caine returned. "I needed to hear that."

"What can I do, Gracie?" Joe offered.

"I'm not sure. I guess if you could just come everyday you are here in Tallahassee and stay nearby, in case Nick wakes up. I'm awfully tired and could use a break. The kids should be home tonight, and maybe if I just go home and rest a bit . . ."

"Sure! I can stay 'til the end of the week! I need to be with my brother. Politics be damned. Nick is more important to me. You go on home. I promise I'll call if anything comes up. You go on now. Do you want me to call you a cab?"

"No, thanks. I'll be fine. Claire Barlow is coming over to the house later. She said she wanted to bring us a meal. She is real upset by all this. She wants to come down here, too, but I asked her to wait. And . . ." Grace seemed to be rambling in a hopeful way. Joe just listened and nodded his head in an understanding manner.

"She seems to think that . . ." Grace couldn't finish, but the tears showed the words in eyes that filled with love for her hero husband, now so helplessly bedridden. "Claire told me that her son, James Barlow, came to her. It was in a dream. And she said he was there in a room, speaking to Nick and had put his arm around him and then the two walked off together. Claire said she woke up right after and called me to tell me everything will be in good hands. But I . . ." Her voice broke again. "He won't die, will he, Joe?" she cried.

"Yes," came the broken vocals from behind her. "I saw Jimmy, and I will die," Nick sighed. He had stirred to the conversation. "I will die, but not my heart. It belongs to someone else. Jimmy told me so. Hello, Joe."

"Hey, there, Nick!" he replied. "See? See, Gracie, how strong he is? I walk in, and Nick can't even stop yakking."

*   *   *   *   *

Mike was getting weaker day by day, and he and Maggie were running out of time. She had called every resource around the country she could think of. She had done mass e-mails to all her surgeon and hospital contacts. She was down to considering an artificial heart pump. The thought of Mike operating on a mere mechanical pump further depressed her, but it was at least a ray of hope.

"He doesn't deserve this!" she cried into her pillow. "God, where are you!" she demanded as she tossed, seeking sleep to deliver her from this torment.

Her last thoughts were of Mike and their supposed honeymoon. *I want to be a wife and a mother. Michael Stone, don't leave me.*

27

Lawton's flight was still cruising south, and he was thinking deeply about how he would help end one life with dignity while allowing another to continue. He felt like a winner, though. With all the power over life and death, all the intrigue, all the battles to fight, fires to put out, and fires to start, he felt like a man in control of his destiny. Some would call his position as a kingmaker lucky.

Lawton didn't believe in luck. He felt a man made his own luck. Intelligence, timing, and expert execution of carefully made plans—those were the things that ensured success. But in this case, he couldn't take all the credit for the way things had lined up.

He was about to save a life; something he rarely did. It would please Jackson Lyon, the leading contender for the American Alliance Party presidential nomination, that Mike Stone would be getting a new heart, and to Lawton, that was worth some political hay.

Jackson Lyon had worked hard to establish himself as the national "poster boy" for national security. The events of 9/11 and the subsequent war on terrorism had created an unprecedented necessity for new ways to track people and communications, and Digiwatch Corporation's surveillance technology was on the cutting edge of a growing, international industry.

As a member of Digiwatch's board of directors, Lyon could go on the same television and radio talk shows where he had been welcomed for years as a spokesman for The Gun Club, a national, ultra-conservative proponent of the Second Amendment and an organization that had found increasing favor with the American people.

Lyon had parlayed his native Southwestern charm and philosophy of fast shooting but fair play in war and politics into a growing national, personal popularity. The polls bore this out, and enthusiastic crowds met him everywhere he spoke—something that was not lost to the television cameras that covered his every appearance.

The national organization he had started and simply called The Gun Club had given blue-collar, patriotic, promilitary voters across the country an effective lobby.

For strategic purposes, he now needed to distance himself a bit from The Gun Club, focus his attention on Digiwatch, and become the champion of the growing public acceptance of the idea that in times of war, personal liberties sometimes had to give way to national security.

"Guns first, identifying people second, control third," he had told Ron Lawton in a Digiwatch meeting just one week before. Lawton, who had shown himself capable and more than happy to offer his expertise and service to Lyon's cause, had gotten it and agreed it was a brilliant strategy.

Reading the political winds, Lawton would later in the year quietly transfer his political allegiance from Caine to Lyon and turn over his chief of staff duties to a lesser staffer. He'd still control things in Caine's camp, just be free to run with Lyon to the top.

The confidential files, in the possession of Mike Stone, detailing contributors to both Joe Caine's and Jackson Lyon's past campaigns and other sensitive matters were of vital interest to both men. Lawton knew that the dirt Stone had reportedly accumulated on Joe Caine, if it were to exist, would be of particular use to Lyon. If Lyon had access to such information, he could control Caine in their competition for the nomination of the independent American Alliance Party. To prevent any embarrassing revelation, the senator would gladly agree to support Lyon's candidacy and accept second place on the ticket.

But if those files were to be found, Mike Stone needed a savior—someone to secure for him a good heart to rejuvenate his failing physical body. It was Ron Lawton's good fortune to be in a position to be that someone. He would arrange for that new heart, and in doing so keep Stone alive, but more importantly consolidate his position with Lyon.

Lawton needed those files also to keep Caine in his debt and not come off looking like the senator's enemy. If Lawton could get them from Stone and keep their contents from becoming public, Caine would be grateful to Lawton for helping him escape not only public humiliation but political annihilation.

Joe Caine needed to know that Ron Lawton was doing everything in the senator's best interest. Joe's brother, Nicholas Caine, was dying anyway. No need to let a perfectly good heart go to the dumpster when the old boy permanently checked out.

Giving Nicholas Caine an "early out" from his hospital stay was simple math; one man dies and another man lives. *When Nicholas dies isn't as important as who gets to live because of his heart donation. Even Joe Caine could appreciate that fact,* Ron reasoned to himself.

The stewardess brought him his vodka and juice. "Keep the change," he said as he took it from her and began to mix.

Ron was, ostensibly, coming to Tallahassee to ensure Joe Caine would get the maximum, favorable publicity from the hospital vigil the concerned senator would be keeping at the side of his dying older brother. The popular and much admired, retired Tallahassee minister was "A man with a good heart, if there ever was one," Lawton had coached the senator to say.

It would be a stake in Joe's own heart—in more than one way—when his brother, Nick, suddenly expired, leaving his heart to donor recipient Mike Stone. But Lawton knew the senator. The consummate politician would play the good soldier to the national audience, and he would survive the death of his brother, Nicholas.

Why? Because his good brother's heart would live on.

And laid to rest with Nicholas Caine would be many fears and doubts Joseph Caine probably suffered from, Ron assured himself. *I am their friend. I'm quite the good guy after all,* he allowed.

"Another vodka and any kind of juice you have will do," he said as the stewardess passed his way.

28

GRACE CAINE AND NICK talked earlier in the day. This morning Nick had strongly reiterated to Grace what he wanted done when he died. His acceptance of the inevitability of his death was emotionally overwhelming for Grace, and now she was all but drained. Explaining this to Joe, and then being reassured by him that Nick wasn't in immediate peril, she finally left for some much needed rest.

Joe was now alone with his brother and decided to relax in the reclining lounger next to his bed. Exhaustion overcame him, and he slept by his brother's side through the night. He awoke in the morning and exited the hospital for his downtown hotel suite, face drawn, wearing a wrinkled suit and loosened necktie, only to be confronted by a battery of reporters and television cameras that zoomed in on his haggard face.

"Senator Caine, can you tell us how your brother's doing?" a reporter asked.

The senior senator from Florida faced the cameras and replied, "He is basically stable. He talked to me yesterday when I arrived. Thank you all for your concern and prayers," he said. "Our family is very grateful for the outpouring of love from people everywhere, but especially from Nick's congregation in Tallahassee. That's all I have to say for now. I'll be back this afternoon. Thank you all very much."

News reporters chased him to his car where a new office aide, Barbara Waters, was waiting to take him to the hotel. He slid into the backseat, closed the door, and rolled down the window and waved as the car rolled away.

Joe engaged in no formal or small talk this morning with the pretty lady half his age, other than: "I understand you are new?"

"Yes, Senator."

"Your name sounds like the news gal—Walters."

"I get that a lot."

"Hmm."

"Is there anything else I can do for you, Senator?" she asked as they pulled under the portico of the nearby Hotel Carlton.

He looked at her eyes, now locked on his in the rearview mirror.

"Uh, no. Not at this time. Are my bags here?"

"All taken care of, Senator."

"Who was it who hired you?" he asked. He stood outside the car, turned, and took a closer look at the attractive and petite mixed-race woman. *She reminds me a little of Meredith* . . .

"Ron Lawton," she answered, interrupting his thoughts. "I'm honored to be working for you, Senator. I hope I don't disappoint you in any way," she smiled, displaying a set of dazzling white teeth and a gorgeous mouth.

"I . . . uh . . ." he cleared his throat. "I am sure you will do fine, just fine." He kept his dignified posture and turned to head into the lobby.

Barbara picked up her cell phone and made her first business call of the day.

A gruff-speaking man questioned her sternly, "The package?"

"Yes, the package has arrived."

Click.

Barbara Waters had just delivered the first of many "packages" she'd deliver for Digiwatch.

*   *   *   *   *

Nick's speech, temporarily impaired by the stroke, was already improving. "I just know. Promise me, Joe. Promise me that someone worthy will get this heart when I die. It was Jimmy's, you know. Promise me. Okay?"

"I want you to stop this. You are improving. Look at your chart. I had a doctor explain it to me just last night. All your vital signs are normal. Your speech has returned in nothing short of a miracle. Your headaches, anemia, all under control. Your fever, totally broken."

"Drugs and prayers. It always works. But I will die, Joe. I know it."

"So? We'll all die."

"No, Joe. This is only a reprieve, a gift from a beneficent God to one who has tried to become his servant for the past three decades."

Joe was inside the curtain drawn around Nick's bed.

"Okay, a reprieve," Joe answered. "The reprieve can last five, ten, twenty-five years. You know that. Come on, Nick! Let's not be so morose, for heaven's sake. The good Lord still needs you here."

"Do *you* need me here, Joe? Do you?" Nick reached out a much strengthened hand and grasped his younger brother's arm. "Tell me, Joe. Is there anything you need? Something you want to tell me?"

Joe reached for his brother's hand and gently pried it loose. "No, Nick. I'm fine with my Maker. I'm fine with the past. Let's leave it buried. Can we?"

Nick shook his head and wiped with the back of his right hand at the moisture coming to his eyes. "For years, Joe, I've had nightmares. I've never told you about them. If you won't tell me, then I'll tell you. I see you standing over Jimmy Barlow's body with that baseball bat you always carried."

"Nick, please, don't—"

"Let me finish. Joe, I need to know something before I die. I see you swinging the bat to finish Jimmy off. You aren't yourself. You are about to do something that in your right mind you would never do. Meredith appears in her car and then . . . all goes foggy. I am seeing everything through Jimmy's eyes. You understand? I think I have Jimmy's memory stored in my chest, and now it haunts me until—"

"Stop! Just stop, Nick! I paid my price! I went to Vietnam. I killed in Vietnam! What happened to Meredith was an accident! I swung. I swung with all I had. I had to. Can't you see? I'd been drinking. I had to . . ." he said, voice trailing off.

"And then?" Nick weakly asked.

"I picked her up and took her to the cottage at the beach. I hoped to revive her, take care of her, make her well—make her love me!" he cried. "I was going to call a doctor. I didn't know what to do. Can't you see how everything was done to protect you, me, us? Meredith shouldn't have been there. I wasn't going to be there. I felt bad about what we decided to do to Jimmy and went by the church and—"

"You knew Meredith was going to the church. In fact, you picked her up and took her there."

"How the hell do you know that?" Joe bellowed.

"I saw it."

"I didn't see you there. Were you hiding in the grove?"

"No, Joe. I saw it through another man's eyes. I saw the bat. After you hit Meredith and put her in the car. I saw your rage. I heard your words."

"I, ah . . ." Joe stopped and cleared his shaken voice. "Nick—see here. You can't believe I caused someone's death purposefully. I didn't murder anyone. I made a mistake. Mistakes are different. I cared about Meredith more than I cared about my own life. Jimmy Barlow was in the way. I was angry. You were involved. How do *you* rationalize this? It was *all your* idea."

"And you think I haven't suffered every day since? You think I haven't tried to make up for it? I have been sorry ever since we hatched that plan to intimidate Jimmy. It got out of hand, we all were drunk, but that was no excuse!" Nick cried.

"I know," Joe replied solemnly. "It's okay, Nick. It's over. We can't go back," he added glumly.

"You're right, Joe. We can't go back, but we can ask for forgiveness. I'm afraid for your soul, Joe. You understand me?" Nick asked earnestly, but his voice was weaker than before.

"Yes," Joe softly returned as he sat at the bedside, head hanging down, his eyes fixed unseeing on the tile floor.

Nick said more softly, "Until this latest sickness, I had rationalized these memories, dreams, and fears on the basis that James W. Barlow Jr. knew I was dying from a bad heart. He knew! My story had been in the news. He was hospitalized because of the injuries we caused him. When he saw my story on television, from his own sickbed, he had his mother, Claire, call to the hospital.

"He instructed his mother that I was to get his heart if he should pass on. Somehow he knew he wasn't going to live much longer." Nick's voice broke, "Can you believe it? He knew I was one of those who had beaten him, and yet he designated me to get his heart." Nick struggled to control his emotion, then went on. "Jimmy died days before the doctors expected me to pass on from my heart condition. God only knows why I lived and he didn't. Now do you understand why I feel this heart must go on? That it must still beat for the living—to do some of the good that Jimmy might have done had he lived?"

Nick clutched his younger brother's hand and looked deeply into his eyes. "Well, do you understand now?"

Joe nodded. "I do understand, and I promise you, if you die, the heart will be given to someone worthy to carry on this mission of yours and Barlow's. You have my word," Joe finished.

"It was a heart from a good man," Nick finally said as he relaxed back into his hospital bed.

"Nick, I'm sorry I upset you. I see your energy though; your passion. Nick, you are not dying. Not today. I don't know how to fix this right away, but you aren't dying," Joe insisted.

"You can fix this by going to God and asking for forgiveness. Then it will all be okay. Will you do that, Joe? For years, that's the only thing I've wanted—to have you make what we did right with God."

Joe looked his tired brother squarely in the eyes. He nodded. Didn't say a word. Practicing the art of diplomacy in body language, he nodded again.

"Good. Now I can leave this tired body in peace."

"You aren't dying. I told you, you are still strong enough to carry on."

"Something inside me whispers that's not true," Nick assured.

"What? A voice? A voice from God Almighty?" Joe answered with cynicism. "If there was a God, he wouldn't have let Meredith get hit accidentally and—"

"And He would have stopped you from dumping her body on the rocks at the breakwater near high tide."

"What! I did no such—"

"You did."

"How could you know that?" Joe blurted.

"Isn't it true?" Nick asked. "I saw it in a dream. I'm not sure it actually happened, but I fear it did."

Joe didn't answer but held his head in his hands and took a long breath. After a moment, he forced the air out but didn't respond.

"Then it's true, isn't it?" Nick said.

Joe sat without speaking, neither admitting nor denying Nick's accusation.

The brothers sat in silence for a time. Finally, Nick said, "I am going to die. Gracie is bringing papers for me to sign and for you to witness. I need to know Jimmy's heart will go on. You understand?"

Joe nodded but once again said nothing.

The man who had quietly entered the room a few minutes earlier had heard everything. He now slipped out into the hall before Joseph Caine could come out from behind the closed curtain surrounding the bed of the dying Nicholas Caine.

Senator Caine. You have let your dirty laundry out of its bag. Shame on you, sir, Lawton thought. *Shame on you for what I will now have to do.*

29

SWEETHEART. DO YOU HAVE the papers?"

"Yes, dear," she meekly replied.

"Please, Joe, you sign to witness my signature. I have given you all power over the donation of any organs that might be used to save another life; you know, if something happens to me."

Gracie Caine couldn't take the emotional meaning of this moment as she covered her husband's heart with hers. He received the embrace and wrapped his arms around her frail body, tenderly holding her. She wept as Joe Caine signed the documents.

"Okay. There," he said. "I promise to take care of your request, but that will be twenty years from now. Rest now. Relax. Gracie, he looks good. I'll be back tomorrow."

"Thank you, Joe." Nick was visibly at peace now as his eyes searched for Joe's.

Joe avoided his brother's gaze.

"Do what you can for someone who needs this, okay?" he asked in a tender, emotion-filled voice.

"If," Joe reminded him, "you ever die. Personally, I think that if anyone is getting raised up into the clouds of glory when Jesus comes—that rapture thing I keep hearing about—it will be my big brother, Nicholas. Hope you settle down a bit now."

"You believe in it?" Nick asked excitedly as he held onto Gracie, whose sobs had now subsided.

"No."

Nick couldn't mask his disappointment. He knew now he would die, and soon.

*   *   *   *   *

Barbara Waters answered her cell phone. "I need to know where the senator will be at eight o'clock P.M.," Lawton told her. "Visiting hours end at eight-thirty," he said.

Barbara was seated in her sedan with another man who remained still. "I'm meeting Senator Caine at the hotel at seven o'clock," she said. "He has invited me to dinner. Says he likes to get to know each new staff member on a personal level," she explained.

"Good. Do not—"

"No need to even say it, Mr. Lawton. He will get my smile, and that's all."

"Good. And never use my name on the phone."

"Yes, sir."

"I thought we had covered that."

"We had. I forgot."

"Forget again, and I will have to forget you were hired."

"Yes, sir."

"I'll be in touch."

She quietly closed the phone and looked at the man seated next to her. "So?"

"So you will have dinner with Joe Caine."

"And then?"

"Senator Caine will interview you, and you will rise to the occasion. He will finish dinner, but not before you extract a promise, or at least plant the idea strongly, that you should become his new chief assistant to replace a Miss Beth Benoit who quit over some silly incident in Mexico."

"That's your plan?"

"As you rehearsed with Mr. Ron Lawton . . . yes."

"How do you know all this?"

"I'm an expert. And I'm always watching. Just remember that, and it will all go well in your new job and the other one at Digiwatch that Lawton promised you. I've got the same contacts he does, just a bit younger and more hip as to how new intel is gathered and massaged. Twice the salary and power is coming your way. Just do as I ask and keep me informed, my dear."

"You da man," she teased.

"You got that right, baby. Seems Ron Lawton has taken a liking to you," he said as he used his hand to softly stroke her slender arm.

She pulled away but smiled.

"You know, you are in this pretty deep, a key player," he told her. He got out of the car and opened the door of his rental car parked next to hers.

"And so are you," she said to herself as she pulled toward the exit of the parking lot.

TJ Mattsen got in his car and adjusted the rearview mirror, watching her as she drove away. *You have no idea how deep,* he thought.

*   *   *   *   *

Ron Lawton sat staring at his phone as if he could sense something at work besides the call he had just concluded with the new girl, Barbara Waters. He had checked her background and had personally cleared her for this job. Someone would be needed to take Beth's place as Senator Caine's chief office assistant. This girl had the charm, the wit, and the dusky good looks to play the senator for all the information that Lawton would need.

But I'll need to keep a close eye on her, he thought as he flipped the cell phone shut and continued putting on his makeup and disguise.

Tonight he would become a doctor—a heart specialist—in order to save the man who was the caretaker of Senator Joseph Caine's greatest and darkest secrets—the near-death Mike Stone.

30

IT HADN'T TAKEN LONG and was almost too easy. Wearing a white lab coat over his dress shirt and suit pants and carrying a stethoscope in his pocket, Ron easily passed for an "on-call" physician. No one questioned him as he officiously studied the charts, head down, engrossed in the information, as he walked briskly down the hall to Room 301.

Nick had been given a sedative to help him sleep and was now groggy. He squinted in an effort to focus on the face of the man standing next to his bed.

"Hello, doc," he forced out.

Lawton nodded but said nothing.

Nick's eyes were too heavy to attempt to converse with the new physician. He watched numbly as the man injected something he had taken from his lab coat pocket into Nick's IV line. The preacher's eyes grew wide at the sudden sensation and then relaxed. *It doesn't feel too bad,* Nick thought as his eyes closed for the final time. *In fact, it feels real good,* he decided. *This man—his face, it has another kind of evil . . . But I . . .* Nicholas Caine's brain was shutting down.

Ron Lawton put the needle and syringe back in the plastic bag from which he had taken it just seconds before. *The neurologist will determine massive intra-cerebral hemorrhage,* he thought, knowingly.

Lawton studied the monitors and noted the sudden spike in heart rhythm. *Kills the brain, not the heart. Well, actually, just makes a person seem to be in a brain-dead state,* he thought as he watched the man's lights go out.

Epinephrine is a naturally occurring hormone, Mr. Nicholas Caine. Doesn't show up in toxicology reports. Sweet dreams. If it's any consolation, you are doing a valuable service for the country.

Ron wasted no time stepping into Caine's toilet and shower closet, where he took the lab coat off, stuffed it into his satchel, and then put his best Ron Lawton face on.

There was no need for Lawton to hide the fact that he had now arrived in town. He picked up the hospital courtesy phone and called Joseph Caine directly from Nick Caine's hospital room.

"Senator!"

"Yes. Ron, where are you? What is it?"

"I got a flight after a layover in Atlanta. I came directly to the hospital. I thought I'd find you here, sir." His tone was urgent.

"What's wrong, Ron? Is something wrong?"

"Sir. I think you should come immediately."

"Ron . . . I—"

"Immediately, sir!"

Ron hung up the phone as two nurses followed by a physician now rushed into the room, responding to the sound of an alarm in the vital sign monitors. They quickly began working over the almost lifeless body of Nicholas Caine.

"Another stroke?" a nurse asked.

"Could be. BP up. Spiked heart beat," the doctor said.

"Arrhythmia?"

He shook his head. "Something else going on here," the doctor answered as he checked Nick's pupils.

"Temperature slightly elevated," a nurse added.

"Do another full blood workup. Check for IV drip abnormalities, anomalies in procedure, virus, bacterial infections; the full range. I want to know, to make sure he didn't get some bug here in the hospital that set this into motion. The last thing we need is Senator Caine suing us."

"You mean *you*," the head nurse offered from the door.

He gave the nurse a look of disapproval but didn't deny it.

Both attending nurses made knowing eye contact with each other but said nothing as they watched Doctor Rand Chester continue his cursory examination of the patient. Doctor Chester was not a popular physician. Known for a bedside manner that bordered on the warmth of an iceberg and an arrogance only exceeded by his nasty and ill-tempered manner with staff and patients, he didn't inspire much loyalty.

"This man is on his way out. We're talking scrambled eggs for brains. Come on, people! Let's get it down," he said, referring to the skyrocketing temperature.

Ron quietly left the hospital room and quickly exited the hospital. Once outside, he took a cell phone from his satchel and dialed the preset number. A female answered.

"So?" Lawton asked.

"He took the bait," Barbara answered.

"So you are moving to D.C.?"

"Monday. All set. Allows me to get back and forth to Philly and Digiwatch much easier."

"Meet me at The Canteen Grille. You know the place?"

"I do."

"One hour." He clicked the phone off.

It had gone much easier than she had imagined. Barbara Waters had Caine in the palm of her hand and was already working Jackson Lyon's ego over as well at Digiwatch. *Some powerful girl,* Lawton smiled, satisfied. With her resumé contrived to meet the needs of each man, Lawton now had her in place to handle Caine's personal business while at the same time consulting with Jackson Lyon on PR.

Lawton had first noticed Barbara Waters at a Digiwatch luncheon, when she was sent in to deliver some papers Jackson Lyon needed. She was a dark-skinned beauty with a stunning figure, who apparently wasn't at all intimidated by the high-powered company officials at the table. When he later asked about her, Lawton was told she had recently come to work for Digiwatch, following a two-year stint as an aide to the mayor of Philadelphia.

Intrigued by her beauty and self-confidence, Lawton immediately scheduled an appointment to get to know her, then had her transferred from the communications department to office staffer in Lyon's office for security. Her background checked out, but Lawton was still curious about how such a young woman had become so politically savvy. She seemed to instinctively know who really held the power and how to manipulate it.

Lawton's mind rolled on to the day ahead, but also to what he had done to get Mike Stone primed for a new heart and positive publicity from all this.

He would hire a reporter—a little cash and a promised "scoop" on a politician's private affairs always worked. The reporter was a man he trusted at the *Washington Post.* He'd pay him to give good PR on the upcoming heart donation of one Nicholas Caine, as orchestrated through the goodwill of Senator Joseph Caine.

Well, Senator Caine. You have enough time to get here and invoke the donor organ rights you recently signed off on, he thought. *Mike Stone, you unworthy political hack, you are getting a preacher's heart.*

*   *   *   *   *

"Doctor Miles Hall! I have some exciting news! A heart is becoming available," she said excitedly. "I know this is short notice and I can't be sure what day," she added as she paced with her cell phone to her ear.

"I'll keep you posted," she replied and then clicked the cell off. She turned to look at Mike as he lay ashen and weak in his hospital bed.

She took his hand, and he opened his eyes, smiled, and squeezed her hand weakly. "Hey, babe. You look absolutely mahvelous," he said, imitating comedian Billy Crystal's famous line.

"Mike! I've got good news!" She stepped closer to his bed and took his hand in both of hers and bent to kiss him tenderly. "You, my dear, are getting a new heart! A very good heart. And making history!"

"History? Someone important must have died and given me the nod to have their pump."

"Something like that. I feel terrible to be so happy. But I can't help it. The person passing is so good for doing this! You have no idea how difficult it is to get a heart donor to specifically will that lifesaving organ—it's like a miracle!"

"Who is the donor? Can I ask?"

"Mike, darling. The donor is a fellow Floridian. He knows you. He got suddenly ill and asked his brother to donate his organs to whoever might need them. You have been in the news down there."

"Who is it, Maggie?"

"Nick Caine. His brother, Senator Joseph Caine, was given charge over his estate, his affairs, and specifically, if Nick should die, over his organs. Pastor Caine wanted to make sure someone special would be blessed with his heart."

"Pastor Nick Caine?" Mike whispered.

"Yes . . . and . . . Senator Caine wants you to have his brother's heart. Isn't that wonderful?" Maggie added. "Isn't *he* wonderful?"

"Wow." Mike couldn't think of any other response. "When?"

"In a matter of hours; days at most, we think. Are you ready, Mike?"

"I don't want to leave you, Maggie. Of course I'm ready. One question? Why is this historic?"

"Well, it seems Nicholas Caine received the heart he's donating to you from another man, another minister, whom he replaced at the pulpit in Tallahassee. It's strange, really. Surreal."

"So this double heart transplant is history-making because this is the first time ever for a heart to be in three different bodies?"

"It's never happened before," Maggie smiled, and then clearing her throat, said, "and it is rather controversial."

"Because I'll be getting religion?" he smiled weakly.

"Mike, stop," she said, poking gently at him.

"Soooo . . . controversy. That's nothing new. Just getting a third-hand heart . . . Do you think I'll take up the pulpit?" he weakly offered. "You know—"

"If you repent enough; I suppose even that is possible," she offered playfully.

"Don't," he chuckled. "You're killing me."

"I love you, Michael Stone. You are going to live!"

"With you. Forever," he whispered.

"For as long as two hearts beat; for as long as God gives us. His hand is in this, Mike. I just know it."

"I suppose I owe Him—but Senator Caine is no small part of this," he added meekly. "I suppose he gets free political advice after this?"

"Mike. I won't let you go back into politics."

"I was hoping you'd say that. So how do I thank Senator Caine?"

"Forget Senator Caine. The publicity from this whole thing is payment enough. Good Nick Caine's name should never be forgotten though. I'd say we support his wife, his entire family, with our gratitude."

"And the man who originally owned the good heart?"

"Pastor James Barlow. A young, African American minister who was active in the 1960s civil rights movement."

Mike let that settle in and then thought to himself how ironic it was that a politico like himself should inherit such a life. Maggie had preached to him the medical theory of heart memory.

He had been curious about losing his own identity by receiving some other man's, or woman's, heart, and had started reading from books Maggie had brought to the hospital on heart transplant memory, therapy for heart transplant recipients, and the like.

Now Mike wondered what he might inherit from the man, Nicholas Caine.

31

I WANT THE JOE CAINE and The Gun Club contributor files found and secured! Damn all this stuff about Mike Stone and his transplant, and that goes for his secretary's accident as well! I DO NOT CARE! You understand? SECURE the information, man!"

Jackson Lyon slammed his cell phone shut. Ron Lawton had left Lyon's backside vulnerable. In military jargon, Lyon had been flanked. He didn't like information that could prove damaging just hanging out there in a storage locker, or worse, in cyberspace—information on the loose—for someone not allied with his American Alliance Party ambitions to tap into and use against him.

"Damn these men!" he said as he flung the cell phone against the wall. "Don't they know what is at stake here?" Lyon allowed as he paced his office near his home in Santa Fe, New Mexico.

"No one knows the importance like you do," Barbara Waters cooed into his ear as she gently stroked his silver hair. "Come and sit on the couch. I'll fix you a drink."

He nodded and obeyed. "I'm going to have to deal with Lawton now. Too much power."

She didn't agree or disagree, just smiled as she handed him the mild sedative—juice and gin, his favorite.

"Ron has been a great asset to Digiwatch, to me personally, but his ambition has gotten the best of him. I have seen men like that in the military. They'll get an entire platoon, company for that matter, killed just for advancement. I'll be damned if he will ruin my chances for the presidency."

"Wouldn't it be best just to let all this Lawton business run its course," she said as she used her strong hands to massage his neck from behind the sofa.

"I need people I can trust."

"Do you trust me?" Barbara asked.

"You know I wouldn't be speaking like this if you hadn't proven yourself . . . I can judge a man or woman quickly."

"What if you get tired of me? You worry me, Jack. I am giving my entire life up . . . my deepest secrets—for you, and I have nothing to show for it but these rare moments together. People are getting suspicious."

"Life demands choices. I've loved you since you first walked into my office at Digiwatch one year ago. Hell, you can even handle a gun. When I watched you fire that twelve-gauge shotgun at the Albuquerque Gun Club range—my word, woman, the way you hammered in each round with the pump action—I knew we had to be together."

"What are you saying, Jackson?"

"I need a strong woman with me. Jean—she's tired of all the politics. She can't hold up; not that I blame her. It's just that she isn't strong—not like you.

"I have to make sure my power is set and firmed up. You are helping me with that. My wife knows about us, about me, about my weaknesses. She's always known. It's always been a matter of time before she is granted what she wants."

"The ranch at Rio Diablo?"

"That, and a small fortune."

"Is it about the money so much?" Barbara asked as she moved around the couch to sit next to him.

"No. I just said it is about the power. Power attracts money. I can always get more money. It is about the presidency. I want you with me in the White House, not a wishy-washy matron who only wants to entertain, hates politics, but a real woman with . . ."

"Chutzpah?" she asked nuzzling his ear.

"Something like that," he said, turning his full attention to her.

Barbara quickly broke free, stood, and crossed the room to the bar, pouring herself a drink.

"What is it?" he asked.

"You won't divorce her. You can't. The press would eat you alive, and right before the political conventions this summer when you seek your party's nomination? I'm not dumb, Jack."

"There are other ways," he mumbled.

"What?" she asked.

He gulped the last of his drink. "Ways. People don't only get divorced," he replied.

"Like?" she asked.

"Separations. Agreements . . . Death . . ." he added.

"Hmm," she posed as she mixed him another drink of gin and juice. "I suppose there are ways people work out their love lives," she said.

"That's my girl talking," he grinned as he took the full glass from her hand. Their fingers met, and the exchange lingered until she pulled away.

"I need you to help me take care of Lawton," he muttered as he took another sip from his glass.

"Whatever you say, Jack. I'm just a humble Digiwatch employee looking out for my boss's best interests." She thought about the three men she worked for; each giving her assignments to carry out in the

name of Digiwatch or national interests: Ron, TJ, and Jackson Lyon
. . . she could only be true to one; two she would betray.

"I'm falling for you, Barbara," Lyon offered huskily.

"I know," she cooed in reply.

*　　*　　*　　*　　*

Troy Price visited Lizzy everyday now. He had been released from
the hospital after that first week, and even though she was still quite
weak and still only semi-conscious most the time, the miracle of faith
seemed to be supplying what a medical remedy could not.

"It's love, babe. That's what is bringing you back to me. It's healing
you. I love you so much!" he said as he kissed her on the cheek,
squeezed her hand, and then put his ear down to her lips.

She whispered. "I love you, too, Troy! Thank you for not giving
up!"

"Never," he whispered in return. "I'm taking you home soon.
You'll see."

She smiled weakly and then with closed eyes drifted off once more
to a place that she had come to know all too well.

He straightened the sheet and blanket over her, looked into her
face, then turned and left the private hospital room to head for the elevators. He and Bill were closing in on the guy who had caused this.

Troy's friend Mac Richardson from CID days was none other than
Jackson Lyon's son-in-law. Troy hadn't known what that meant, didn't
care, until all this took place.

Mac was a true patriot—almost too patriotic, if a man could be
called such. He was wrapped head to toe in the flag, God, and his
family. He was an honest man and one, who when Troy had worked
investigations with him years before, was always someone you could
count on to be the first one in the office and last man out. He'd been

a combat officer and then became CID after Gulf War wounds sidelined him.

Retiring after fifteen years, he put in for and received an appointment as a Special Agent with the FBI.

The world truly is a small place, Troy thought. *How weird that Mac should end up working with the Bureau and be a supervisor in Virginia and work Lizzy's case with Bill Maxfield, an assistant director of the FBI.*

Troy had wanted revenge; still did he supposed. But he also knew his strengths and limitations. He felt fortunate that fate had lined up these two players—Mac and Bill—so that he could quit worrying about finding Lizzy's assailant and focus instead on her recovery.

I almost blew it, he thought. *The priest had given Lizzy the last rites, and we were even planning to donate her organs to save someone else. Now she's alive and getting better.*

"True love," the voice of the woman behind him in the elevator happily said.

"Maggie! Hey, I was just thinking about you and Mike. I'm headed up to see how he is doing. I heard he has a donor."

"He does. Can you believe it? Things are working out."

The elevator door opened and passengers got off. As the door closed again, Troy moved back to be beside Maggie.

"I'm so happy for you, Troy," she said. "Lizzy is a lucky woman."

"And Mike is a lucky man."

"Think so?"

"Know so," he replied. "What did you mean by 'true love'?"

"It makes all the difference in healing, and you have given what Lizzy couldn't get from us—the physicians."

"Oh, they did their best. I can't argue that. I'm just grateful she's getting well," he said. "So when is Mike getting the transplant?"

"The news just came in," she said as the door opened to the fourth floor, and they both exited. "His donor just passed away. The heart and other vital organs are being prepared for transportation, and Mike is being prepped as we speak."

"Maggie! This is great news!"

"I'm so nervous, Troy," she answered as they stood outside the ICU. "One man dies so another can live; and I feel guilty about . . ."

"Being so happy?"

"Yes," she quietly replied.

"It would have been hard for both of us had Lizzy . . ." he didn't finish.

"I know," she said in a hushed, almost reverent tone. "Life is so full of unforeseen events: life, death, and all the implications. Well . . . I'm just stunned by all this. Who would have thought that Lizzy and Mike would be in the situations they are today. Just months; weeks ago, I mean . . ."

"Doctor Stone," a nurse called. "It's Doctor Hall on line two."

"Doctor Stone, she says to me. I'm still not used to it," she smiled.

"We'll be praying for Mike, and for you," Troy said. "Let Mike know."

"I will," she assured with a quick hug. "Thank you for being such good friends!"

Troy nodded, Maggie walked away, and Troy took a seat in the waiting area. He had agreed to meet Bill Maxfield here with Mac Richardson. Bill wanted to visit his cousin Lizzy and also show support for Maggie and Mike.

He thumbed through today's *Washington Post,* and his eye fell on the article almost immediately. "The Senator and a Secondhand Heart," the heading read. "A reporter has been on this already," he muttered. "Man, nothing is sacred," he said under his breath as he read on.

Troy was shocked and disgusted by what he read. The reporter made it out that Joseph Caine was a savior to Mike Stone—that Joe was the hero when it was his brother who was the real one. It sickened Troy how the article lauded the senator for simply carrying out his dying brother's wishes. As he read on about the history-making aspect of the situation, he hoped the reporter had that right.

Washington Post—Weekend Edition:

This morning one man died but in that passing another man received the word of hope—that he will receive a lifesaving heart transplant from the deceased.

Most people are unaware that over 50,000 people each year go onto a national waiting list to receive a heart from a donor. The math is staggering if one considers the sacredness of each life. One person must die for one person to live. Yet every year only 1 in 100 in need will find a suitable match from a heart donor, giving them a second chance to live.

This week Senator Joseph Caine of Florida made the toughest decision of his life, as he put it. With power of attorney and the blessing of the dying man's family, he authorized the removal of his older brother's heart upon his death. Pastor Nicholas Caine of Tallahassee, Florida, who would have been sixty-six years old next week, failing for more than a week, died this morning, but not before receiving the assurance just days before he began to slip away that his vital organs would help save other lives.

He had every reason to live a long and happy life after having retired just months ago, but a sudden stroke and resulting irreversible brain damage brought hope of a good man's wife and family to a final conclusion:

Pastor Caine's life was soon to be over, and his heart was still good.

It had been his final wish to make sure that the gift of life would go to someone in desperate need, and that his brother, Senator Joseph Caine, would be the one to decide who that recipient should be.

According to Grace Caine, the retired pastor's wife, Nicholas Caine had been extremely concerned that his heart receive a new home following his death. Normally the National Center for Donors, a clearinghouse with long waiting lists, would be notified, and the heart would go to the next person in line.

This was not just any heart, however. This heart has a history that precedes Nicholas Caine. In fact this heart had been transplanted into the body of Nicholas Caine thirty years ago.

For more on the amazing story and journey of a good heart, check back with us tomorrow as we follow the man, Senator Joseph Caine, in his quest to save another man according to his brother's final request.

Troy considered what he had read. *So, Joseph Caine. You run Michael Stone into the ground for twenty years and now get him a pump to keep him working for you and in your debt. Hmmm.*

Troy appeared to be mesmerized by the print on the page, but his mind was racing through mental files by the thousands a minute.

"Troy. Hey! Troy," Bill said as he waved a hand in front of Troy's face. "What you reading that has you so hypnotized?"

"Oh, hey, Bill. Sorry. I was miles away."

"I could tell."

"Here, read this," Troy offered.

Bill took a seat in the waiting room chair next to Troy and scanned the newspaper article. "Amazing."

"The heartless getting all the glory for the good-hearted," Troy said.

"Isn't that an understatement?"

"Bill, what do you have?"

"Mac Richardson couldn't make it. Something to do with a family gathering. Being Jackson Lyon's son-in-law carries its own stresses."

"Richardson is so honest," Troy said.

"He works for the Bureau. He'd better be."

"Yeah," Troy offered.

"Well, seems our friend Ron Lawton is doing double duty."

"Two jobs?"

"Right. He was security chief until he left Digiwatch to work as Caine's chief of staff. But, here's the kicker. He never entirely left Digiwatch. The Bureau has an interest in what goes on at Digiwatch; and that comes direct from the top."   ·

"The White House has federal agents placed inside Digiwatch?"

Bill didn't acknowledge the statement with anything but a nod of the head.

"FBI types undercover as employees?" Troy asked.

Bill offered a furtive smile to confirm Troy's conclusion.

"So, Mac Richardson has the dirt on this guy Lawton? What does he have to do with Lizzy's attacker, and mine, and the kid's?"

"Follow the trail. Lawton wanted Lizzy to get him certain Jackson Lyon files—files that had the same contributor information as Senator Joseph Caine's. These files could be incriminating—if they exist. Jackson Lyon sits on the board of directors at Digiwatch. Digiwatch has its own hired goons—a la Ron Lawton and company. What Lawton can't do directly, the heavies from Digiwatch can. Lawton's hands are technically clean, and the thugs from Digiwatch do not officially exist. And—"

"Got it. No need to say more. So where does that take us?" Troy urged.

"Hold on. There's more you really do need to know. Seems a man fitting the description of your convicted murderer from one of your CID investigations; you remember—the escapee from military prison a few years back? You know—the case you and Mac Richardson last worked on together two years ago, before you left the Army?"

"Right. Go on . . ."

"Well, he, as you know, was a black ops specialist in making himself and others disappear. He got sloppy a few times. Mac took it on as his personal off-duty hobby to find the guy, track him, and see if he could trap him. He's still alive and a dangerous character."

"So? Where is he?"

"According to the news people of Northern Virginia, one TJ Mattsen had rented a small bungalow in the farm country outside Manassas. Seems the Bureau was starting to notice the activities of TJ Mattsen; had found him through their contacts inside Digiwatch. Ex-Army CID investigator, now FBI Special Agent Mac Richardson, was in charge of the investigation. This Mr. Mattsen arranged the deaths of a couple of Mexicans the DEA were interested in, and rescued a beautiful but very scared Beth Benoit from their clutches in Acapulco."

"Beth Benoit? Senator Caine's personal assistant?" Troy asked.

"*Ex*-personal assistant. I'll fill you in on that story in a minute. But the Beth Benoit adventure kind of put the missing TJ Mattsen puzzle together for them. She talked to someone during a phone tap, and our leads were connecting this TJ and Lawton to your train station assault. We have a very capable female agent working at Digiwatch who has collected the information on Ron Lawton and Mattsen. She will be helping out on this from now on."

"So my buddy Mac, from the Army CID, is now with the FBI and stumbled upon this with the help of this female agent?" Troy asked, trying to keep the people involved straight in his head.

"Right. This Mr. Mattsen rigged it to look like he had died in a fire that burned down his rented bungalow. The dead man turned out to be a transient. Mattsen fooled everyone but Mac. Suffice it to say, Beth did a lot of talking and even provided some personal items that TJ had handled when he rescued her in Acapulco—another part of the story I'll fill you in on. They matched his prints and DNA—if you know what I mean—similar to what was gathered from Lawton at Digiwatch by a certain female agent working as an assistant to Jackson Lyon."

"So we have Mattsen? He's the one who did the job at Union Train Station?"

"You recognize this? This? This?" Bill asked as he threw down photos one after another.

"Holy crap! That's Jon Gilbert! The guy I put away in Leavenworth. It just came to me. He's the same guy I saw in the train station and I'm guessing the guy who hit me with the two-by-four. Do you know where he is?"

"He seems to be something of an expert at staging his own fake death. After that house fire in Virginia, he went under deep. Real deep. We hadn't been able to raise any information on him until this last week. The good news is he has interests and contacts at Digiwatch, as I mentioned. He thinks he's smarter than the rest of us; you know, another cerebral criminal egomaniac at work. He also wants Ron Lawton's head on a platter, and Ron wants his. Bad guys fighting under the guise of the flag and country."

"Never liked those kinds."

"The world's full of them, Troy. You don't even want to know what—"

"I've been there," Troy cut in. "Part of the reason I got out of Army CID."

"Well, we still need some 'good guys.' Where would we be if we all surrendered our jobs to the bozos who'll do anything for their power?"

"What can I do?"

Bill Maxfield took Troy for a walk—a long walk—during which he laid out a plan to trap both TJ Mattsen and Ron Lawton and also recover any information Mattsen and Lawton might have on presidential aspirant Jackson Lyon and his conspiratorial running mate, Senator Joseph Caine.

"It'll take months. It'll take a healthy Mike Stone," Troy answered after learning the entire plan. "But I like it."

32

Falls Church, Virginia—Inova Fairfax Hospital

GREAT. THE WORLD'S ONLY LIVING heart donor," Mike weakly answered after Maggie told him about the Caine heart donation.

"No, Mike," she laughed. "Not that Caine, the other one."

"What other one?" Mike answered, playing it out.

"Stop it, Mike. This is serious."

"How'd the senator get his brother to give his heart up?" Mike asked.

"How does one give one?"

"By dying?"

Maggie just smiled and nodded. "We are running a match, and you should be in surgery tonight."

"Uh, don't I have to sign or approve this?"

"Nope. You gave me power of attorney. Remember?"

"Oh, yeah. We're married, too. I keep forgetting that."

"How can you forget? Mike, that was the most important day of my life!" Maggie replied.

"I was very sleepy. Getting worse by the day I guess. Seriously, Maggie, sometimes this all seems like a dream, and that part of it is the only good part."

"What can I do to make you remember?" she asked as she held his hand and snuggled close to him.

"Bring a bed in and share the room, I guess. Like Ozzie and Harriet; you know, the quintessential morally and politically correct bedroom—twin beds. Very cozy too."

"I don't remember that show."

"Oh, yeah. I forget. You are just a girl. I'm married to a girl born in the seventies."

"Late sixties," she corrected him, as she reached for his charts.

Mike was weak, and even that much banter took its toll on him. He closed his eyes and concentrated on taking in enough air.

Maggie was going through Mike's charts now and called out to a nurse.

"Yes, Doctor Stone?"

"Has anyone located Doctor Hall yet?"

"No. We have tried everything. He was supposed to be back from the conference in Atlanta this morning. We'll keep trying."

"Heart transplant physician, I presume?" Mike asked in a tired voice.

Maggie nodded. "Not to worry. He promised. He'll be here."

"Great. I get a perfect heart while fifty thousand other people are waiting on the national lists, but no doctor to put it in."

"There are other physicians, equally qualified," she said. "Just none I trust as much as Miles Hall. Except for . . . " She thought about the ramifications. *What if Miles doesn't show? What if he had an accident or some other emergency that has him stuck somewhere?*

"Maggie?"

"Huh?" she rejoined—shaking her thoughts loose from the many "what ifs."

"That was real thoughtful of Nicholas Caine. How did he die?"

"Cerebral hemorrhage. He had suffered a stroke a week before, and then was getting better. Suddenly he suffered a major bleed. No one caught it in time."

"So Joe Caine worked it out even though hundreds of people in the area of this hospital are already waiting for a new heart?"

"Joe Caine is a senator. You know the 'one call, that's all' slogan of the ambulance chasers on late night TV? Senator Caine needs to make just one call, and he gets what he wants."

Mike lifted a heavy arm and massaged his eyes with his fingers. "I guess I am a pretty lucky man."

"You deserve it for what you've put up with over the years."

"Oh, I got paid well."

"The man is a political animal and wouldn't shed a tear for you, Mike, if . . ."

"If what? Maggie, are you insinuating that Joseph Caine wouldn't have done this for me out of the goodness of his heart?"

"Goodness of his heart? Mike, are you putting me on? I grew up in a political household. Senator Caine wants you alive so you can serve him, or to get something out of you."

"Like?"

"Like a lifetime of indebtedness, so he can use you however he needs on his climb to the top."

Mike stopped talking. He was tired. He wondered if Maggie was right. Something had changed the way he viewed life. Maybe it was the love Maggie had lavished on him or the care that was being given him in the hospital. He was grateful for the kindness that had been extended to him, and that gratitude had caused him to make saints out of everyone, including Joe Caine. He felt nothing but kindness toward the people around him and couldn't see how anyone could go around conniving. Except, he'd been the same kind of self-serving conniver himself, and there were of course Ron Lawton and the thug who had nearly killed Lizzy and Troy.

"How's Lizzy?" he finally asked.

Maggie put the chart down and picked up her cell phone. She seemed not to hear him. "Please get me the number for Dr. Kenneth Miller—University Hospital."

Mike waited until Maggie finished, had written down the number, then asked again. "How's Lizzy?"

"Huh?" Maggie's concentration and energy was miles away. "Lizzy did you say?"

"Yeah. How is she?"

"Oh! Better. Much improved. A miracle really. Did you know she wanted you to have her heart if she died?"

Emotion gripped Mike spontaneously, and he found himself suddenly tearful.

"Mike, honey? What's wrong? Did I upset you?" Maggie asked. She took a tissue and tenderly blotted his eyes. "I'm sorry, Mike. Tell me what's wrong," she asked softly.

He just shook his head. The irony had hit him hard. Lizzy had been willing to sacrifice her heart for him. She was nearly murdered because of him. And the man she was keeping the information from was none other than the man now in charge of seeing Mike survive—getting him the heart he needed. Mike had brought this heart problem upon himself by years of bad living. Lizzy was innocent of her near death.

He turned his head away from Maggie, closed his eyes, and drifted to a safe place. *Maybe I'll wake up and this will all go away. Maybe it's a dream. Maybe . . .*

*   *   *   *   *

"Hello, Bill, Troy," Maggie said as she entered the hospital waiting room. "I've been meaning to ask about Lizzy. How's she been since last time we talked?" Maggie asked Troy.

"Progressing. She's off the ventilator, but I guess you knew that. She is trying to speak. I think the drugs keep her so sedated that she can't. But I'm hopeful," Troy answered.

Maggie gave him a soft buss on the cheek and a friendly hug and whispered something in his ear.

"Thanks, Maggie, I needed that," he said, smiling.

"Well, this is it," Bill interjected.

"Yes, the heart is on its way from Tallahassee, and I'm so . . . so . . ." Maggie was suddenly speechless.

Bill held out his arms and offered. She accepted his caring embrace. "He'll be fine," he whispered, patting her back and holding her close.

She nodded, but the clinician barrier was broken. She was a wife and loved Mike and knew he could just as easily be dead as alive by the end of the day. She also understood something she hadn't ever known to this degree—gratitude for the love and support of people.

Troy added his supportive hand to her shoulder as she pulled away, nodded, grabbed a tissue, and assured them both: "We have the best there is. Doctor Ken Miller, a renowned heart specialist—world-class, really—will be here shortly and perform the operation."

"What about Hall? I thought Doctor Hall was going to do the surgery," Bill said.

"He's missing. I'm sure it is just a foul-up on his schedule. He was due in from Atlanta, a medical conference, and no one has been able to reach him."

Troy looked at Bill, and Bill returned the silent question: *Do you think Ron Lawton has anything to do with the doctor being missing?*

"What did you say the name was of the heart surgeon?" Troy asked.

"Miller, Ken Miller. I've known him for years, and he's the best there is. Why? Is something wrong?" Maggie asked.

"No. I just wondered. A little nervous. You know, when a last minute change occurs—for Mike's sake," Bill explained.

"I can understand that," Maggie chuckled nervously.

"So is Senator Caine due in when his brother's heart arrives?" Bill asked.

"Yes. Any time now. A medical conference and press conference is being set up. I guess you know that this is a first."

"How's that?" Troy asked.

"He's getting a secondhand heart," Bill answered for Maggie.

"Yes, but a very good secondhand heart. Nothing wrong with that pump, I can assure you. It has passed all tests, but even if it hadn't, it's the only chance Mike has," she said with a hint of voice cracking. "I'm so, so, . . . grateful. I just wish I could do something for Nicholas Caine and his family."

"Well, you are. Seeing that Nicholas Caine's heart lives on is quite a tribute," Bill assured.

She nodded. "Well, I'd better go."

"We'll stand by," Troy promised.

"Right here, if you need us," Bill added, holding up his cell phone.

She smiled and turned to leave, then turned back to the two men. "Please pray," she asked before entering the double doors to the operating corridor.

Bill winked with a nod.

Troy smiled. "We will, Maggie."

After the doors swung closed behind her, Bill said, "Shall we run a background check on Doctor Ken Miller before he cuts Mike's old heart out?"

Troy nodded. "And while we're at it, why don't we find our missing Doctor Hall."

Bill motioned with a side movement of his head.

"Where are we going?" Troy asked as they walked down the long corridor toward the elevator.

"You ever been inside FBI headquarters in D.C.?"

"Nope."

Bill smiled and winked. "We are going to do this one right—for Mike, Maggie, and our Lizzy."

33

Tallahassee

CLAIRE BARLOW HEARD ABOUT the historic heart transplant on a news channel, not from the mouth of her beloved pastor's wife, Gracie. But she understood. How could she expect anyone to remember her? She was sure they would invite her to the funeral and that she would be given a place of honor. *After all*, she thought, *my pastor and part of my son are being buried.* But it suddenly hit her that that wasn't quite true. The part of her son that had lived in Nicholas Caine would now be missing, gone to sustain another life.

With Nicholas Caine's passing there would come also the end of her own reason to live. Her will to go on lived in direct proportion to her knowledge that she was needed, and she had always felt needed by Nicholas and Gracie Caine. But with her beloved Nicholas gone, she too might as well lie down and surrender.

Sure, her daughter visited, and the grandkids, too, but they were so busy, so tied up in living with work, schooling, getting ahead; she ached to see them, but couldn't force it.

Nicholas Caine had carried her son within him. When he visited, so did her son, James. And her husband, James Sr., seemed also to be part of the beating going on inside of Nicholas's chest.

Thinking of Nicholas's demise, she prayed for him, for Gracie, and for herself. She wondered how the church would go on.

A temporary, interim minister had been found, and certainly a new permanent pastor would be named. He would doubtless do his very best and in time might make his own niche, but it was an awesome thing for someone new to try to fill shoes that Nicholas had worn at the pulpit for thirty years.

It seemed to her the end of an era, and she didn't know if she could live on with that feeling. She pondered on this finality and of not knowing the man who would be getting her son's and Nicholas's heart. *Will I ever be able to hear James's heart beat again? Lay my ear upon the chest where it will reside?*

"Dear, Lord," she finally cried as she knelt by her bed. "May I hear his heart beat once again? Just once, before I too die? Please, Lord? May I hear him?"

34

Tallahassee Hotel—present day

For Joe Caine, this moment brought everything into focus. He sat at his desk in the hotel room. Two Percocets, a vodka watered down with juice, and a headache that was only matched by the pain in his heart. He'd have to be the hero again tomorrow; watch Nick's heart packed in an ice chest to be shipped off to Inova Medical Center in Falls Church, Virginia.

At least it is getting a good home; one I know, he thought as he considered Mike Stone. The effect of all the painkillers and alcohol was causing him to get foggy—and lost in fog was what he wanted to be right now.

He kicked off his shoes, threw his tie into the corner of the room, un-tucked his dress shirt, and fell back onto the hotel bed.

Losing Nick meant losing his living conscience. Joe had teased Nick about Nick being his Jiminy Cricket. He smiled in contemplation of that . . . He was the bad boy Pinocchio of the two, with a long nose and jackass tail, never realizing the promise made by Geppetto the toy maker, that if he always did what was right and told the truth, that he could someday be a "real boy."

But losing Nick was the end of a family era, too. With their parents gone, except for himself, no one was left now. To lose Nick also meant he had lost his ability to make things right.

He had always planned to talk things over thoroughly with Nick. He would do it, he had promised himself, when the time was right and it was more convenient. His mind went back to the day that had changed everything for him.

January 3, 1969—Tallahassee

The car skidded to a stop on the graveled road, and dust swirled in the headlights as they shone on the prostrate man lying on the ground.

Meredith rushed to the open window on the driver's side of the car. "Joe! You got to do something. Jimmy's bleeding bad," she cried.

"What happened?" Joe slurred. Joe had been drinking. Unusual for him, even on weekends. He prided himself on being in control, keeping his wits, and not letting others see him as a fool. Drunkenness did all that, yet he had allowed it.

"Is he hurt bad?" Joe asked as he stumbled out of his car.

"Joe! You're drunk. And when I need you most!" Meredith cried as she sat to cradle Jimmy Barlow's bleeding head in her lap. "Go call someone. Hurry! Get an ambulance."

Joe was carrying his baseball bat; a trademark he had created for himself. Joe always had a baseball glove, bat, and ball bag in his car and was eager to get out and hit some, almost daily now. A former college player, he found hitting a baseball took his anger away, he had told Meredith once.

"For heaven's sake, Joe. Put that bat away, and will you get some help?"

"You want help?" he asked. "What about me? Why don't you help me? Jimmy is dying, and you couldn't care less about the man standing right here in front of you!"

Meredith raised herself from the ground to face Joe, and Joe roughly pushed her aside. She fell to the side of him in the dark, and he took a batter's stance over Jimmy's limp body.

"I'll show you who is a man! The man who made your child! I deserve you! Not this, this . . . crumpled, powerless, toad in the road! You know what I do with toads?"

"Joe, you wouldn't!" Meredith cried, rising to her feet.

He smiled wickedly, as one does when he thinks he is in control, and looked into Jimmy's open but glazed eyes. Jimmy couldn't speak, but his eyes begged. Instead of mercy, Joe felt only rage. He'd show this upstart nigger who was the better man and obliterate the heartache that being tossed aside had created in him.

Again taking the stance of a batter and thinking only to frighten Meredith, he swung the bat in a wicked arc above Jimmy's head, just as Meredith dove to shield Jimmy from the blow.

"NO!" Joe cried from his hotel bed as he jerked upright, perspiring profusely, and trying to focus his eyes in the darkened room. "Meredith? Oh, Meredith!" he cried as his head hit the pillow in a semi-aware state that he was never to rid himself of the haunting, the torture, and the knowledge that he had killed the only thing he had ever truly loved.

"If there is a God, then make it all right," he slopped out as he reached for the nightstand to finish his drink. He chased a handful of aspirin down with the fruit-flavored alcohol.

"You know, I been square on lots of things, Mr. God," he added slowly in his drunkenness. "I didn't mean to do nothing to hurt anyone—not . . . ever! Not Mer . . . dith, my girl. I only killed . . . Charlie Cong," he slurred, "in Viet-damn-nam!" he sang to an old soldier's refrain. "And, Sir . . ." he said, his eyes glazed over, "I respectfully request, THAT be taken to mean . . . I . . . all . . . read . . . dee . . ." he sobbed as he paused for each syllable, "did . . . my . . . time . . . in HELL!"

He rolled onto his side as tears wet the pillow that cushioned his tired mind. He drifted into darkness but allowed himself to talk to Nicholas once more as his voice choked on his deeply stirred emotions.

Like a boy losing the most important love, the most important thing he'd ever cared about, he cried: "I am going to be the commander in chief, Nick; and I order you to come home! NOW! You can't go with Jimmy! He can't hurt me! Meredith can't hurt me! We don't need nobody else!" he sobbed. "Just you and me, big brother. Just you . . . and me," he repeated, as blessed numbing sleep descended over him, cloaking the light once more.

*   *   *   *   *

Ron Lawton was thoroughly frustrated in his search for the files containing Mike Stone's twenty-year history on Joseph Caine and supplemental information on Jackson Lyon's past campaign contributors.

That Lizzy chick . . . if TJ hadn't messed her up . . . I'd like to go one-on-one with that punk. "When I find him . . ." he swore under his breath as he carefully tore Mike Stone's home apart. He knew the place didn't have a false wall, door, or safe. His expert detection team had already been through the place three times; but he hadn't. So now it wasn't just a matter of being sure they hadn't missed something, it was going through Mike's computer files, once again, and looking for any trace of an address that might lead him to a storage facility or a safe deposit box.

Troy and Lizzy Price's town home had also been thoroughly searched. And he had also gone through Troy Price's parents' home in Sterling, Virginia. To mask his intent, Lawton had instructed his team to make additional random burglaries in both neighborhoods, so that the break-ins wouldn't automatically be connected to the attacks on the Price couple.

"Voila!" he exclaimed as he did a random search on Stone's banking "bill pay" site. Arlington Mini Storage. Lawton noted that the last payment, made just three months before, was for a year's extension. Wearing rubber surgical gloves, he covered his tracks and left through the town house's back door.

It was dark and raining. The best time for operations entering private residences—not too many people outside, and few poking their noses through open windows.

He knew he would have to give up some information to Lyon to assure him that the confidential files—containing the names of "soft money" campaign donors whose contributions were in violation of federal laws and statues—were being adequately protected.

Of course with Mike Stone dead, no one would talk, and yet Mike Stone needed to live so that Lawton could either make him tell him where the files were kept or at least keep the threat of death—the only other way to assure silence on the information in those files—alive . . .

Death threat to keep him alive, he thought as he turned the ignition to his car. *Oxymoron.*

35

Washington, D.C.

Because of its rapid growth and the nature of its business, Digiwatch Corporation had attracted the attention of the federal government. Though the listening devices and surveillance equipment the company had developed and were manufacturing were not illegal, uncontrolled use of them might constitute violations of the First Amendment. There were also unsubstantiated but serious charges that the growing company had obtained unfair advantage by negotiating "sweetheart" deals to supply government and private agencies. So, though Digiwatch appeared to be in compliance with all federal and state regulations, their meteoric growth and concern over the gathering of private and governmental data had alarmed many within the Justice Department as well as in the White House. From the vantage point of the government, it was a company that for several reasons bore watching.

Barbara Waters was in deep cover. She had been placed inside Digiwatch by the government. No one but her private handler and higher-ups at the FBI even knew of her operation.

Barbara had never worried about working alone until now. She had three male egos at stake: Lyon's, Lawton's, and TJ's. Her feminine wiles were at work, and literally only God knew where these yo-yo's were coming from. Watching her back had made her sleepless, and she was exhausted and edgy.

Lyon, Lawton, TJ Mattsen, she thought. *Loose cannons, renegades, formerly All-American military types, now on personal quests for power. Ruthless . . .*

She called her handler on a secure line. Didn't even know his name.

"Yes?" the male voice answered.

"I'm in over my head," she said. "Someone is going to get killed."

"And?"

"I think it is Joe Caine. I really think one of the other nuts—Lawton or Mattsen will personally be the trigger puller, but something is also happening with Lyon. He wants Ron Lawton out and TJ in. That is messy. Ron Lawton is Joe Caine's right-hand man, personally placed by Lyon. What's going on here? You got any intel I should have?" she asked.

"Lyon is still clean by all accounts. Remember that. The government wants to follow him around some more. His run for the top seat, his driving influence behind Digiwatch . . . it all will lead us to others we need to expose," the voice answered.

"So am I right? Caine's removal from the living would take him out of the running for the nomination and eliminate the potential embarrassment of whatever secrets are contained in Mike Stone's files?"

"You got it," the voice on the other end of the line answered. "And, yes, Lyon is preparing to remove Lawton . . . a major blunder for him, especially if Mattsen is chosen as his successor."

"So what now?" she asked.

"Mattsen is technically dead. We have him on the run, however. Seems Lawton placed a nifty Digiwatch device—in some dental work Mattsen had done."

"I thought—"

"Nope . . . They have more than heart surgeons who do this stuff. Scary, huh?" the voice said.

"Yeah," she replied, suddenly fearing she was also being tracked. "Who knows where I go?"

"What?"

"Does Lyon know? Lawton? TJ?"

"You mean, have I, your private handler been compromised? I am the only one, and no, you do not have an implant—unless you've been to the doctor in the last year who works under the health plan of Digiwatch."

She was silent.

"But if that had happened, I would have let you know."

"I don't know you."

"And you are scared."

"Of course."

"Take a time-out . . . This isn't a sci-fi thriller, it's government surveillance work."

That's what I'm afraid of, she thought to herself.

"Besides. You have the gut instinct thing. You've proven it over and over. That's why you were picked."

"Who knows up top? I mean, outside of you?"

"That's classified."

"If you choke on a fish bone and die tomorrow, where does this go?"

"Is this instinct working on overdrive? You are letting yourself get too carried away."

"I'm an American first. I'm loyal. I don't know your name, and I'm still loyal. It's not about instinct. It's about safety, and knowing I'm on the right side. Am I on the right side?"

"What do you think?" the male voice asked.

"I think if the American public knew about people and documents carried on their persons being tracked by a privately held corporation—legally—that they'd go berserk. I think that my life isn't worth much right now to certain parties, and that you are aware of that. I think I'm underpaid and undervalued. That's what I think."

"We're working on that. Listen to me carefully. I am giving you an order. You watch Lyon—he's clean—for now. The other two you already know wouldn't lose sleep if something were to happen to you. You have more than just my eyes watching out for you. I'm sending an inside man, a company man, to meet with you at location 'Sixties.'"

"When?"

"Same time as before."

"What do I look for?"

"Brooklyn Roads."

Click.

Bill Maxfield had gotten a call from a fellow deputy director at the FBI. He was made aware of one of their own who was going to get a partner—him. He hadn't worked a field case in years. As a deputy director with the Bureau, it was very unusual to be involved in any details of cases, outside of supervising agents, their work, and diplomacy on behalf of the Bureau with Capitol Hill or other D.C. bureaucrats like himself.

This was a special assignment for Bill for two very good reasons. One, he was already involved as a friend to Troy and Lizzy Price and Mike Stone. The second reason was that his knowledge of the players would undoubtedly finally lead him to a certain female agent that he needed to know was planted at Digiwatch. He needed to not interrupt an ongoing investigation or he needed to be included in it. The Bureau chose the latter.

If Bill were to accidentally connect her as a bag handler for TJ Mattsen or Ron Lawton, he could misinterpret her role with Digiwatch and Jackson Lyon. The Bureau had too much at stake to have Deputy Director William Maxfield trip up on this without full disclosure to him of the ongoing investigation and operations. So they were making him a part of it.

Bill had the feeling that tonight's rendezvous with Miss "X" would involve more than a little music; it would become either a career ender for him, or one that led him into a new world of FBI work—one he never relished being personally involved in—government sponsored, corporate espionage.

*   *   *   *   *

Barbara Waters left the office a little before five o'clock. She had finished her day by contacting Ron Lawton and assuring him she had Jackson Lyon fully in her confidence. Then she met with Jackson Lyon and persuaded him to leave Ron Lawton alone; to back off. He'd agreed, but was still worried about how much Ron had on him, and would prefer, he had said, to bring TJ Mattsen back into the fold to replace Ron.

"Can't," she reminded him. "He's officially dead. Besides, that's his call. The way he wants it."

"Of course," he said. "Of course, you are right. That's why I like having you around, Barb. You have the female touch, the intuition, and make it a pleasure at the same time. When are we . . ."

He closed the gap between them, put a hand on her shoulder, and she responded by brushing her lips against his cheek and whispering, "Soon."

Now, she was playing after-work-career-girl; running errands to the grocery, dry-cleaners, drugstore—just in case she was being tailed or, even worse, being "Digiwatched" by some plant she didn't know about. *I'd better have the car cleaned,* she thought, thinking of scouring it for an electronic bug rather than road grime. She was worried about a digital device that would have been kindergarten-like easy to place in the cushions of the passenger seat of her BMW coupe, or on the dash, under the hood, anywhere really—while the car was in the garage or parked on the street. *If the average citizen knew how easy it is to track, to get to them if we wanted . . .* the thought chilled her.

Barbara Waters was still a believer, though. Her beautiful African-American mother and the father she never knew—some marine her Mom had met in Jacksonville, North Carolina, at a nightclub—had given her the looks but also something else. Somehow she had been given a genetic propensity to embrace the flag, the country, and the cause.

She now shuddered at a growing technological war that was hidden from the public even as virtually every American household embraced digital technology with appliances, cameras, sound systems . . . Perhaps that was the insidious nature of growing up in a digital world—you get used to it, and even if it were used for something wrong—you just shrug, go online and order a pizza, giving out personal information through the air at the speed of light.

This whole digital world was a new opportunity for governments, and a corporation like Digiwatch, to profit by what micro-digital implants could do. Now anyone, anytime, could be tracked. In a war on terror, that was not only good for intelligence gathering, but necessary. In espionage, the playing field was leveled once again because the technology wasn't morality based—it was neutral. If the bad guys had it, the good guys would need it.

But it gave Barbara the creeps to think about her every move being observed from some uplink to a satellite signal.

Barbara pulled her sports car slowly to the curbside parking spot just vacated. She grabbed some quarters from the change holder in the center console. Popping out of the car, she flitted over to the meter and fed an hour's worth of change in.

The Music That Rocks You music store was "Sixties," a coded location outside of D.C. in a suburban Maryland town northeast of the capital. Barbara coyly glanced over each shoulder, pressed the lock alarm button on her key ring, and then nonchalantly entered the music store, focused upon the code and keyword: *Brooklyn Roads.*

She went to the patron's computer—used for identifying song and album titles—and typed the keyword in. *Neil Diamond,* she thought as she saw his name pop up next to the song.

Pop Music Section, she said to herself. She noticed the several people browsing in that section but didn't see anyone who even remotely resembled a fellow FBI agent. She picked up a couple of albums from the rack and read the play lists, then looked specifically at the Neil Diamond bin. The first album in the rack was the singer's "Sixties Hits," with a scratched up cover and the plastic wrapping gone.

"I'm sorry," a gentleman said to her. "I shouldn't have put that back after listening to it. I took the shrink-wrap off to play 'Brooklyn Roads.' One of my favorite Neil Diamond tunes."

"Hmm. Well, thank you. I think I'll keep it . . . unless of course you want to purchase it." She raised her eyebrows.

"No. I think you'll like everything on that particular CD. Have a nice evening."

Bill Maxfield had just met his contact.

So had Barbara Waters.

36

Doctor Ken Miller was a nationally renowned heart transplant specialist and had just taken the good heart from a soldier whose family had asked that their son's final wish be granted. The young man had been grievously wounded in a firefight in Afghanistan weeks before and had just expired following unsuccessful surgery to repair his wounds.

A marine, and an admirer of the retired USMC colonel, U.S. senator, and ex-New Mexico governor Jackson Lyon, the young warrior had also been a charter member of Lyon's New Mexico Gun Club. The thirty-year-old marine captain had signed a release before his death stipulating that Walter Reed Medical Center find a needy person for each and any of his organs, should he succumb to combat injuries.

When the young captain did die from after-surgery complications, Jackson Lyon took notice. He was genuinely touched by the young marine's selfless, final act. Now the marine's vital organs were already on their way to Boston, where a young woman who had been on the national waiting list had been found a match for a heart-lung transplant.

The news cameras followed Jackson Lyon to Boston, where Lyon would speak glowingly about the great work of Doctor Miller, the selflessness of a young marine who had died of wounds sustained in the service of his country, and the spectacular history of an emerging company, a watchdog for national security—Digiwatch, Incorporated.

Digiwatch, he would point out, was the leader in microchip tracking technology, which was now being used, with a patient's permission, when he or she received a transplant. Digiwatch, he would say, was also providing America even greater security against terrorism, by virtually eliminating document forging and completely validating all U.S. passports as well as visas granted to visitors from other countries.

This was an irresistible opportunity to spotlight for the nation everything Jackson Lyon held dear: Digiwatch, The New Mexico Gun Club, and most importantly—political power.

"Your heroic son and husband did more in death to ensure the security of this nation than one hundred men will ever do in a lifetime!" he had told heartbroken parents and widowed spouse while ABC News broke the story by gaining access to the private meeting Jackson Lyon held with grieving family members at Walter Reed Hospital.

The family and the fallen marine's comrades took Jackson Lyon's eulogy as a fitting tribute from a fellow warrior. But for Jackson Lyon, the event meant more than that. The dead marine's selfless act provided publicity of inestimable worth to Lyon and his causes. With NBC, CBS, CNN, and FOX all waiting in line for additional television interviews and a chance to retell the heart-wrenching and heartwarming story, there would be opportunity as well to advertise Digiwatch Corporation's DW Charitable Foundation.

This public focus on organ transplants also benefited future vice presidential candidate Senator Joseph Caine, who seized the opportunity to further his own political agenda. The story of Pastor Nicholas Caine's beneficent willing of his heart to Mike Stone also tugged at the nation's heartstrings and gave Caine's politician brother a chance to keep his own name in the headlines.

Jackson had told his confidante and assistant, Barbara Waters, to contact Doctor Ken Miller, offer him every service Digiwatch could provide, and make sure also that Mike Stone got anything he needed, courtesy of Digiwatch's DW Charitable Foundation.

Of course, Jackson Lyon wouldn't fail to mention that Digiwatch's Charitable Foundation had paid all expenses for the transplant donation, including the heart surgery in Boston. And he would add that Digiwatch was so moved by Michael Stone's need and Senator Joseph Caine's dilemma that they were flying Doctor Miller on their corporate jet to Florida to help Doctor Mullins harvest Nicholas Caine's heart, then bringing him back with it to Falls Church to do the actual transplant surgery.

As the principal surgeon in these celebrated cases, Doctor Kenneth Miller would stand side by side with Joseph Caine as the senator mourned the passing of his brother and rejoiced in his friend Mike Stone's good fortune. Having the celebrity physician "on their team" would provide credibility to Digiwatch and its campaign to get each organ transplant recipient to accept the company's offer to implant in him or her one of the company's latest generation micro-identification chips. This would be a huge win for the company and Lyon as well. It would show the American public the benefit of monitoring vital organs, once donated, and how the tiny microchip would potentially save the "life that was saved by the transplant," as Lyon liked to say.

Identification implants were a tricky and sticky business to talk about these days, especially with so many rabid defenders of personal privacy calling in to conservative radio talk shows. The religious right, who Lyon admired, also linked the idea of any implanted ID with the ominous prophecy from the book of Revelation that in the last days Satan's minions would bear the "mark of the beast." Fearful of the government tracking them, even under the rationale of needing to identify who was an American and who wasn't in a time of war on terrorism, these conservative citizens were justifiably uneasy. Lyon understood all those misgivings and even sympathized with them.

But to his way of thinking, those concerns were outweighed by the terrorists' declared intent to destroy his country. As an ex-military man and a candidate for the presidency, he understood the importance of control. Knowing who was on America's side, and who wasn't, was vital and could swing the struggle in favor of the United States. Control of the borders through proper registration of citizens could also be easily facilitated by technology now available in Digiwatch's systems and devices. If America was to survive, such controls were simply too vital to dismiss because of First Amendment concerns or religious bias.

Lyon's goal and legacy was to leave behind him a safer and more secure America. Digiwatch implants could make all that possible.

"They save lives, protect our freedoms, and identify the true patriots," he had explained the night before to the host on *Larry King Live.*

Now he could use the power of the American media to show the world what the nation was up against. The other governments and the terrorists—those vowing to destroy America—would be able to read between the lines and perceive what they could expect when he was elected president on the American Alliance Party ticket. Jackson Lyon was not about to allow the American people to go unprotected, not on his watch. It was a foregone conclusion for him—all Americans were headed for simple, inexpensive security implants to be installed as a part of their routine dental and medical visits.

"And it started with one good preacher and one good marine heart," he whispered in satisfaction to Barbara, who sat at his side watching the evening news. "God and country . . . It doesn't get much better than that!"

The Good Heart

*   *   *   *   *

Inova Medical Center, Falls Church, Virginia

It was time to prep Mike for the surgery. Maggie was right beside him, but Doctor Miles Hall was still missing. Her former beau and heart transplant colleague, Doctor Kenneth Miller, was on his way to the rescue. A personal favor to Maggie, of course, but coincidentally linked to the cause of Digiwatch Incorporated, which Miller was newly allied with.

The process of harvesting Nicholas Caine's heart itself required sophisticated surgery. It had taken place at the University of Florida Medical Center, and the good heart, the first heart ever to be transplanted for a second time, was on its way now, packed carefully in a freezer-style container, accompanied by Doctor Tricia Mullins, a visiting transplant physician and cardiology staff instructor from the University of California Medical Center at UCLA, who just "happened" to be at the University of Florida and available to help. Dr. Mullins, another of Maggie's good friends from the medical community, had come through, reinforcing Maggie's conviction that prayers in behalf of Mike were being heard and answered.

The stage was set, and Doctor Ken Miller was being rushed to the hospital from the private jet, provided by Jackson Lyon and Digiwatch, which had flown him to Virginia.

The head surgical nurse came into the prep room and told Maggie, "The missing Doctor Miles Hall has finally been located. It seems he had a series of mishaps in Atlanta. It's hard to explain, but he profusely apologizes for not being here."

"Thanks, Jan. It happens. Anyway, Doctor Miller is world-class, and we are fortunate to have him. Has he gone over the procedure with you?"

"He has. He instructed me about a monitoring device that is to be implanted. He showed me where it goes and what it's for, but this is all new to me. Haven't read about it in the journals, JAMA. You know, you'd think—"

"If Ken Miller says it's okay then there must be a reason. He was telling me about some Digiwatch thing used to track heart transplant progress. If he's approved it, it can't hurt. Anyway, no need to worry about the small stuff. My husband is getting that heart and, Jan, I'll owe you for the rest of my life for what goes on in there."

"He'll make it just fine. We're the best, aren't we, Doctor Sanders?" Realizing her blunder, she stammered, "I . . . I'm sorry, I meant Doctor Stone."

"Thanks, Jan. Yes, we are the best. Just follow Doctor Miller, and I'll be there with you."

They hugged, donned their surgical scrubs, and went through the meticulous washing routine before entering the sterile environment where Doctor Miller was already busy inspecting the donor heart, which had just arrived at the hospital after coming on a flight from Tallahassee, escorted by Doctor Mullins. Now they waited for the new owner to be wheeled in—one Michael Stone.

37

Hᴏᴡ ᴡᴇ ᴅᴏɪɴɢ, ɴᴜʀꜱᴇ?" Doctor Miller asked.

Jan responded by reading off the data from the heart/lung machine that was keeping Mike Stone alive.

"I did one of these two days ago. Lasted eight hours. Kept springing leaks. This is rather amazing," he said.

"What?" Maggie asked anxiously.

"I keep forgetting that this is the second transplant procedure for this one heart. To look at it you'd think we just harvested a heart from an athletic twenty-five-year-old. No significant scarring, no coronary buildup—nothing more than I would expect from anyone who had reached the donor's age. The immunosuppressant drugs the donor took should have left their mark, but this heart is clean!

"I honestly thought, even if the heart did beat, this man wouldn't see a year with a secondhand heart. Amazing," he added once again.

Maggie had been praying as she had never prayed before. She knew there is always the chance of some sort of spontaneous rejection of a new heart going into the system of another person. The age of this heart—its two lifetimes behind it—also posed a major concern. There was a very real possibility that Mike Stone could die today. *If the heart chooses not to beat, I could lose him!* Maggie thought.

"We've got to tie this one off and then we'll see," Doctor Ken

Miller offered. He was just completing the meticulous work of attaching each artery and vessel with the new heart seated on the old atria.

From the glassed-in viewing station over the operating room, the med school students and specialists who had been invited to observe the delicate procedure were more than impressed. During one of the critical junctures, a young intern declared to the others, "Man, what technique! This guy can thank God that Doctor Miller is in the Jesus seat on this one."

Though she was caught up in the medical technicalities of the procedure, Doctor Maggie Stone had never forgotten that it was her husband on the table, and live or die she belonged to him. Her involvement was limited today to assisting on monitors, making sure the heart/lung machine was not only operating but being read with two sets of eyes.

The rest of the members of the surgical team watched the surgical calisthenics with a detached but professional interest.

Will the heart choose to beat? Maggie posed over and over again. *Please beat. Please pick up Mike's nervous system signals—God, please. It's all in your hands.*

"That's it, folks," Surgeon Miller declared as he backed away from the chest cavity and allowed the nursing staff to clean up the opening. "It has to beat now. Let's see what happens as the blood gets her heated up."

Miller understood the historic significance of what was happening this day and how Senator Caine's prominence in this on the national level would serve Doctor Miller's growing name recognition. Ken Miller quietly reveled in the esteem of his colleagues and the admiration of aspiring young doctors from the three medical schools this hospital served, along with the national publicity this operation was receiving—thanks in part to Jackson Lyon and Digiwatch.

He now turned his attention to the implant. The assigned nurse knew what to do. She presented a microchip that came on a tiny, clear adhesive style bandage, Doctor Miller accepted it and quickly attached the device to the muscle and tissue of the sternum. His patient was thus easily and painlessly "Digiwatched," and Doctor Miller was guaranteed his work would continue to be funded by the major corporation.

For Maggie, this was the most critical few minutes of the procedure. She had observed it a number of times, and it never ceased to amaze her. The patient on the ventilator, attached to the heart/lung machine, which made possible immediate survival, was now about to receive a second chance at life. The transplanted heart, seemingly dead and inert, was about to be tested. That it could be revived from the cold storage it had been suspended in for so many hours and turned again into a living organ was to Maggie simply a miracle. It left her in awe, proving her feeling that a greater physician was in charge of humankind.

Because it was Mike under that sheet, her interest was much more than academic. This was real. Warmed by Mike's blood, the heart would either commence to beat or it would not.

Her reverie was suddenly broken by Ken Miller's urgent command.

"Nurse, stat! Give me a . . ." he rattled off terminology that meant "jump start" drugs, and Maggie was instantly alert to Mike's life-and-death struggle.

Maggie moved to Mike's head and spoke into his ear. Her voice was shaky with emotion and her eyes welled with tears as she said: "Live, Mike. It's Maggie. Please live! I need you. Take the new heart. Oh, Mike! Please? Live!"

38

J. Edgar Hoover Building, Washington, D.C.

Troy, I'd like to introduce you to Assistant Director Don Kelly. Don, this is Troy Price." Bill pointed in the direction of a man seated behind a large mahogany desk in offices of the FBI Headquarters, 935 Pennsylvania Avenue, NW.

"It's a pleasure, sir," Troy greeted as he reached across the desk to shake hands.

"The pleasure is mine, Mr. Price. I apologize for not greeting you at the door. That was the director on the line. Seems he has taken an interest in the discussion on our friends in Philadelphia, Bill."

Following hand gestures from Mr. Kelly, Bill Maxfield nodded and took a chair beside Troy.

"Bill, Troy, I'm glad you were able to meet with me today. Troy, I want to express my sorrow at the trials you have gone through recently with your hospitalized wife, Elizabeth. I'm sorry the two of you became victims of a vicious crime and that you had to be brought into this investigation."

"Thank you, sir. But frankly, I'd rather be involved."

"Well, I know revenge is a temptation, Troy. It would be for me if I were in your shoes. But you are a former Army CID investigator, and I know you understand that emotion must be capped if we are to get the goods on the bad guys and string them up as they should be."

"I'm willing to do my part," Troy answered.

"Good. Bill, perhaps you can let Troy know what we have planned for a certain senator, his chief of staff, and a slippery fellow by the name of . . ." Mr. Kelly searched through the file in front of him.

"He went last by the name of TJ Mattsen," Bill offered.

"Yes. Here it is. We think we have a handle on his whereabouts, but he is the big question mark and seems to come in and out of the picture quite easily."

"I've dealt with him before," Troy answered. "Once this year at Union Station and once, along with Special Agent Mac Richardson, when we worked CID together. He went then by the name of Jon Gilbert and was a special ops guy—trained to kill and evade capture, and an expert chameleon."

"That sounds like our man. And you sound like the citizen we'll need to trap him," Don Kelly agreed.

"Troy," Bill began. "We have an agent at work inside a corporation called Digiwatch." Bill explained the undercover work he was doing with Barbara Waters without revealing her name. He went on to explain the intricacies of an operation where just one or two agents were at work under the FBI's jurisdiction. The dangers to the agents were explained, along with the undercover angles being used to gather information that could implicate Senator Caine in fraud and illegal contribution activities through corporations like Digiwatch. He also described the government's suspicion that Digiwatch might be using illegal tactics to influence the awarding of government contracts.

Bill also told Troy about the suspicious death of Sherman Johnson, Senator Caine's former chief of staff, who had conveniently been replaced by Ron Lawton.

While ex-governor and former senator Jackson Lyon remained at this point "clean," there was mounting evidence that he had conspired with Ron Lawton and TJ Mattsen in a number of illegal activities.

"Troy," Kelly said, "in short, we need Lyon where he is. He needs to feel secure while we gain any incriminating evidence of conspiracy against him. We have checked your military status out, and it appears you still have 'reserve' standing. Is that correct?"

"Yes, sir. I agreed to stay on active reserve with the Army. A weekend a month," Troy answered.

"We'd like you to go back on active duty. We've taken the liberty to see to it that CID will accept you back, assigned out of Fort Meade. We understand what this might do to your present employment and income," Don Kelly said.

"I'm sure we can work things out. My employer is actually my father-in-law, and he has been very supportive so far. Would this be a temporary duty?"

"Just as long as it takes to bring Mattsen in," Bill interjected.

"Well, then, I guess I'd better report for duty."

"Welcome back to government service, Mr. Price," Assistant Director Kelly offered with his handshake.

"Let's get you across the Potomac to Fort Meade, put you back in business, and get that new CID badge and side arm," Bill offered. "Then I'd like to go over to the hospital. We need to see Lizzy and support Maggie. It's Mike's big day, you know."

Troy nodded. He was single-minded now. He'd follow Bill's lead and make sure to lock his emotions away if they had a chance of screwing this up. He knew this was the only chance he'd have to rid himself of his and Lizzy's attacker. He knew Jon Gilbert or TJ Mattsen or whoever he was calling himself now was a man who wouldn't hesitate to finish the job once he felt threatened.

"Welcome aboard, Mr. Price. Ready?" Mr. Kelly asked.

"I'm ready."

*   *   *   *   *

Philadelphia

Ron Lawton had made an early morning direct flight back up to Philadelphia with an exhausted but heroic Doctor Ken Miller. The good doctor had performed two highly publicized heart transplant surgeries in three days; one in Boston that had saved a girl's life, with the donor being a young marine, and one at the Fairfax County Med Center where Mike Stone lay improving but in guarded condition, the recipient of Pastor Nicholas Caine's secondhand heart.

"Show me how the organ donor tracking is monitored," Ron Lawton ordered the young woman in the Digiwatch control room.

"Yes, sir. We have each digital implant for every organ coded so that, like files, we are able to locate the individual implant. Then the device is triggered via our digital uplink. It's simple really. The technology has been around for years. It has just been a matter of legality, as you know, sir," the technician said.

"Of course. So find me Michael Stone."

She responded, and in less than one minute had his file pulled up, all his medical charts, and had initiated the automated tracking procedure to locate him via GPS.

"Here you go, sir. He is now in this building here . . . and the address is . . ." She gave Lawton the location of the Medical Center in Virginia.

Ron Lawton felt the stir of triumph as he realized he had control of Mike Stone and his entire life in the palm of his hand. No longer were mere threats and extortion the game, but actual and deliberate action could be taken against any individual carrying such an implant. And the war on terror, global commerce, exigencies of the day, made the implant ID system all the more reasonable to sell to American citizens.

He knew what he had to do now. One, he had to win back the

trust of Jackson Lyon. That meant taking Joe Caine, his boss, out of the picture. It meant blackmailing the senator with the information Lawton had overheard when Joe confessed to his dying brother, which conversation Lawton had been conveniently present for before the untimely and sad demise of the good pastor.

Lawton also knew he had to find TJ Mattsen and destroy him before Lawton was destroyed. And finally, Lawton had to secure all the dirt Mike Stone held on Joe Caine and Jackson Lyon, to make sure those two ambitious politicians were completely in his control.

Mac Richardson, beloved son-in-law, is getting a little snoopy, too. I'll need to deal delicately with that one, he decided.

As usual Ron Lawton's plate was full. But with Mike Stone as bait, he was sure he could kill more than two birds . . . with one Stone. *Maybe three birds,* he cheerfully told himself. "Ron, they don't come better at this game than you do, old boy," he whispered as he adjusted his rearview mirror after sliding into the company car.

I'll have my files now, Mike Stone; if it's not too much trouble.

39

MAGGIE CONSIDERED THAT DAY two months before when she had held her breath, waiting for Mike's new heart to decide to beat. She had experienced the "high" of watching a life saved through an operation of this type before, but never like this.

"Mike, I'm so excited!" she squealed into her cell phone from the hospital. "I've just gotten off the phone with Ken Miller. We went over your test results, and he says your recovery is one of the fastest he's ever seen in a heart transplant patient. But what he still can't get over is that your heart previously served two other men. You, my dear, have made history."

"I don't know about the history part of it, but I feel great. Better than I have for years," Mike replied.

"Are you up to the drive to Florida?" she asked.

"Absolutely. The movers have already left, I've given the keys to the realtor, and the Suburban is all packed. How soon can you be here?"

"An hour. I've got to finish up a few things, and then we'll be on our way. Are you ready?"

"For the drive? Or for your new job?"

"Both. Oh, Mike, I can't believe how fortunate we've been—your

245

new heart, a great new job for me at the University of Florida, a new life for both of us, away from the pressures of politics."

"I know. It's pretty incredible, isn't it? Going home to Florida is perfect for me, my health. I've never felt so good or been so ready." He felt a sudden rush of emotion. "I love you, Maggie, with all my heart! Don't be long."

"Love you too!" she said as she hung up.

With all my heart, Mike thought. *With all* our *heart. Whose heart?* he questioned. Mike Stone had turned into a philosopher. Something had changed him. He wasn't willing to totally accept the notions of cellular and heart memories derived from the previous owner, but he had experienced more than subtle changes in moods, tastes, and desires. And the dreams!

He hadn't told Maggie about the dreams. But they had discussed the changes he had experienced in his enjoyment of certain foods, his willingness to exercise, and most profoundly the sudden disappearance of his cravings for alcohol and cigarettes. Those old appetites seemed to have vanished when his broken-down heart was tossed in the dumpster.

But the dreams. . . . He seemed to be seeing life through someone else's eyes when he let his own close to sleep. The dreams were foreign to him and vivid, and he wondered if they weren't those of his heart's prior owners. He needed to know more about Nick Caine's personal life.

Specifically, he wanted to put to rest a long-standing nagging suspicion (that ate at him now more than ever) about an incident that had cropped up from an anonymous source during the first Joseph Caine campaign he'd worked on in the 1980s. The information wasn't specific but indicated that as young men, the two Caines had had some involvement in the deaths of two young people—one James Barlow and Barlow's fiancée, Meredith Little.

For his peace of mind—and to rationalize the dreams away—Mike needed to know more about those vague accusations from the Caine files. The name of the sheriff's deputy who had worked the accidental death case of Meredith Little was in the file, and Mike decided to hire a private investigator friend to track the man down—see if the deputy was still alive, and if so, would he share what his investigation had uncovered back in 1969.

Mike's PI pal in Florida specialized in closed files, cold cases. Mike sent off a check and instructions to research Nicholas and Joseph Caine's lives beginning in 1965, and the few years following.

The first packet of information had just arrived from Eagle Eye Private Investigations with offices in Atlanta and Tallahassee.

Ross Reynolds, owner of Eagle Eye, had uncovered some old sheriff's records thought lost during a 1970 hurricane. It appeared that County Sheriff Blaine Lockhart had some very delicate issues regarding personal behaviors he needed to cover up, and young Joe Caine was one of the few privy to Lockhart's sordid dual life.

So Joe Caine had the man over the barrel. Why? Mike asked himself as he picked up the crisp new folder containing photocopied pages from old, typed police investigation and autopsy reports.

Sheriff's Report

Date: Jan. 3, 1969

Case: A1969–03

Victim's name: Meredith Little.

Cause of Death: Blunt trauma to the skull.

Scene of Death: Fort Walton Beach Marina. Levy area at breakers. Body found upon rocks.

Suspected Cause of Death: Accidental fall, resulting in blunt force trauma to front of skull.

Investigation: Continuing. Autopsy ordered.

Mike flipped to the next page and read: "Cause of death ruled accidental. Case closed."

Signed by Sheriff Lockhart himself, not the investigating officer, Mike noted.

He then read Eagle Eye's findings:

"There appears to have been a cover-up. Lockhart was compromised by Joseph Caine, who was in possession of potentially embarrassing information about the sheriff's personal life. (See attached copy of Lockhart's handwritten notes from a telephone conversation the sheriff had with Joseph Caine, who was at that time a former congressman's aide and then assistant to the Mayor of Tallahassee.)

"Joe Caine would bury it, if he, Lockhart, made sure Meredith Little's death was classified an accident. We have been able to determine that the investigating officer, Charles Stillman, followed the trail and ended up temporarily arresting Joe Caine, who was never charged with any crime. Joe Caine got his 'one call,' and it went to the home of the sheriff himself, and not an attorney. Soon after, Joe was freed, and an autopsy report subsequently classified Little's death as accidental, as Joe Caine had reported, and the case was officially closed.

"Joe Caine's version: While strolling with Meredith Little along the rock levy, following dinner at a nearby restaurant, Meredith stumbled, Joe reached out to grab her, but she fell headfirst onto the rocky boulders below. He immediately called an ambulance.

"Investigating officer's version: Because of the severity of the trauma to the deceased woman's head and the relatively short distance she had fallen (approximately six feet), he immediately suspected foul play. He made some calls, found Meredith Little was supposed to have been in Tallahassee with her fiancé, one James Barlow, who then lay in the hospital, critically injured from a beating.

"Stillman noted in his report that the time of death estimated by the coroner was earlier than the time of death reported by Joe Caine.

Notes in the file also indicated that the cause of death was a massive fracture on the side of the skull, rather than a secondary and less traumatic injury to the front of the skull, which the coroner concluded was likely caused by the fall onto the rocks.

"When Stillman protested Sheriff Lockhart's failure to take into account the incriminating report, he was taken off the case and transferred to traffic duty. Stillman subsequently left the sheriff's department and put it all behind him (he rationalized that Barlow and Little were 'only' African-Americans) until Eagle Eye recently found him and he gave the above version. More information on the way.

"Respectfully,

"Ross Reynolds"

"Joe Caine's secret torment . . ." Mike said as his eyes focused far from this place. *If this information is accurate, then the reason Joe fled the state and joined the Army—even tried to get himself killed in Vietnam—has its roots with Jimmy Barlow, Meredith Little, and whatever really happened on the night of January 3, 1969.*

Mike closed his eyes and tried to recapture the images that had been coming to him in the night. He had seen things only dreams concoct, and they hadn't made sense . . . until now.

40

Tallahassee

MIKE AND MAGGIE HAD BEEN SETTLED in their new home in Tallahassee for three months. Mike was continuing to make a remarkable recovery, and they were enjoying life. Maggie was thrilled. It didn't matter to her that credit was still being given to the man in the "Jesus seat," as they called the doctor in charge of the operation, Ken Miller.

The good doctor was in the news constantly now. No doubt his skills were exceptional. But the Jesus seat? Mike knew something about that with his heart that he couldn't express in words or intellectualize with the mind.

The troubling, recurring dreams had continued. He would fall asleep in the easy chair during the day and see Pastor Nick Caine doing something, talking to someone, and earnestly trying to convince him to make things right with God. He would see a black man he had never met, running, and then lying in a pool of blood. Then Mike would awaken.

Mike had never dreamed much before the surgery, or if he did, he had difficulty remembering the dreams after he awoke. But these dreams were different—frequent, vivid, and always easy to recall.

It was as if some spiritual or personal trait of the deceased who had owned this heart had passed along not only memories but abilities to

250

see things in the dream state. Mike was exhausted by them and reluctant to share them with Maggie.

Sometimes his dreams were nonsensical, about things and people and places that had no meaning to him—old political events he was too young to have witnessed but had grown up hearing about, a restaurant he had never seen before, people he didn't know. In one dream he was dating a beautiful, light-skinned, African-American woman, and he actually kissed her!

He didn't dare talk to Maggie about all this, especially kissing another woman—even in a dream. That had been pleasurable, but otherwise, he couldn't make any sense out of the frequent, almost daily occurrences.

He was afraid of two things really. One was getting Maggie, his new bride who as Mike Stone he was just beginning to enjoy, mixed up with the strange thoughts he attributed to having Nicholas Caine's heart. Was he loving Maggie with all his heart, or with someone else's? Confusing.

Second, he was afraid, and this was absurd, that by having another man's heart he wasn't really Mike Stone any longer.

He often sought relief from these fears by going to sleep, only to meet there what he assumed were Nicholas Caine's memories.

Michael Stone was grateful for the second chance at life and love, but he couldn't help searching for someone he used to know: the-devil may-care man he used to wake to in the mirror each morning. That man seemed gone now . . . forever.

*   *   *   *   *

TJ actually went to Afghanistan, did Lawton's dirty work, met his would-be killers, and instead of becoming their victim, sent them on to their "big adioses." Then he e-mailed Lawton, requesting that his

$50,000 be deposited in his regular drop-off bank in Switzerland, and waited for a reply.

"Congratulations," the reply came. "You passed. What say we call a truce? We can work together. R."

TJ Mattsen then flew to Switzerland, spent a week relaxing, made sure the money was deposited, watched to see if he was being tailed, and decided Lawton might come around to seeing things his way.

But the guy has tried to kill me, not once, but Mexico, Afghanistan . . . Naw, better to have the old man permanently retired, he finally decided. *Can't risk working with the old-school chump.*

TJ decided to call Barbara.

"Hello?"

"We on for this weekend?"

"Date's been changed. I'll contact you," she said and then abruptly terminated the call.

TJ really liked this girl. She was not only a looker, but she had spunk. He wondered where she had really been trained for this kind of intrigue. She wasn't your average Digiwatch employee or hadn't simply been pulled from some temp agency into Joe Caine's office by Ron Lawton.

I could really fall for her, he thought again.

TJ Mattsen was en route to meet Barbara whether it was "on" for this weekend or not. Now would be the time to strike and move Lawton aside, and anyone else, including the senator if needed, to secure his position with Lyon.

TJ knew Ron Lawton was up to his eyeballs in problems, worried about files surfacing that could expose secrets that Joe Caine and Jackson Lyon could ill afford to have out. Lawton was also an old dog in a world full of new tricks. If any, that was the edge TJ had on Lawton. Mattsen had mastered technology and methods of operation

that were changing with the speed of computer tech upgrades . . .
almost daily. Lawton was still stuck in the dark ages on that count.

TJ thought again about pretty Barbara Waters. *I wonder who she
really works for,* he posed in quiet reflection as he allowed his eyes to
shut.

Then he thought of Ron Lawton again and wondered if Barbara
had followed through on his orders. *You had better be upgraded to some
new hardware, Mr. Lawton,* he thought as he relaxed in the cushioned,
firstclass cabin seat of the Delta Airbus headed for JFK.

*　　*　　*　　*　　*

Barbara now knew TJ had been implanted with a Digiwatch chip
during routine dental work the year before. Lawton, probably Jackson
Lyon, too, continually knew where Mattsen was. Although dealing
with paid killers played on her mind and robbed her of a sense of security, Mattsen was at least less dangerous, in her mind, now that he
couldn't just appear without some sort of notice.

Her next call was to her new partner. She got to her new car that
was provided courtesy the FBI and swept daily before she used it,
called her partner, and filled him in on the developments.

"I've contacted Mike Stone about this, but he doesn't know you
are involved."

"Good," Bill answered. "He can know the day of."

"Mike told me that he's got some new information on Caine. He
paid a PI to do the research. Something about Joe Caine's reason for
leaving Florida in a hurry in 1969. He wants to talk to you about it."

"Hmm. Guess I'd better go ahead, give him a call, and not wait to
let him know how deeply and personally I'm involved in all this."

"One more thing. TJ. He's 'digiwatched.' Do we have someone

inside who can keep him located for me? I get a bit nervous when killers show up on my porch unannounced."

"I'm working with your handler now. I'll make sure you get an A.M. and P.M. call on TJ's location from our people inside Digiwatch headquarters. How's our man, Lyon?"

"Still clean as a whistle. Hasn't ordered a hit job yet, anyway," she said.

"Staying clear of it, huh?"

"Keeping his little former senator and governor fanny out of it—yes, sir. Ron Lawton, on the other hand . . ."

"I have some information you will be interested in regarding him. Drop off at location '1' this time. Bavarian Duke. Same hour." Click.

She snickered at some of the coded nonsense old school bureau people like Bill Maxfield held dear. *Some things never change. Duke Street and Route 1 in Alexandria is where I'll have a Bavarian, cream-filled donut tomorrow morning.* "The original Krispy Kremes," she smiled.

*   *   *   *   *

Barbara stood in line for her coffee and Bavarian. She hadn't seen Bill yet but knew he wouldn't let her down.

The door chime sounded and in walked the tall Bureau man with a *USA Today* under his arm. He appeared to look over the menu and then gazed at the newspaper. Barbara went ahead and placed her order. Bill followed and then carried on a friendly conversation with Barbara about the news of the day.

She struck it up. "I see you have a *USA Today.* I think I'll run outside and get one, maybe catch up on the story you were talking about."

"No. Don't do that. Take mine. I'm finished with it."

"You sure?"

"Certainly. No need to spend money on a newspaper if I'm tossing it anyway. Have a nice day, young lady," he said as he took his bag of donuts and left the newspaper with her.

Barbara went into the women's restroom and locked the door before opening the *Lifestyle* section of the newspaper, delivered to her by Bill Maxfield. Inside was a single page of thin paper, containing a handwritten note:

"It will go down like this. Mike Stone will be at the church building where Nicholas Caine and James Barlow both served as pastors in Tallahassee. Maggie Stone is going to ask Joseph Caine to meet Mike there—to visit with Mike about some files that Mike has told her about. She plays the 'nervous wife' who lets the senator know that for the sake of Mike's health, she wants her husband out of all Caine's past dealings. (All true, by the way.)

"The reason Mike is going to be at the church is that he has joined the congregation and taken over some administrative duties there. Since there is no new pastor yet, just an interim substitute from another ministry who serves only on Sundays, Mike is handling finances, the church newsletter, and some other things, pending the appointment of a permanent replacement.

"Mike will be in Nicholas Caine's old office at the church. This might seem odd to Caine, but he'll have to accept it.

"In that environment Mike will determine what Joe wants and why, regarding the long sought after files, and then promise him information Caine wants in exchange for information the government wants. Mike will promise anything he has to.

"This should infuriate Joe Caine. Ron Lawton is sure to monitor or know of the meetings and become increasingly pushy. Pushy makes for careless people. We want Ron to be the fall guy for both Caine and

255

Lyon, so that we can continue our investigation into Lyon's secret dealings with Digiwatch and uncover any illegal campaign contributors.

"With the pressure Joe Caine will put on Lawton to 'do something' and Lawton's own desire to prove his worth to Jackson Lyon, we feel he will trip up, give us cause for a federal indictment.

"With his desire to displace Lawton as advisor to Lyon and Caine, TJ Mattsen will most likely take advantage of any Lawton weakness and seek to be spoiler. He'd play more hardball than Lawton would with Mike Stone. He's not as concerned about old and missing files as he is in making Lawton look bad to his two bosses—Lyon and Caine.

"This is more about information than anything else—but we do have reason to believe TJ may seek to eliminate anyone in this circle who is posing him the most problems.

"Contact me at 'Sixties' today to discuss. Same hour."

Barbara took a cigarette lighter from her purse, set the handwritten note on fire, and held it over the toilet as it burned. Then she flushed the ashes away.

Her job was simple. Facilitator. She would continue to keep Lawton and Mattsen informed regarding Lyon's activities. Then, when Bill called for it, she would deliver to him all the instructions given her by the two would-be political advisors and by the Digiwatch champion, candidate Lyon.

Bill Maxfield would now work with her "handler" at the Bureau, and she would be updated daily. If things got murky or sticky, she always had Bill's direct line.

She took a deep breath. *Maybe this thing is coming to a close,* she thought. *Just in time, too.* Barbara was good, but she didn't know how long she would be able to continue keeping all those balls in the air.

*　　*　　*　　*　　*

"Bill, I'm eager to get on to the surveillance."

"I know, Troy. We are working you in. It should happen tomorrow."

"I've told Lizzy I'll be away for a month. Is she going to be safe?"

"She's in no danger. In her condition, she poses no threat to Lawton or Mattsen. Besides, we've got people watching her around the clock. Hey, she's my cousin. I won't let anything happen. Don't you worry."

"What about my getting hired by Digiwatch?"

"We've got a female agent working in HR. She's moving things along as rapidly as possible. Once you are in, you will be assigned to surveillance, spend a week in Philadelphia going through the normal hiring procedures and workshops for new employees—being briefed on all the standard OSHA, federal, and state laws you will need to know. Then you'll be assigned to their D.C. division, which is filled with ex-government spooks, like yourself."

"I was never a spook. I only did regular law enforcement type investigations."

"That should help you, Troy. The one or two bad guys, the moles placed by Lawton, and the one guy on TJ's personal payroll, should not expect a lot from you. They'll find out from you that you were just a gumshoe type, and they won't feel threatened. That is to your advantage and strength. We need to identify them, even as you track Mattsen."

"My new name and ID?"

"Here you go." Bill handed Troy the driver's license, Social Security card, and former Army CID papers that had been prepared by the Bureau. Troy glanced at his new name. "Charles 'Chuck' Norris? Who picked that name?"

"It fits you," Bill grinned. "Besides, people will laugh, poke a bit of fun, and it will set you apart as someone who is easy to get to know.

Use it to your advantage. Now, down to more serious matters. You should have no problem learning how the Digiwatch surveillance technolgy works. Be lighthearted, easygoing, serious when called for, but not too stiff, and we'll get what we need. Welcome to the team," Bill said as he shook hands.

"So how long am I to be here at the Marriott?"

"You don't like Residence Inns? We can change you."

"No, I'm just wondering about the cover."

"Tell folks you just transferred from the West Coast and you're looking for a house before you move the family. You'll find your former job history in the file, including NCIS service in L.A. and San Diego."

"Navy Criminal Investigative Services," he smiled. "Why not stick with the Army CID?"

"TJ," Bill answered.

41

M̲IKE, MAGGIE, IT'S GOOD to see you," Bill offered as the couple welcomed him into their new single-story rambler outside of town. "You look great, Mike!"

"I feel great. I'm eager to get back to work, but Maggie is keeping me on a fanatic's schedule. You got anything for me to do?" Mike teased.

"In fact—"

"Here, come on in, have a seat on the sofa," Maggie offered after a quick hug and a buss on the cheek.

"Mike doesn't deserve you, Maggie," Bill said.

"I know," she laughed. "But he'll do for now."

"Hey! I may not have my old heart, but it's lovable. What you got cooking, Bill? I smell something more than a friend's visit for old times' sake."

Bill came to the point. "I guess you know Lizzy and Troy will never be off the hook, or you for that matter, until we do something about the files that are haunting Ron Lawton, Jack Lyon, and Joe Caine. I need to ask you for them, Mike. I have an official court order, and I hate to do this, but our investigation is stalled until we can secure them and then get you into some position of safety."

"Safety! Court order! What is going on here?" Maggie exclaimed angrily.

"Calm down, Maggie," Mike said softly.

"Maggie, I—" Bill tried.

"No! You two, listen here! I'm done with Washington and all the political intrigue. Give him the files, Mike!" she sternly ordered.

"Maggie, it's not that simple." Mike fidgeted before continuing. "Bill, I—"

"Mike, I can get you immunity if that is what you are worried about. Maggie, Mike is in the clear. We just need cooperation," Bill said, looking to her.

"Mike! Cooperate! Now!" she said.

"Bill, I'd like to give you the files, but as I was trying to say, it isn't that simple. See, I have them with me and all, but . . ." Mike paused and searched the floor for a way out. He didn't want Maggie upset or involved. He saw how he was being slowly dragged into a case built upon substantial evidence of fraud and misconduct, and knew he had to work with Bill.

"But what, Mike?" Maggie finally insisted in a more tender tone now. "I didn't mean to upset you, honey. I just don't want to be involved in political things! I want Joe Caine out of my life! I am grateful for Nicholas' Caine's heart, but Joe Caine is deceitful. You've said it yourself! He'll hurt you, Mike!"

Now it got deeper for Mike. *How can I ever have Joe Caine out of my life?* he pondered. Bill was respectfully quiet, the assumed posture of a man who had interviewed countless people and knew when to be quiet and listen.

Mike thought of the nightly dreams and having Nick Caine's heart—not to mention James Barlow's. Joe Caine was forever a memory there and things were starting to add up, even now. It appeared that the devil would have his due, and that the heart he carried would never be still or truly be his until he had dealt fully with Joseph Caine's past.

"Bill . . . I know I have to get Caine out of my life once and for all. But, Maggie, I need your support. I need you to go through something with me. I have the files, but I can't exactly hand them to Bill," Mike said, turning his attention to his FBI friend. Then he went on for several minutes to explain his dilemma.

Bill nodded, summed up what Mike and Maggie were in for, and told them how Troy Price was now involved. He laid out the plan, told them who Barbara Waters was and how the key players were involved, and asked officially for Maggie and Mike Stone's personal involvement in a "sting" that would bring down Senator Caine and the opportunist Ron Lawton.

"If we get those two, the Lyon situation will fall into place. As for TJ Mattsen, he is being covered by my partner and Troy Price. I feel that unless you go through with this, you are going to be forever under the menace of Lawton or Mattsen and that now is the time for the FBI to reel this big fish in," he finished.

"I don't like it," Maggie responded. "For the record, I'm upset. But if it means that we can get on with our lives, then I don't see that I have a choice," she quietly responded.

"The files are safe as long as Maggie and I are. Are we safe, Bill?"

Bill didn't answer. He stood, smiled, and said, "Thank you, both. I've got an extra pair of eyes on both of you. Take these," he said, handing each of them a cell phone. "I'm number 'one' on the dialer. All you have to do is click, and I'll be on the other end or standing by."

* * * * *

Church offices, Tallahassee

"Mike, can you hear me?" Bill asked through the tiny earpiece Mike was wearing.

Mike was seated behind the pastor's desk. "Yes, I copy."

"Good. Please get up, talk to Maggie as you move from room to room."

"Maggie, honey. You out in the foyer?"

"Yes, Mike," she answered.

"I'm going to the kitchen to grab something to eat." He rose, walked from the office to the lounge, and then winked. Maggie sat on a sofa in the foyer, reading a magazine. "You nervous?" he asked.

"I've been nervous since I met you. What's new?"

"That's my girl," he smiled. As he walked toward the kitchen he asked, "You want a sandwich or something?"

"No. I just want this over with."

"Mike. That's good," Bill said into his earpiece. "Can you also walk outside to the ball field and back? Take your cell phone. Leave it off and put it up to your ear like you are making a call and let's just talk and see how good our reception is."

"Copy," Mike answered. "I'm headed out to make a call," Mike told Maggie.

She nodded, frowned, looked at her watch, and crossed her fingers.

"Mike," Bill said. "I need to go over some things. Look out into the grove behind the church building. Do you see anything unusual or out of order?"

Mike scanned the line of citrus trees and didn't detect anything unusual. "All looks like lemons to me, Bill."

"Mike, I have men out there."

"Where? Are they dressed in lemon costumes or something?" he chuckled.

"Funny. Now listen. We have lost Mattsen."

"What?"

"Not all bad. After all, skunks hang together. If we've lost him then Ron Lawton has probably lost him. That means he'll show up and so should Mattsen."

"Why?"

"Rotten minds think alike. Trust me."

"Mattsen's a killer!"

"So is Lawton," Bill replied.

"I can't have Maggie involved in this!" Mike protested.

"All she has to do is take any call from the media about the newspaper story of your healing and how you now have missing files from Senator Caine's life and Jackson Lyon that you are releasing. Trust me, she will be totally guarded until this is over."

"I don't want her involved anymore, Bill!"

"How do you suggest we uninvolve her?"

Silence.

"So, Mike; just be cool. It's all going to be okay. Mattsen doesn't want anyone dead except Ron Lawton and possibly Senator Caine. He wants Lawton's job in security at Digiwatch and to be alongside Lyon in Lyon's run for the presidency. That's his ambition. It isn't necessarily about money, it's about power."

"Yeah—power is money . . . I remember that one from Poli-Sci, 'Mud Slinging 101.'"

Bill interrupted. "My partner just confirmed when Caine is arriving. She is dropping him off at 1800 hours."

"When?"

"Six o'clock. She will then leave, since he requested this be a private meeting. We will record the conversation, and you know what we need. Barbara will then appear and drive Caine back to the hotel, where he will promptly be arrested—that is, if we get what we think we will."

Mike was thinking. "What about Lawton and Mattsen?"

"Both will want the files. We take you and Maggie to a safe place and follow them. Mattsen will show and we'll get them. Mike, have faith."

"Do I have a choice?"

Bill was silent.

"Bill?"

"Copy that, Mike."

42

BARBARA WATERS HAD HER HANDS full, trying to sober up Senator Joseph Caine. Apparently he had fallen asleep dead drunk the night before and had then awoken to drink some more.

She'd gotten some hot coffee in him and waited while he took a shower, shaved, and changed clothes. Now she was driving him to his appointment with Mike Stone. "Senator, are you sure you will be alright? I mean, leaving you alone?"

"Odd that we would be meeting in Nick's office. I haven't dealt well with his death yet, and to have Mike Stone meet me there—with Nick's heart. I haven't had a good night's sleep for a full week, thinking about it."

"Sir, with all due respect, you have been drinking heavily."

"No, Barbara, I drank heavily and was drunk. I'm good when I drink. Loosens me up. You just watch and learn, young lady."

Perhaps it will help, she thought. *We need this dope to loosen up. I just wish I knew where Mattsen was.*

"Here we are," she said as they drove into the church parking lot and pulled around back. "Shall I wait in the car, or will you be a while?"

"Oh, you go get yourself something to eat. It's going to be a while, I'm afraid. I'll call when I finish." Joe Caine stepped out of the car.

"I'll wait for the call, sir."

"Barbara?" he asked, leaning down to the driver side window.

"Yes, sir?"

"Do you have any kin around here? Say, last name of Little?"

She smiled. Didn't answer. She knew he was comparing her again to the woman his heart had ached for, for so many years. His reflective mood wouldn't hurt when it came time for him to talk.

Joe Caine stared at her now, trying to see in her lovely face the phantom female from his past. Half-drunk or half-sober, he'd been here before, seen that face before, and he was instantly back to January 3, 1969. "Meredith?" he whispered. Then catching himself, he straightened and turned to enter the church offices.

* * * * *

TJ had shadowed the senator for days. He now knew Barbara was working for the feds, just not sure which agency, but suspected she was far more than Lawton knew; the benign female companion and aide to Senator Joseph Caine, replacing the desirable, and now gone into hiding, Beth Benoit. To take Barbara out along with the senator was a temptation that Lawton couldn't resist. *Maybe winging Lawton would be a better message,* he mused.

The feds had staked this out well. He'd flown over the site in a rented plane earlier in the day, spotted the agents in the grove, one on a water tower nearby—they weren't taking any chances.

He was sure they were after what he and Lawton both wanted—Stone's confidential files, so that they could close the conspiracy and fraud case building against Lyon and Caine. To go after those guys required more than witnesses, it required hard evidence, paper trails, or at least a computer disc with the names, dates, and amounts.

Today Mike Stone would cough it up, a woman and her boss

would pay up as well, and then TJ Mattsen would come out in the open to Lyon, reveal Lawton's ineptitude, and move the guy aside. He didn't have to eliminate Ron, just allow Ron to do it to himself—in a permanent sort of way.

*　　*　　*　　*　　*

"Hello, Barbara," she heard in the private cell dedicated to Digiwatch calls.

"Hello, Mr. Lawton," she replied. "Are you in town?"

Silence greeted her, but it was an angry energy coming through the quiet line.

"Where is he?"

"You tell me."

"You are awful testy, for office help."

"Trained well. Lyon, you, Senator Caine . . ."

"TJ Mattsen . . ." he added, with the voice of experience and suspicion.

Barbara was quiet, then gathered her composure. "What can I do for you, sir?"

"Just give me Caine's location. I'll handle the rest. I am chief of staff."

"Yes, sir. I am aware of that. First Congregational Church of Tallahassee. You know the place?"

"The late Pastor Caine's church. Thank you very much."

Click.

She dialed the private number to her partner. "He took the bait. Number '2' is on his way with number '1' in place."

Barbara was hungry. A quick Subway sandwich was in order. She pulled into the Regal Lanes Strip Mall nearby, got out of her car, went into the sandwich shop, and ordered the vegetarian special. *Better to look completely at ease,* she thought.

TJ Mattsen noted Barbara's car parked in front of the Subway as he pulled through the lot and found the location he would need—a straight line of sight to the church parking lot. When the senator exited the church, Mattsen would do his magic. *The senator needs an early retirement. Kind of ruins things for Lawton, though,* he smirked silently.

It was a perfect set-up: a clear line of fire and easy freeway access. This job would be a piece of cake.

He parked, removed his weapon from its case and mounted the sniperscope, climbed the access ladder to the roof, and took his position. *Thank you very much, Miss Waters.*

*   *   *   *   *

Troy had been operating on remote location under the jurisdiction of Digiwatch surveillance. He had suggested a month-long and boring assignment to his superiors. Monitor a recent implant, in this case a very famous one, known nationally for having been the only man to ever receive a heart two other men had used.

They liked it. After all, gathering more data on organ donor monitoring could only further substantiate the Digiwatch claim of caring for the donor recipient and show the value of their product for general uses.

Lyon had been kept out of the loop. Troy, aka Chuck Norris, had suggested very tactfully that Lyon had taken quite a bit of publicity on this recently and it would only serve for publicity purposes once the data was in. It would provide far more ammunition to Mr. Lyon in that regard than his knowing about the surveillance beforehand.

Troy coached his driver, a young agent with the Treasury

Department, now cooperating with and assigned to the FBI on this and other cases. They had been zeroed in on TJ Mattsen since this morning when he arrived in town. They had lost him for awhile and then realized he may have been airborne. That was a weak link in the system; a "digiwatched" person needed to be on the ground or moving upon it for GPS to work in its present configuration.

Mattsen was now stationary, within five miles of their present location, and they were bearing down on him.

"Not even Mattsen would be stupid enough to try anything if he even suspects we have a fix on his location," the driver accompanying Troy offered.

"Hope you are right."

43

"HELLO, MIKE. HOW ARE YOU?" Joe Caine said. "I enjoyed your wife's informative newspaper article on your recovery. How is Maggie?"

"She's fine," Mike said as he got up from his seat behind the pastor's desk and shook hands with the senator.

"Maggie not present?"

"No. She is busy running some errands."

"Oh! I would have thought she wouldn't let such a famous man out of her sight."

"Well, sir, I have you, expert caregivers, doctors, and of course your magnificent brother, Nicholas, to thank for the fame. Otherwise, I'd be a dead man, but it's all up to God, I suppose."

"Funny you should say that. Nick always said that."

"What?"

"That it's all up to God."

"I'd like to talk to you about that someday. Since the transplant, there are lots of things I seem to have inherited from your brother."

"Oh?" Joe Caine asked with what seemed to Mike a sincere interest.

"Would you like some lemonade? With ice?" Mike asked.

Joe Caine turned somber and stared into the mahogany desktop as if it held a deep answer to the simple question.

"I'll just go get us something to drink." Mike stepped around the desk and into the adjoining kitchen, whispering into the concealed microphone. "He's moody. I think I can work him."

"Good," Bill replied. "Maggie is with me. No fears."

"Thanks," Mike replied as he opened the refrigerator door, poured two glasses of lemonade, and filled one with extra ice.

"So?" Mike posed as he set the drink in front of Joe Caine. "You go first."

"Okay, Mike. First, why here? What's this all about? Seems rather clandestine and hurtful. I mean, you know my history with Nick, this place, the suspicions, the files," he emphasized.

"The Sheriff Blaine Lockhart files, you mean?"

"Yes," Caine stressed. "If they exist and more. You have managed my affairs for years. I trusted you, Mike. What's this about files your wife mentioned in the newspaper article she wrote? She's ostensibly talking about your history-making heart transplant operation and then all at once she's going on about some mysterious political files. Does she have some sort of anti-Caine agenda now? Talking about her husband's file work for the senior senator from Florida?"

"I'll be blunt. She meant to stir things up—to get you and me to resolve some history. She hates politics. Wants me totally out. I'll back her off. But that was a coded message for your benefit, Senator Caine. Glad you took note."

"Okay. Honesty. I like that. Always could trust you, Mike. So what do you want to tell about me? Have you got some deep dark secret in those files that is eating at you somehow, hmm? Maybe something to hold over me?" Caine said with his best poker face.

The senator took a sip of lemonade and sat back, smug and in control.

Mike suddenly experienced a feeling of pity for Joe. It was an emotion Mike hadn't expected. It was almost as though he were recalling some sadness, a past loss, a kind of mourning. He struggled to answer each of the senator's interrogatories.

"First, let me answer your question, 'Why here?' Why not here? I needed something to do while recovering. The church needs a business caretaker of sorts. The church board asked me to help out until a permanent pastor can be hired. I agreed. Simple," Mike allowed.

"Yes," the senator responded as he munched on ice. "Simple."

"You were present at both men's deaths," Mike offered casually.

"What are you talking about?" Caine blurted back. "This is an outrage! That has nothing to do with anything we have met to discuss!"

"Just wondered if it still bothered you," Mike answered calmly.

Mike watched Senator Caine stand and begin to pace. His face was florid and he raged, looking and sounding like a man who was losing his sanity.

He turned to face Mike. "No!" Joe said, slamming his hand down on the desk. "No, Nick! I was not there! You know I was not at Jimmy's side when he died! I was in the Army in Vietnam when he died, and I tried to pay the price. But he died, and I didn't! You know that. Why do you try this with me? You think I am guilty when it was YOU and your boys who roughed him up! That's the price you paid—getting his heart! Ha!"

Mike sat without speaking, stunned by Joe's rage. It was as if both he and Joe Caine were being transformed; as if a destiny were unraveling from inside both of them, and he knew he had to simply ride it out.

Totally disregarding the hidden mike and listeners, Mike answered: "But you never admitted to your part, Joe. Why? Why didn't you simply get it out in the open. Talk with me about it? Jimmy forgave you. And there was Meredith," he said softly.

"Damn it all, Nick!" Joe roared, looking about him wildly. He went to the corner of the room. There was a canvas sports bag standing against the wall, and Joe reached in and pulled out a baseball bat and brought it crashing down on the desk.

Hearing the commotion through Stone's microphone, Bill got alarmed, but waited . . . "Get ready to move a man in," he instructed the supervising agent in charge of his men in the grove.

A voice came back. "Someone has pulled up. Looks like Lawton. He's out front in a car, talking on a cell phone."

"Keep an eye on him," Bill answered. "Come on, Mikey . . . Get what we need. Where are you going with this? Come in, Mike. You copy?"

Mike ignored the voice in the earpiece. He was reliving the dreams now. "You did it out there," he said, standing and calmly putting a hand on the bat. Joe Caine was now sobbing, begging for understanding.

"I didn't want to. I mean. Why? Why did she have to jump in the way . . . ?" he moaned.

"Brother Joe; come with me now. I'll take the bat. Come on. Let's take a walk."

"Good, Mike—that's good," Bill assured into the earpiece. He was sure Mike Stone was now using his head, getting the man driven near insane by guilt out of the office and into the open where his agents could help him if needed. Bill wasn't so much worried about Lawton and what he might do as he was the missing TJ. He felt open space was safe. Even TJ wouldn't take a shot with the potential for so many witnesses that might drive by or simply be out and about on a warm Tallahassee evening.

Mike Stone was not paying any attention to Bill or the present moment. He was now in 1969 with Joe Caine. He knew exactly what

Joe needed. "Let's show Jimmy you finally understand," Mike said as he reached an arm around the taller man and walked slowly with him into the early evening and the dusky parking lot.

"It was right here she died, wasn't it?" Mike tenderly inquired as they reached the spot where thirty-five years before, young Joe Caine had pulled his Impala convertible to a stop and had seen Meredith leaning over the prostrate man.

"I didn't mean to, Nick," Joe whimpered. "I didn't know what to do. You weren't there," he moaned. "I took the bat—I was drinking— like you used to. I was worried that we had done the wrong thing. I took the bat," he said as he yanked it from Mike's hand.

From his parked car, Ron Lawton saw the indistinct figures of two men in the dark parking lot and watched as one man calmly stood by as another screamed and swung something through the air, over and over. Lawton exited his car and cautiously approached.

Barbara was clearing her table of papers and the remains of a sandwich when her cell phone chirped.

"Barbara!" Lawton almost shouted.

"Yes, sir?"

"Get over here, now!" he ordered. "Pick this man up and get him back to the hotel!" He clicked his cell phone off.

"Stay where you are!" came the voice of Bill Maxfield into Barbara's earpiece. "Stand by ready to retrieve Number 1 at the gate," Bill said in reference to a location one block from the parking lot and well hidden by trees, "but stand by only."

"Copy," she confirmed.

TJ Mattsen peered through the infrared scope, of a design that didn't give his weapon away and provided ample night visibility. *This is choice,* he thought. He could clearly see Ron Lawton cautiously approaching two men in the church parking lot, and one of them was clearly Joe Caine.

Like killing two birds with one Stone, TJ Mattsen thought as he fingered the trigger.

*　　*　　*　　*　　*

Our man is being compromised! Move two men into position," Bill ordered. "Snatch Senator Caine and leave Stone and Lawton alone."

"Copy," came a voice from a man in the grove.

"Nick, who is that?" Joe Caine asked.

Mike stood frozen as if caught in a trap. He knew who he was but was spellbound as he lived the dreams he had repeatedly seen. His heart had shown him what was important, and now everything was coming together.

Mike had been in an almost trance-like mode, with Joe Caine seeing Mike as his deceased brother, Nick. Now Mike became alert to the present moment. "Uh, Bill," he whispered, "trouble."

The man coming toward Mike and Joe halted. "What's going on here, Stone?" Lawton angrily demanded.

"Hey, Sheriff Lockhart?" Joe Caine asked. "Where you been, you SOB! I wanted help. I wanted Meredith taken care of! Damn you to hell, Lockhart!" he said as he raised the bat to strike Lawton.

Ron moved aside. "You're drunk, Caine. Stone, what have you done to the senator? What's your scam here?"

"Nick, Lockhart is a bad man," Joe cautioned. "You know, Nicky, he doesn't deserve to live for what he did to me. But I got information on him," he laughed bitterly, suffering from a week of continual alcohol consumption and now clear delusions.

Ron Lawton reached to take possession of the bat just as a car pulled up with blinding lights shining upon the trio. A female exited the car and called, "Joe?"

"Meredith?" Joe said, looking beyond the approaching man. "Meredith," he whispered again as his hands loosened their grip on the wooden ball bat.

"Joe," a woman's voice came again from the night.

Joe Caine blinked and wiped at his fatigued eyes.

When Ron moved furtively for the bat, Joe quickly reared back, poised to strike.

"Joe Caine!" came the female voice again.

"I didn't mean to hit you, Meredith," Joe said. "You tried to help Jimmy, and I pushed you out of the way. That was all. I wasn't going to hurt Jimmy," he cried with outstretched hand as he walked past Ron toward the woman.

Lawton snatched the bat from his hand.

"Where's Jimmy?" Joe asked. "Meredith, I—"

TJ Mattsen squeezed off one shot, followed by another, which both found their targets and dropped the men. He quickly surveyed the area through his scope, then laid the rifle in its case and calmly descended the roof stairs to the store parking lot below.

He had it all completed in fifty-eight seconds, including being behind his wheel and heading out of the parking lot. In ninety seconds TJ Mattsen had "taken care of business" and was headed out of town.

Troy Price and his partner were already closing in on the sandwich shop and now weren't far behind.

44

BILL ROLLED UP IN HIS VAN. An agent from the grove covered Mike with his body as another took the position over the dying senator. Lawton lay sprawled on the ground as Barbara and a half dozen other agents appeared with side arms, scouting for the shooter.

An ambulance was on station in the event it would be needed and was quickly on the scene, following Bill Maxfield as he pulled his vehicle into the lot.

"I didn't even hear the shots. Did you hear the shots?" Barbara asked Bill as he exited the van.

He shook his head, ordered his men to cordon off the area.

"It was Mattsen. Troy is on his tail. Missed him by mere minutes. Barbara, take Mrs. Stone and Mike into the building, set guards at the door. I'm following Troy."

He ordered the supervising agent to dispatch all available agents and gave them the channel to tune to as they joined the pursuit.

"Troy," he said on his private line.

"Copy," came the familiar voice.

"I've alerted all agents. Mattsen will probably attempt to lose his car. If he feels trapped he'll kill and will take hostages. He isn't headed out of town by air. Probably trade out the car for another, try for the coast, and then a boat. But we've got him," Bill assured. "Your job is simply to monitor his movements and keep us on his track. Do not try to take him yourself. Do you copy?"

"Ten-four, copy." Troy wasn't about to lose TJ Mattsen. And he would follow instructions, unless threatened. He felt only the surge of adrenalin and no fear.

Mattsen had already abandoned his car. Troy was far enough behind that he didn't see the actual exchange and was surprised when the tracking device revealed Mattsen returning in their direction. "I have him on Apalachee Parkway, now East Pensacola. He's stopped. Must have entered a building."

The surveillance van pulled up slowly, stopped, and Troy reported the find to Bill.

"Good work, Troy. We have a lot to do. Be alert. We don't know what he's wearing, what his appearance is. We have agents within a mile."

"Copy that. We're on it."

"Can you give me an educated guess which building he entered?"

"This Digiwatch monitor doesn't give you pinpoint exactness until the subject actually stops. Then it generates an exact location."

"Send our Treasury friend down the street. Tell him to act casual. Have him take up in a café, store, wherever he can find a place to observe. Have him head towards Monroe Street."

"Copy, out." Troy instructed the new man, a young and anxious agent in his mid-twenties. The agent eagerly set out for what he anticipated was some adventure and a part in this important capture.

Troy waited. Five minutes passed.

"Hey, Fed? You missing someone?" a voice came over the van radio.

Troy didn't answer.

"Hey, I understand. I wouldn't answer either. So you found me.

Well, I found you. Don't send a boy to do a man's job. You a Digiwatch plant? You'll be the first to die if I go down. Out!"

"Mattsen," Troy whispered. There was nothing he could do now but hold on for Bill Maxfield and reinforcements.

He lay down on the front seat of the surveillance van. The man was good. He had a sniper rifle and scope. Mattsen knew he was in the van, and could easily pop a round in the door and kill him. *In fact, he could be outside the van now,* Troy thought. *I'm not going out like this.*

Troy decided to take a chance outside the van. At least he'd die fast if he guessed wrong. He supposed this man was not a fool and had no personal axe to grind against him. Mattsen didn't know who he was.

On the other hand, Troy did have a score to settle with the man who had nearly killed his wife and who had tried to kill him and the boy who was shot months before at Union Station in D.C.

"Compromised, out," he offered to Bill over his secure line. Troy released the brake on the van, started the engine, headed it down Monroe Street, scouted for a place to exit, then jumped out between a parked Chevy Suburban and a Ford sedan. He didn't bother to set the brake or watch the van continue down the hill where it collided with a car in the intersection.

He picked himself up and dodged the crowd rushing down the street from stores and restaurants toward the sound of the crash. His heart was beating out a rhythm of a sprinter, but he knew he had to be cool to survive.

Troy hoped there weren't any injuries to anyone but couldn't worry about that now. He assumed Mattsen would probably take the opportunity to mix with the crowd and confusion—and so he would as well.

Troy exited the darkness of a narrow alley where he had hurried and made himself the perfect picture of an interested citizen. He calmed himself by asking a stranger what had happened.

"Not sure. Maybe some guy just lost it. Didn't see the red light. Doesn't look too bad. Lucky suckers."

"Yeah," he sighed while a man with a sniper's rifle and scope was on top of the corner building scanning the crowd for his next agent target.

"Come on. I know you're in there," Mattsen muttered. The kid he had just killed was a dead ringer for a new agent. *Dumb luck,* he chided. He felt bad for the young man. It angered him to have to kill someone who had gone into government work as a good guy—someone who had done exactly as he had done a dozen years before.

"Well, chump . . . time for you to go to work. Bye-bye," he said as he allowed the young man's limp body to tumble down a staircase and spill out onto the sidewalk below.

Troy turned to a woman's scream and fought the urge to run to the aide of his fallen comrade. Instead, he played the stunned onlooker from across the street in a crowd of stunned onlookers. There wasn't a thing he could do for the young agent now.

Troy backed into the open door of a pizzeria behind him. He needed to contact Bill. He was failing in this assignment.

He took a deep breath and pulled his weapon, a Glock 9mm, from his leg holster, checked to see it was loaded, then crossed the street and joined two cops who had arrived at the young man's body. He pulled his ID and told the officers to contact the FBI. He gave them his name and the name of one Bill Maxfield, then moved people aside and stared up the dark stairs.

45

BILL MAXFIELD WAS IN A CHOPPER and had the city and county police and state troopers involved. They had enough men to cover the four-block-square area, including the capitol building, and screen most people leaving. It was a waiting game now. He hoped that Mattsen hadn't gotten through the line of cops and agents looking for him.

It looked as though Senator Caine wouldn't survive the gunshot to his head. Ron Lawton was wounded in the neck but had a fair chance of recovering.

"Barbara, Troy has disappeared. We don't know if he met the fate of our Treasury agent, but the van has been in a collision and is pulled off to the side of the street. Can you go in and see what the monitors show? Troy would have left them going if he had to abandon the vehicle. Can you check it out?"

"Copy. I'm with our party at the church. What shall I do with the Stones?"

"I forgot. This Mattsen is bad, and I made a promise to Mike. I'll leave you with them. I'll see what I can do. Keep them safe. Out."

Handgun drawn, Troy edged along the wall of a building. The loud hammering in his chest was echoing in his ears. He had done this once before. Union Station. Pursuing the same guy. Then, Troy didn't have a gun. Then, he also hadn't known what he was up against. Now he knew. He was up against an evil mind, and he hadn't ever thought like this guy. In fact, he couldn't outthink him. He would need luck and prayers to survive.

He found himself breathing hard and trembling as he ascended the stairs and rounded each dark corner, fully expecting another two-by-four to come crashing into his face, or a bullet to catch him squarely between the eyes.

Think, Troy. Where would you go? What would you do? God, what should I do? I need some help, he prayed.

He reached the top floor, tiptoed to the end of the hall, and cautiously exited to the roof.

"Huh!" he exclaimed, spinning to confront a spitting cat that suddenly leaped away from him and disappeared in the darkness. "Geez!" Troy allowed. Mattsen should have had him by now. He hadn't even been able to sneak up on a cat.

Where would you go if you needed to get out of the public eye? He asked himself. Then it hit him suddenly and squarely. It was the old reliable "hunch" investigators learned to trust over years of checking leads, trying to think like the criminal.

Yes, he said to himself. *I'd do that too.* He looked down and saw a short, club-length piece of two-by-four studding, lying near the stairwell entrance. *Strange,* he thought, remembering the stairwell in Washington, D.C., where he had very nearly lost his life to the same weapon.

A swift chill swept through him, prompting him to pick up the piece of wood. He holstered his handgun and did so, then reentered the darkened staircase, headed down from the roof and to a rendezvous with fate—and TJ Mattsen.

*   *   *   *   *

The man was acting nonchalantly, just another member of the crowd that had gathered to gape at the wrecked van in the intersection.

"Is this your vehicle?" an officer asked.

"No. I was just in this restaurant and heard the crash. What happened?"

"We're trying to sort that out. Why don't you either go back inside and finish your meal or show me some ID? I can't let you out of this area until I see some ID."

Mattson complied as he strained to see inside the van. He desperately wanted to see if the monitor was on and still tracking. He felt his back pocket and assured himself his side arm was still there under his coat.

"Starting to rain. Mind?" he asked the officer who turned to take another ID. He slipped past four others who had been stopped by the police and found the backdoor of the wrecked van they protected was ajar.

My man left from the back. Smart, he thought. He made no attempt to hide as he simply opened the door, acted as if he owned the van, and entered. The monitor caught his eye. He took a stiletto from his pocket and quickly disabled the system by slashing the wiring.

Got to find out where they put that thing. Doctor, dentist . . . had to be an implant. SOB's! he sneered.

Mattsen turned to exit the back of the van.

Armed with the length of two-by-four, Troy waited.

"Hey!" an officer yelled.

Troy was angry. Angry for Lizzy. Angry for himself. Angry for the kid who had taken a bullet for him at the Union Train Station in D.C. He was angry that his younger partner had just been killed by this maggot . . . and knew he'd die before letting Mattsen get away.

"I'll shoot!" the officer from behind him yelled.

Stooped forward to exit the back of the van, Mattsen glanced up to see both the officer with the gun and a man standing before him, wielding a club.

Troy saw the sudden fear in Mattsen's eyes. He had him by surprise. Troy watched the solid piece of wood smash into the man's face. As if in slow motion he saw the blood spatter and watched Mattsen crumple as officers drew their guns on Troy, who was standing over the fallen man, screaming at him.

"Get up, scum! Gilbert or Mattsen . . . or whoever you are!" He was completely lost in rage.

"Drop the club!" an officer ordered.

Troy ignored him, continuing to glare at the man he had just savagely bashed.

Suddenly strong hands grabbed him, tore the club away, and threw him to the ground. He felt his arms being wrenched behind him and handcuffs being clamped onto his wrists. He didn't resist as officers lifted him roughly to his feet.

One of them knelt to check Mattsen. After a moment he announced, "This guy's dead."

Standing in the rain, with police emergency lights reflecting off the wet street and the bottled up fury finally released, Troy was trembling. He felt numb and shook his head in disbelief. He'd never killed anyone before, not in the Army, never.

He closed his eyes. *How strange. That our paths should cross again like this.* He felt as though he had been on a mission that was now concluded, that everything had come full circle. He'd caught Mattsen once before. Known then by the name of Gilbert, Mattsen had been a vicious killer. He'd proven himself to still be the same—in the train station in Washington, D.C., and here again tonight. Troy didn't know how he should feel.

"What's the chance?" he asked himself in a muffled tone.

"What'd you say?" an officer asked.

Troy was too tired to explain. All he wanted to do was go home.

46

WAITING FOR THE DONOR'S HEART to arrive at the Walter Reed Medical Center, Doctor Kenneth Miller had the potential recipient of the replacement heart prepped and waiting. A young soldier, barely twenty years old, the recipient had arrived only hours before from Iraq, with a badly shot-up heart. Emergency surgery in Iraq and again in Germany had kept him alive, but his damaged heart needed replacing. Tests had indicated the match for this donor heart was apparently a good one.

Senator Joseph Caine, mortally wounded by an assassin, was giving up his heart to save another life, in the same city where his brother had done the same thing just three months earlier. It was a coincidence the press was calling, to use an old cliché, "stranger than fiction."

Maggie Stone, though shaken by the event, helped harvest the beating heart of the brain-dead U.S. Senator. Now, instead of making national headlines for authorizing his brother Nicholas's heart be given to Mike Stone as the first "secondhand" heart ever transplanted, Joseph Caine was himself giving life to another.

For Jackson Lyon and Digiwatch consultant, Dr. Ken Miller, these two transplants and the resulting publicity were a dream come true. Lives saved, a bad guy tracked, and a sad but inspiring parting with their associate, Joseph Caine. It all made for a heartwarming story.

Following his historic surgery, Mike Stone had acquiesced to his wife's request and had sworn off politics. He delivered the confidential files that had been the subject of so much interest to Bill Maxfield. Barbara Waters took her next assignment with the FBI and moved to Philadelphia where she worked faithfully for Jackson Lyon. And the war for truth and power went on.

47

Two years later, Tallahassee First Congregational Church

THE NEWLY MINTED PASTOR MIKE STONE was at the pulpit.

" . . . That all happened over twenty-four months ago now. Reliving these events over the last two hours has been cathartic for me, though I fear the memories might almost be too much to endure for those who were hurt or who lost a loved one or associate. I feel sorry for any who might have failed to get himself right with his Maker before leaving this life.

"I am also grateful beyond expression for the grace of God and the good fortune that allow me to stand before you, literally 'born again.'"

Members of the congregation began to stand, and a chorus of gratitude began with Andrew, the aged church caretaker, in the back of the chapel. "God bless you, Pastor Stone!"

"We love you, Michael!"

"Hallelujah!"

Holding their newborn, the pastor's wife nodded her approval and fought back the tears.

Mike searched the crowded hall for other familiar faces. His "best man," Bill, was there. So were Troy Price and Lizzy, not fully well yet, but able to stand. *Thank, God,* Mike thought as he smiled and nodded toward his friends.

Perhaps I will tell them more, over time, about how the transformation from political advisor to minister takes place; about my change of heart, and the study and prayer that have been involved.

The organ commenced playing, and the congregation began to sing: "What a friend we have in Jesus . . ."

Mike looked from the dais to the back of the chapel, and his eyes froze as he caught sight of a young man standing next to Andrew.

Strange. I wonder if . . . His heart skipped a beat at the musing. It was a dark beat with an ominous rhythm accompanying it.

He let the feeling go as he refocused on the glow and warmth of this day. His eyes fell on aged Claire Barlow, one of his newest and dearest friends. Mike reflected on the aged woman. It saddened him to think it wouldn't be long now until she too would lie in quiet repose. He of course knew something of her charitable support of the church, but more than that he was aware of her remarkable gift, to have bequeathed to a man responsible for her son's death that boy's heart. He could not imagine any greater demonstration of love and forgiveness and was certain that whenever she passed she would surely hear that other-worldly commendation: "Well done, faithful servant . . . enter into your rest."

Claire's heart was also full. She reflected gratefully on the momentous and historic change experienced by this congregation of believers. Not only did they now have another beloved and able pastor, but he was also a living testament. The torch of life, the gift of flesh and blood, had again passed to a new man. As another door closed she could now be at peace, knowing it was all in God's hands after all.

As the congregation departed, Claire gazed around her at the chapel that she had loved so well. The national media crews had wrapped up and were gone. Her life could quiet down now.

She would go home and note this day in the journal she had diligently kept since James's death in 1972, after he had endured three long years of suffering from the effects of his brutal beating. He had been the first pastor here at the church their family had quietly built from dreams decades ago. Because of Jimmy's good heart, he had not lived nor died in vain. A good soul's influence had rippled down through time.

With the aid of a solid oak cane, Claire walked slowly to the exit. She turned to gaze upon the fine workmanship of this building, and a feeling of gratitude swept over her. *So much tragedy turned to joy.*

Both her husband and her son lived on in here and in the many lives they had touched. She and her husband, James Barlow Sr., had given their boy a life. And God had given the son, James Jr., something more!

One heart, dear Lord, she silently prayed. *You gave just one heart! And, oh, Lord! How much one good heart can do!*

MAGGIE, I LOVE YOU!" Mike said as he kissed her fully upon lips that eagerly greeted him.

"Oh, Mike. You are everything I hoped for. You know, women really like ministers. Something about them."

Maggie's mother had arrived earlier that morning and attended the service. She now came forward to offer a gift. "Please take this. My husband used it often. It was his Bible. He was very political, but he found solace here." She held the well-worn book out to him.

"Mom," Maggie exclaimed as tears formed in her eyes.

Her mother had wanted to patch feelings up for some time but had been embarrassed. "I, uh . . . I'm proud of you, Mike," she simply said.

"I love you, Margaret. And I love how a Mom and daughter share a name I love," he said as he warmly embraced his mother in-law.

"I love you," Maggie mouthed.

"Keep that thought," he said. "I'll be home soon. I've got to meet with a young man who called. I still can't get used to this minister stuff. Pastor Stone . . ."

Maggie smiled as she left the building, carrying their infant son in her arms, blowing him a kiss and raising an eyebrow. "See you later, Minister Mike."

He waved then turned to respond to a voice.

"Pastor Stone? Sir?"

"Oh. I'm sorry. I didn't see you. Did you see all that?" Mike asked.

"Yes, sir. I hope I can earn that from a woman like her some day."

"Thank you! Can I do something for you?"

"I'm the one who called, you know, this morning?"

"Oh, yes," Mike said, motioning him toward his open office door.

"Thank you, Pastor."

Mike still wasn't used to the title. Wasn't sure he would ever get used to it. He felt so guilty, as if he were presuming he was worthy to be called by a title he had always held out to holier men than he could ever be.

Mike gestured to a chair in front of his polished mahogany desk, the same chair that Joe Caine had occupied not so long before, on that fateful night that had set Mike on this course. Then he sat down himself behind the desk. "What may I do to help you?" he asked.

"You don't know me, but I have been attending for about four weeks now, and I heard your sermon today. I hope you don't mind that I came in for a chat."

"No . . . I'm pleased." Mike waited for more.

"I'm not sure how to start," the younger man added as his eyes darted nervously around the office.

"Oh! You like baseball?" he cheerfully asked as he reached for the softball equipment bag and pulled out an aluminum bat. "I love baseball; softball, too. I didn't always like it until about two years ago. I'm a better golfer actually."

"Yes, well . . . we have a church team. You're invited. We play every Saturday morning. Eight o'clock."

"Gee. Thanks!"

"Yes—of course. So! What . . . what is it you need? What can I do for you?" Mike asked as he gingerly reached for and took the bat from the younger man's hands and laid it on the floor behind the desk. Then he moved to a chair next to the door and motioned for the young man to swing his around to face him. He was a little nervous and didn't like the idea of being trapped behind the desk. Not after . . .

"Oh! I'm sorry. It was your sermon today. I can't get it off my mind."

"You'd like to become a member of our congregation? Is that it?" Mike asked. "I'm as new at joining as you. There is nothing to be afraid of, I can assure you."

"Sure. I guess I'd like that. I just thought if I went to a church now and then it couldn't hurt."

"Okay. Then, you have my standing invitation. Is there something else?"

"Yes, sir. Yes, there is. I . . . uh, don't know where to begin." He licked his lips. "Do you have some lemonade or maybe some ice water? I seem to get a dry mouth when I get nervous."

"You like chewing on ice or having lemons in your water?"

"Yes, sir. I do." the visitor replied. "Strange how that is."

"Why's that?"

"Until I got my new heart, I didn't like anything sour, and I never chewed on ice. Now I can't seem to get enough of it."

Mike raised an eyebrow, pointed to the kitchen. "Yes. Certainly. Well, there is no shortage of lemons with that grove out back. The church kitchen is always stocked. Help yourself. Paper cups are on the counter and there's plenty of ice in the fridge."

Mike smiled as his congenial young friend slipped by him into the hallway and through the open door of the kitchen.

Mike waited for him to return. *There's something about this fellow . . . I know him . . . Maybe in the chapel last week . . .*

The happy visitor returned. "This is good ice, Pastor Stone. Real crunchy."

Mike froze. He had heard that voice before. In fact that annoying crunch of ice reminded him of the years he had worked for . . . "Who did you say you are?"

"Joseph King. I go by Joe, actually. Joe King, and I have something in common with you. Although I don't know why I feel this way."

"Sit down. Here on the sofa next to the door. Let's keep this door open, shall we? The breeze feels good." The kid seemed a little flaky, and Mike felt uneasy, though he couldn't say why. Joe was certainly friendly enough. "So you want to learn about God?"

"Well, more about my place in the scheme of things, I guess. I am trying to decide what to do with my life. I was in the Army up until two years ago. Got sent to Iraq, where I was wounded. Bullet went through my armpit actually. Hit a rib, rattled around inside real good, and hit a major valve. I was in bad shape. Walter Reed Medical practically wrote me off for dead. Well, sir, I really wanted to stay in the Army. I was good at it. And funny thing is, I'd been shot before, once in downtown Washington, D.C. and—"

"What! Where?" Mike cut in.

"In the back, up high—"

"I mean, where were you when you were shot?"

"Oh, right. It happened at the Union Station Galleria down by the Capitol. I was only eighteen. You know? I think I was in your story today. This man in a car drove by and was trying to kill this other man and . . ."

Mike's face went ashen.

"Is this troubling you, sir?"

"No. Go on, please!"

"So, there I was shot, and a hero for getting in the way of a bullet, and it made me all the more determined to join the Army. Once I recovered, I went straight through Basic, then Advanced Infantry Training, and shipped over with the 1st Cavalry Division. I was there only three weeks when me and three other guys got caught in an ambush. It got pretty hairy. Two died, and me and another guy got shipped home to Walter Reed. It was all I really wanted to do . . . you know, the Army, and once I was discharged for health reasons, I just sort of went downhill."

Young Joe King stopped talking, took a long drink from his cup, swirled the ice around in the bottom of the glass, and then started chewing on it. He looked up to see Mike Stone's discomfort. "Oh! I'm bothering you. I'm sorry, sir. Nasty habit, but not as bad as the alcohol I used to drink by the gallon," he said. "That would have killed me if the bullet didn't."

"Of course. So, you were saying?"

"Well, you had a heart transplant. So did I, and—"

"When?" Mike interrupted.

"Sir?"

"When did you have the transplant?"

"Well, what is amazing is that I had it a little bit after yours, from what I can tell from today's speech, I mean sermon. Quite a story, sir. I've tried to find out who the donor was, but the medical records are sealed. I think he liked ice and lemons though," the young man said with a chuckle. "Sir, that's what I came here to talk to you about."

Mike sat forward on the edge of his seat. "You had a transplant, and now you feel like you know things. Things you never knew before, like how you enjoy the ice. The lemonade reminds you of someone you knew and loved but you don't know who? And—"

"Sir! The dreams! I have these dreams . . . And I am always trying to do something good, but I fall, and then I get up and my brother is talking to me about how I need to change, but I don't have a brother.

And then this thing about baseball . . . I liked football, played soccer, but not baseball. I don't know why, but I'm even thinking of getting into politics. I used to hate politics. I don't know what is happening. In here, I mean," he said thumping his chest. "Sometimes I think I'm losing my mind. Am I making any sense?"

Mike would have been frightened of this man, had he not felt the comforting assurance that this was someone with a heart he knew.

"Do you want to do what is right, Joe?" Mike found himself asking the young man.

The younger man's eyes welled spontaneously with salty moisture. "I do, sir. I want to be good and give back for all my bad years. I want to change. With my heart transplant came a new desire—a desire to be better, and I like all of these new things . . . I just can't put it all together, and somehow, when I heard you speak, I knew you could help me."

"I understand you, Joe," Mike kindly offered. He then closed his eyes and softly offered a whispered prayer of thanks and blessing.

"How did you know I needed that? Those words?"

"Because I know your heart, Joe," Mike smiled.

"How?"

"Your new heart, Joe . . . your transplanted heart gave you more than life. It brought with it the true desires of another man, Joe. He was a brother to the man who gave me *his* heart."

"You think?" the startled younger man said excitedly. "They wouldn't tell me. And I really wanted to know because I was afraid—even more than just curious. I was afraid that—" Joe King stopped.

"Of what? Afraid of what, Joe?"

"Afraid I'd get . . ."

"A bad heart?" Mike cut in.

"Yeah! I'm superstitious is all. And I thought maybe, well . . . maybe I'd become what he or she was . . . I guess."

"I understand. I worried over the same thing. But I feel here," Mike said as he touched his chest, "that when hearts connect there is a reason. I knew Joseph Caine as a man, but my transplanted heart knew him as a brother. And you know from my sermon that I am the third man to occupy this pulpit with the same heart beating in my chest."

"I knew it! When you spoke? I just knew it!" Joe King declared happily. "I know who I am now! I know!"

Mike smiled, stood, and they gave each other a hearty and brotherly embrace. "You are Joe King, and it is your heart, Joe."

Mike stood back and could see something in the younger man's eyes that he had never seen in Joe Caine's. It was a feeling of peace, of contentment, at long last.

"We are brothers, Joe," Mike said. "And you are where you should be." He held out his right hand in greeting. "Welcome home, Joe."

*   *   *   *   *

Ron Lawton and heart transplant specialist Doctor Ken Miller stood watching the large color monitor in Digiwatch's tracking station.

"Uncanny," Doctor Miller whispered. "Two men who I did the heart transplants for, implanted with the Digiwatch microchip, finding each other and now in the same room at some building in Tallahassee, Florida. Mr. Lawton, do you know what this means?"

Lawton nodded, smiled, and shook hands. "Well done," he acknowledged. "I'll let Mr. Lyon know. He'll be delighted."

Ron was satisfied. His scheme was working. He could see the White House, the power, and the control over lives that he would help direct in the way that would make Americans supreme in every sense of the word—financially, in health, and security—free from the threat of terrorism. And he and Jackson Lyon would have engineered this transition to a new world order.

Nothing would stand in his way. He had just this morning issued a mild threat to Pastor Michael Stone, just in case Stone ever got an urge to get back into politics or for some reason share the information from the files.

Lawton had gone to Mike's home after the sermon, and before Maggie and her mother got there, he had left the threat where Mike would be sure to get it—on the bathroom mirror. *Hope I didn't scare Maggie,* he grinned. He had a private Digiwatch jet waiting at the airport and in a few hours was back at corporate headquarters.

The files, he reflected. *Just a mind game. The guy actually stores the most vital files in his head, like a computer. I just about get killed for something that didn't even exist. Well . . . never too late to live and learn . . . for most of us anyway.*

*   *   *   *   *

Regarding the matter that so troubled him, Claire Barlow had many times reminded Nicholas Caine, "It is all in God's hands" and to believe this:

"And I will give you pastors according to mine heart, which shall feed you with knowledge and understanding."

—Jeremiah 3:15